THREE GIFTS

Kyra—who had the gift of the spirit, alone able to travel beyond the body to seek the wisdom and aid of the Lords of the Sun

Karne—who had the gift of the flesh, the strength and courage to face and fight against the most fearful odds on earth.

Fern—who had the gift of love that made her one with all nature and life

Only by joining together could these three hope to survive and triumph over the darkness descending upon their world in the shadow of—

THE TALL STONES

Be sure to read the second volume in Moyra Caldecott's
THE SACRED STONES trilogy—
TEMPLE OF THE SUN
soon to be available from Popular Library

THE
TALL STONES

THE SACRED STONES TRILOGY #1

by Moyra Caldecott

POPULAR LIBRARY • NEW YORK

THE TALL STONES

Published by Popular Library, a unit of CBS Publications, the Consumer Publishing Division of CBS Inc., by arrangement with Farrar, Straus & Giroux, Inc.

ISBN: 0-445-04365-2

Printed in the United States of America

10 9 8 7 6 5 4 3 2

For Rachel,
Stratford, Julian and Oliver
with love

The Discovery

KARNE AND KYRA lay on their bellies in the long grass within sight of the tall Stones of the Sacred Circle, but well hidden from view themselves. They were about to commit an act of blasphemy. They were about to spy upon a priest.

Behind them, some distance to the east, was the straight silver line of the sea from which liquid strangeness the Sun came each day to watch over them.

The Sun!

It was said that men of power had built a Temple to the Sun in the South that contained within its circumference the answer to all the secrets of the Universe. It was to this Temple Karne longed to go; it was these secrets he longed to learn.

But first there were matters in his own village that needed explanation.

The priest of their community knew many things. He stood alone within the Circle of Stones and learnt answers to questions that most ordinary people never dared to ask. Karne dared to ask, but Karne was a boy among other boys supposed to work the fields and not question the ancient mysteries. He did not know why he felt compelled to question. The other villagers seemed content enough to follow the daily routine and accept whatever the priest told them, but Karne always found himself discontented, wanting to know more.

The rituals satisfied the others. They chanted the words, beat the drums, lit the fires, did everything the priest commanded and found that that was enough for them. But to Karne there was an invisible part to the ritual which he knew was the most important part of all, understood only by the priest.

Why?

Why were these things kept from him? His mind felt capable of grasping much more than he was given.

"These things are no concern of ordinary people," his father told him. "Maal is special. He was chosen in the ancient days and born to bear the burden of knowledge for our people. It is not an easy way. He has nothing of the love and companionship we ordinary people have among ourselves. He lives alone and carries all our lives upon his back. See sometimes how he bends with the weight of it all."

Karne thought about the priest. He was old, bent and shrivelled like a withered fruit. Surely Death itself walked not far behind his back. But—and now another picture of the priest came to the boy's mind—on holy days when he walked the processional way towards the Standing Stones upon the hill his back straightened and he carried himself tall and steady, like a young man. He entered the Sacred Circle and he was transformed. Karne had seen him, his eyes burning with a sudden fire as though he saw things they could not see that made him young again.

Karne was silent, thinking on these matters, but on another day Karne asked his father, "What if Maal dies? There is no one in our village or in the land as far as any of us has ever travelled who is trained to be a priest. What

8

will become of us without a holy man who knows the mysteries?"

"These matters are not for us to think about," his father replied. "It will be taken care of."

And he would say no more.

"It will be taken care of!"

How that sentence irritated Karne.

How?

How would it be taken care of?

By whom?

When?

In what manner?

Karne felt his head would burst if he did not get some answers.

Maal lived alone and, as he aged, hardly ever spoke except on holy days. When it was the turn of Karne's family to provide food for the priest, Karne volunteered to take it to him, hoping to have an opportunity of conversation. But the old man was not at home and Karne was forced to leave the food and go back to his chores before Maal returned.

But one day when Karne had forced himself between the adults crowding beside the processional way to see Maal pass during one of the rituals, he fancied he caught Maal's eye looking into his. He had a strange feeling that the eyes of the priest could see right into his head, see what he was thinking. He fancied the priest's lips moved slightly in a smile, but it was all so fleeting and so quickly past that Karne could not be sure he had not imagined it. All he knew was that he was trembling and his head felt as though it were buzzing.

It was just after this that he first noticed there was something unusual about his sister Kyra.

Up to that time he had been aware of her as one of his family, two years younger than himself, female and therefore of not much interest to him. His brothers were more fun to be with, companions on hunting expeditions, helping him by taking his place when he wanted to escape

9

some planting or some ploughing, coming with him when he explored beyond the village to the far hills or the forests, even helping him with the building of a boat of wood and hide which he was planning to take down to the sea one day in an attempt to find the fabled Temple of the Sun. He did not believe it was as impossible as the Elders said it was and he had managed to persuade at least two of his younger brothers to be companions in the adventure.

It was on one of the days when he was working on the boat by himself that the thing happened with Kyra. She came looking for him with some bread she had baked and, while he finished what he was doing, she sat on a log and watched him, breaking off pieces of the bread bit by bit and popping them into her own mouth.

He had told everyone he was making the boat to go fishing. Only Ji and Okan knew what it was really for and he had forced them to draw blood and swear they would tell no one. He did not want his handiwork broken up by some irate Elder on the grounds that it was against the will of the Holy Ones that he should go looking for the Temple.

Karne pulled one of the hide thongs tight with all his strength, binding it again and again round one of the ribs. He tried to hurry, smelling the delicious hot bread and feeling annoyed with Kyra for breaking off so many pieces.

"The journey to the Temple of the Sun requires more than just a boat, you know," she said suddenly.

"What do you mean?"

He finished the last knot hastily and shot out his hand for the last piece of bread before it vanished down his little sister's throat.

"It is a journey on many levels," she said calmly.

He stared at her astonished. Her face had a strange expression.

"You know I am right," she continued patiently, "there is no need for you to pretend."

He swallowed a lump of bread unchewed and it stuck

10

in his throat. He choked and thought bitterly about his two younger brothers. But even as he thought up suitable punishments for their betrayal of his confidence, he knew there was something more to Kyra's knowledge than it was possible for the boys to have given her.

She was staring at him calmly and for a second he had the same peculiar feeling that he had had when he had met the eyes of the priest.

Kyra could see into his head!

She also knew things that he did not know.

He was horrified and dismissed the idea immediately.

"Get going!" He was angry with her. "What do you think you are doing interrupting me like this? I am busy! And besides," he added with extreme irritation, "you have eaten all my bread!"

He picked up a stick and pretended he was going to throw it at her. She laughed and jumped lightly to the ground. As he watched her running and leaping across the field she looked just like an ordinary little girl again and he was sure he had imagined that she could see into his thoughts.

He returned to his work disturbed and disgruntled.

Somehow it no longer went so well. He lost confidence that the boat was ever going to be able to sail across the sea. The hides, however taut and oiled, would not withstand the buffeting of the really big waves. He had seen sea-going boats, in fact had modelled this one upon them (though his was smaller) and he knew this one was not good enough.

Perhaps that is what Kyra had meant.

No, it was not what Kyra had meant.

"The journey to the Temple of the Sun requires more than just a boat," she had said, and she had said it with authority as though she had secret knowledge.

"Nonsense," he said loudly, packed up his belongings, pulled his boat under the awning of leaves and branches he had built for it and left, marching and striding back to his home as though he were being watched by someone he was trying to impress.

Some days passed without much of note happening. It rained a great deal. He saw Kyra but she seemed such an unexceptionable little girl that he thought more and more he had been mistaken about her.

And then on the next ritual day something happened to renew his suspicion that his sister was not quite as she seemed.

The people gathered as usual along the processional way on the night of the full moon to watch the priest tread his slow measured way to the Stone Circle at the top of the hill. They bowed their heads as usual as he passed, whispering softly the names of the gods so that their voices sounded like wind through the leaves and the air vibrated gently to a kind of rhythm. This was not to be the Spring ritual when they brought the branches of blossom, nor the Winter ritual of fire, it was the Moon ritual when the priest stayed alone with the spirit of the full Moon and listened to the messages of Night. For the Rising the people stayed with him, the vibrations of their voices important for his work.

"Why is it so important?" Karne thought defiantly. "What are these sounds that they matter so much?"

He knew they were the names of gods, but there were many gods and these were only a few of their names.

"What would happen if I whispered different names?"

"Do not," Kyra whispered in answer to his thought, "it would be dangerous for him."

He spun round and stared at the dark shape of her face. The moon had not yet risen and it was too dark to see clearly, but he had the feeling her eyes were upon him and that she could "see into his head". A chill ripple passed under his skin, but he said nothing. He made sure he whispered the correct words.

At moon rise the momentum of the vibrations changed and finally stopped. With the first glint of brilliant light the whispering became chanting which grew louder and louder, faster and faster, until the time when the enormous disc of blazing light was in full view, its lower rim resting on the horizon. At this point the priest raised his arms in a sudden splendid movement, and with that the immense vibrating sound of the chanting cut, stopped, utterly ceased. In dead silence the visible counterpart of the invisible Moon Spirit lifted clear of the horizon and sailed majestically into the realm of the stars.

The villagers watched with an awe that never grew less no matter how often they took part in this ceremony.

After a timeless moment of watching, of worshipping, the priest moved again, his arms lowered to shoulder height, cutting the air sideways with a sharp movement. The villagers turned to go, leaving their priest to communicate with the spirits and the gods.

In the morning, when they gathered again at the coming of first light, Karne noticed that the priest who normally walked lightly as though he felt no strain stumbled slightly on the path, and as he did so looked up swiftly to see if anyone had noticed. No one, except for Karne and Kyra, had, and the priest's eyes found them out immediately. His sharp eyes penetrated Karne's mind briefly and blazingly, daring him to repeat what he had seen, and then turned to Kyra's, where his gaze stayed, and Karne could sense a shaft of consciousness leap between them like lightning in a stormy sky.

But even as he registered it, it was over, and the old priest was gone, surrounded by the Elders.

This time Karne was determined to find out what was happening with Kyra.

"I did *not* imagine it," he told himself and followed her closely. But she was walking with her mother, their arms linked, and there was no way he could talk to her alone.

It was not till late that afternoon that he managed to corner her.

"I must talk to you," he said urgently, knowing that it was only a matter of moments before their baby sister would tire of playing in the mud puddle and demand Kyra's attention again.

She knew at once what he meant and nodded.

"Where?" he asked tersely.

13

She thought about it seriously for a moment.

"Near the boat?"

She knew this was a relatively secret place and a place he went to often to get away from people. Ji and Okan were far away this afternoon helping their father in the forest, so they would be no bother.

"Good," he said. "When?"

She shrugged and looked at the baby covered in mud from head to foot. It grinned up at her with its little toothless gums black with the mud it had been stuffing into its mouth.

They could not help laughing.

"You had better get it cleaned up," Karne said. "I will be at the boat. Come when you can."

He was glad he did not have the task of cleaning the baby and he wondered how much mud it had swallowed and whether it would be sick as it had been the last time. Poor Kyra.

Poor Kyra?

The priest had looked at her in a way he had never seen him look at anyone else.

The priest had smiled at *her*.

Why?

He had looked at Kyra as though he knew her in some way.

Something was beginning to happen out of the ordinary, and Karne was finding it very intriguing and exciting.

He waited impatiently for Kyra to come to him. If she did not hurry they would have no time to talk, it would be time for the sun to set and the setting sun meant family prayers and then the evening meal. By rights he should be helping now with the animals, but with any luck the rest of the family would manage and he would get away with a mild reprimand from his father. For all his questioning he would not like to miss the evening prayers. The dark was not a thing to face unprepared.

Kyra came at last.

He pounced on her.

14

"What is going on?" he demanded.

She hesitated a moment.

"I do not really know," she said slowly, her face thoughtful, "but it seems to me . . . sometimes . . . I know things . . . I mean I *feel* as though I know things . . . I cannot possibly know . . . like . . . like people's thoughts . . . before they say something . . ."

"I knew it," shouted Karne triumphantly. "You can see into my head!"

"I cannot!" Kyra answered indignantly and vehemently.

"Well, sometimes you look as though you can!"

Kyra's expression was distraught.

"I do not mean to," she said miserably. "It just happens."

Karne was very excited and was walking up and down restlessly.

"It is great! It is the most wonderful thing! Why on earth are you looking so miserable?" He was talking faster and faster as he walked about. "There is no end to the things we can do with a talent like that . . ."

"We?"

Kyra looked astonished, but Karne took no notice of her.

"The priest Maal can do that. I know he can. He looked into my head in just the same way as you did the other day. We will be able to find out all kinds of things this way. We may even be able to find out what *he* is thinking . . ."

"Karne!" Kyra began to be really alarmed. "What are you saying! You will be stricken by the gods for such blasphemy! A priest's thoughts are sacred. All his ways and his knowledge are secret. They *must* be secret . . ."

"Why must they be?" Karne challenged, his eyes blazing at the thought of all the power they could have if Kyra really could see into people's thoughts.

"It has always been so, since the ancient days!" she cried.

"Well, these are not the ancient days! And why do I feel in myself such urgency, such desperation to know the

15

things it is forbidden to know if the time has not come to know them?"

Kyra looked at him with wide eyes. He seemed inspired. Possessed?

"Karne," she whispered, afraid for him. "It *cannot* be! Calm yourself! Besides . . ."

She hesitated.

"Besides what?" He found himself shouting.

"Besides . . . I do not have this great power you seem to think I have . . . only sometimes . . . occasionally I get glimpses . . . only bits and pieces . . . nothing one could rely on. And besides . . ." she said again.

"Besides what?" He shouted again, his voice amazingly loud and unlike his own.

"Besides . . . even if I had the powers you think I have I would not use them the way you want me to use them. Only the priest can know the High Secrets. It is not fit for us to know them."

"Why not fit?" He challenged her angrily, but she held her ground bravely.

"Well, not safe then."

"How not safe?"

"We cannot know the whole, and to know only the parts can be misleading."

He thought about this for a while, somewhat sullenly. He sat on the grass with his head in his hands, thinking deeply.

"You see," she said at last in a very small voice, "I cannot see what you are thinking now. I can never *make* it happen. It just seems to happen . . . by itself . . . sometimes . . ."

He still said nothing.

She strained to catch his thoughts, "to see into his head", but she could not.

She felt miserable and wished that she had never told him. She wished that it had never happened to her in the first place. Before this day she had found it disturbing, but not frightening. Now she was wondering if it was an evil. She had never seen Karne in such a mood.

16

But his mood was changing even as she was thinking this.

"Kyra," he said, raising his head from his hands and looking at her more calmly, but with something in his eyes that had not been there before. "I am sorry. I did not mean to frighten you."

She noticed that there was a hint of respect in his voice, and affection.

She looked at him uncertainly.

"This matter is important. We must think about it. The gods must have given you this gift . . . surely to some purpose?"

She still looked doubtful and unhappy.

"Think!"

She shook her head sadly.

He could see there was no point in pushing her further at the moment. Her pace was not his pace. He would have to be patient with her, but he would not let the matter rest for ever.

They walked home together, and yet not together, two very small separate figures in a huge landscape, the gigantic red Sun god that ruled over their lives sliding past them into the dark regions of the west, the tall Stones on the hill growing taller as they grew darker and sharper in outline against the brilliant luminosity of the sky.

Kyra shivered slightly as she looked at them. They had always seemed holy before, protective, the priest's concern and none of hers. But now it came in to her mind that somehow her destiny was crossing theirs and her life as a little girl minding babies and grinding meal for the family was going to change. She stopped walking and stared at them. They grew longer and longer, dark shapes reaching great distances into the universe, the light behind them growing in intensity of pale yellows and greens to an incredible white. It seemed to her that she was staring into the heart of Light and it was blinding her.

She dropped her face into her hands and squeezed her

eyes shut to avoid the hurting of the light, but she could feel it still.

The Light and the Circle were both within her in some way, and yet, at the same time, outside her, encompassing everything that existed.

She encompassed everything that existed!

She was the circle encompassing everything that existed.

Nothing existed that was not within herself.

Karne was shaking her.

"Kyra! Kyra!" he was calling, his face a study of anxiety. "What is the matter? Kyra!"

The vision disappeared and she was left a shaken and shuddering little girl in the growing dark, her brother's rough hands upon her shoulders, his worried face, very much outside her own, staring at her in consternation.

Still shivering, she looked around her. The light was gone and the sky was dimming rapidly. The Stones on the hill looked very ordinary and were almost fading from sight. A last straggling string of birds was trailing off to the forest in the south, some of them calling mournfully. Friendly smoke from home fires was rising beyond the barley field.

"Oh Karne," she cried, tears streaming from her eyes, but laughing at the same time with the sheer pleasure of the ordinariness of everything. "That beautiful, beautiful smell of wood smoke!"

Karne dropped his hands from her shoulders and took her hand. They ran towards their home together, looking at nothing but the ground beneath their feet.

The Mind of Maal

THEY DID NOT refer to this again for some time, but both thought a great deal about it. They had touched on something they had not understood, about themselves and about the world they lived in. Although there was no outward sign in their daily lives that anything had changed, they both knew there was no going back to where they had been before.

One day the Elders called a meeting of the community.

There was some murmuring and grumbling from many of the villagers. It was not convenient to leave the work they were doing at this point, but a command from the Elders could not be disobeyed.

As Karne hurried from the fields in answer to the call he found Kyra carrying their baby sister on her hip. He walked beside her.

"Do you know why there is to be a meeting?" he asked.

She shook her head.

At that moment they were joined by others asking the same question.

The village gatherings were always held beside an enormous flat stone that formed a kind of natural platform. It was heavily striated from north to south, scratched and gouged in the ancient days by some force the villagers did not dare to contemplate.

While the people were arriving the Elders walked with measured, dignified steps around the outside circumference of the Sacred Circle on the hill and when everyone was present and the expectant chattering had died down, they took their places on the platform, each one standing in a position echoing the position of one of the major Stones in the Sacred Circle. They formed a kind of living Circle, their chief spokesman nearest to the people.

The Sacred Circle of Standing Stones was never entered by the ordinary members of the community. The seven Elders were permitted under special conditions at special times, but otherwise no one dared to go within range of its powerful influence except the priest who had been trained for many years to work safely with its secret energies.

There was something very awesome about the Stones. They had been chosen in the ancient days in ways the villagers did not understand, for purposes they did not understand. They were content to leave them well alone.

Karne was beside Kyra and they put the baby on the grass to play. He noticed that as the Chief Elder, Thorn, began to speak Kyra stiffened slightly and began concentrating on his words in a way that gave Karne the impression that she was hearing more than he was saying. He was so interested in her reactions he missed the whole first part of the message. When he became aware at last of what the man was saying it was something about change . . . and adjusting their lives . . .

His attention was rivetted at once. Was something actually going to *change* in their settled ways at last?

"What . . . what is going to change?" he whispered urgently to Kyra.

She raised her hand to stop the interruption of her concentration and he fell silent immediately. This was not the gesture of his little sister, but of some stranger with authority.

". . . he has been chosen by the gods and will serve us with the dedication that the Lord Maal has shown throughout his time with us. Nothing will be disturbed. It is the natural time for change."

For the first time Karne noticed that the priest was not present in his usual place.

Was he dead?

As the Elder stopped speaking a kind of movement went through the crowd of listeners that Karne had seen in a barley field on a windy day. The hillside did not seem to be covered with individuals but with a kind of composite being that reacted, sighed and moved as one. Only Karne, seeing it, felt himself separate and apart.

He turned to Kyra. She too stood alone.

"Is the Lord Maal dead?" he asked.

She shook her head.

"No, but he is about to die," she said calmly.

"Is he ill?"

Karne remembered seeing the old priest stumble.

She shook her head again, but said nothing. There was a line between her eyes and he could see that she was deep in thought. He tried to keep from asking her questions, but he found he could not hold the silence between them for more than a few moments.

"Who will be the new priest?"

Kyra had picked the baby up and turned to go. She did not reply.

Karne followed her insisting on an answer.

"A new priest is coming to take Maal's place?"

"That is what he said," she replied, but there was something in the flatness of her voice that made him know that there was more to the story.

"What do you mean 'said'? Do you think he will come?"

Kyra walked on thoughtfully for a while.

"Kyra?"

"I do not *know*," she said impatiently at last. "He said there would be a new priest coming from the Temple of the Sun, but . . . I do not know . . . I sensed something else . . . something wrong . . ."

"What do you mean?"

"I cannot be sure . . . but Thorn seemed not to be speaking the truth . . . and it is a strange thing . . ." Here Kyra seemed to be staring at something Karne could not see. "I do not *see* a new priest coming to us . . ."

"Perhaps Maal will not die?"

"Maal will die . . ."

"Perhaps he will die before the new priest has arrived and there will be a period when there is no priest."

"The gods would surely not allow that," Kyra said firmly, but she sounded more like her ordinary self when she said it.

Karne had taken to distinguishing two people in Kyra, the child sister and the stranger who could "see into heads". The stranger had been there a moment before, but already the child was taking over. There was no point in questioning her any longer. He moved off and went back to his duties with much to think about.

The priest in the community was the guardian of the Mysteries, the messenger of the gods. He communicated with a network of priests across the world and spirits across the universe, so that their community could develop in harmony and peace as part of a greater whole.

Maal had served them well for many years, attending to their sick, presiding at birth and death, guiding them on Good and Evil, on rain and drought. They were sorry his time had come to move on to other duties in the hierarchy of the spirit world, but they accepted it.

It was the way.

While the rest of the village was anticipating the arrival of the new priest with pleasurable excitement Karne was worried and intrigued by what his sister had experienced.

It was to find out what was behind that experience that he and his sister came to be lying on their bellies in the long grass within sight of the Circle of Sacred Stones, unseen but seeing, as the priest Maal came alone and without the ceremonial crowds, to commune with whoever he communed with, within the Circle.

As they watched he seemed not to be aware of their presence. His face was thoughtful and withdrawn as he walked evenly and calmly between the entrance Stones.

They had never been so near the sacred place before and Karne could hear his heart beating loudly. At first he thought it was the earth pounding with a kind of deep rhythm, but then he realized it was coming from inside himself. He wondered if Kyra's heart was doing the same, but she looked calm enough. Her head was raised slightly and her expression was one of concentration and intensity.

The priest walked to each Stone in turn, touching it with his forehead and pausing as though he were sensing something from the Stone through his forehead, and came to stand at last before the huge recumbent one in the southwest quadrant that was a different shape to the others and was flanked by the tallest pair of Standing Stones. He stood for a long time in front of it, his head slightly bowed, thinking . . . or was it listening? Then he put his back to it, lay against it, with his arms spread out on either side, the tips of his long and sensitive fingers stretched towards the two uprights on either side. He tipped his head back to lie upon the stone with a sigh and the two watchers noticed the sun was at its highest point of the day and blazed down upon his face.

They dared to creep a shade nearer the Circle the better to observe his face and were startled to see a strange pallor upon it, the muscles relaxed in a way that made them think of dead people they had seen.

"He is dead!" Karne whispered in horror. "He has come here to die!"

But Kyra held up her hand and her inner senses were alert. She shook her head almost imperceptibly and with

23

the gesture of her hand prevented Karne making any further movement or sound. Her face was strained and she was leaning forward as though she were trying to catch some minute breath of sound too small for normal ears to catch. He recognized the stranger in her and waited patiently, watching her more than the priest now, admiring the concentration of her attention, the stillness of her body. She scarcely seemed to be breathing.

As the time went on every muscle in his body ached and itched to move. He dared not and yet he could not stop himself. He sensed there was almost a thread as fine as a spider's web from the girl to the priest and any movement on his part would snap it. But he could bear it no longer. They seemed to have been there for hours and as far as he could see nothing was happening. He moved at last and as he had feared his movement cracked the girl's delicate and subtle concentration.

An expression of loss, followed by irritation and almost dislike, flitted across her face as she turned to him. She seemed at first bewildered as though she had forgotten where she was and looked as though she were about to say something. He seized her shoulder and pulled her lower in the grass, at the same time indicating with a jerk of his head the danger of their situation so close to the Sacred Circle, spying on the priest.

Her face registered recognition, quickly followed by panic. He flung his arm around her comfortingly and they lay flat in the grass. They could hear the priest moving in the Circle now, but were too frightened to raise their heads. Karne could feel his sister's body trembling under his arm. He suddenly wished they were far away and had not done this blasphemous thing. It seemed to him the footsteps were coming nearer and nearer and he braced himself for some terrible blast of wrath.

But nothing happened.

Maal walked calmly out of the Circle between the two entrance Stones and steadily and quietly down the path as though he knew nothing of their presence.

"He knows," whispered Kyra, tears streaming down

her cheeks. "He knows!" She was very much the little girl again.

"Nonsense!" he said, feeling bolder now that the priest had moved off. "He would have said something to us. Come on, let us leave this place!"

He was longing to ask her what had been happening when she had been concentrating so intensely. He was sure something had been going on that was beyond his senses, but the place had become oppressive for him now and he wanted to get as far away as he could from it.

She felt the same and before the priest was safely out of sight the two were scrambling down the hill and running and tripping and sliding down into the valley where Karne kept his boat.

Once there they flung themselves panting down on the grass and tried to collect their thoughts. After giving her what he considered enough time to recover Karne asked her what had happened in the Circle. She was a long time answering and then spoke slowly as though she were trying to find words for an experience that did not really have words to express it.

"Strange," she said, "very strange. He seemed to . . . I mean . . . he seemed to . . . go away . . ."

Karne was staring at her intently, anxious not to miss a word.

"What do you mean? As though he were dead?"

"No. Not like that. As though he had gone away . . . somewhere else. At first when I was trying to reach his thoughts I could not get anything . . . but it was different to the other times when I try to see people's thoughts and I cannot. Those times I cannot because there are too many thoughts crowding . . . making too much 'noise' somehow . . . This time there was nothing there . . . a sort of absolute blank . . . a sort of silence . . . as though there *were* no thoughts to see."

"He looked dead."

"At first I thought he was dead . . . as you did . . . but I knew he was not. I could not make out what was happening . . . and then it seemed to me I was inside his head looking out."

Karne sat bolt upright at this.

"What did you see?"

She was silent, struggling to find the right words.

"I did not see what I expected to see," she began slowly.

"What did you expect to see, for the gods' sake!" cried Karne impatiently. She was so *slow*!

"The Sacred Circle, the sun, the hills and fields all around us here . . ." She swept her arms in an arc to indicate everywhere in every direction they could see.

"What did you see then? Darkness?" Karne prompted.

"Sort of. At first."

"And then?"

"And then . . . I saw other people . . . very dimly . . . I could not make out their faces . . . standing round him in a circle all touching hands . . . in a circle . . ."

"And? . . "

"And beyond them, Standing Stones . . ."

"Ours?"

"No. Much bigger . . . different ones . . . the circle seemed to be enormous . . . and beyond the Stones there seemed to be a kind of hill . . . I suppose a bank that went right round behind the Stones . . . you could not see over it . . . there was no landscape beyond . . ." Her voice trailed away.

"What else?" he cried impatiently.

"I am sorry," she said miserably, putting her head in her hands, "I am trying . . . but it was all so . . . so . . . strange . . . and already I cannot believe I really saw it . . ."

"You *did*. You did see it! Try and remember."

She shook her head.

"That was all."

"Were they saying anything . . . the other people . . . ?"

"No . . . I do not think so . . ."

26

"What were they . . . priests? . . . Elders? . . . ordinary people?"

"Priests I think . . . I am not sure . . . but they were *inside* the Stone Circle and they were trying to communicate with Maal . . ."

"Communicate? You said they were not saying anything!"

"They were thinking . . . they were all thinking the same thing . . . that was why they were holding hands in a circle. They were really *trying* . . ."

"What were they thinking?"

"I do not know."

Karne gave an exclamation of disgust.

"*Think!*"

"I am! I am!" she cried, "but it is so hard. My head is hurting!" She rocked backwards and forwards holding her head in her hands.

Karne pulled himself together.

"All right. I am sorry. Let us see now what we have. Maal enters the Sacred Circle, *our* Sacred Circle, goes round touching the Stones with his forehead . . . goes into a kind of . . . a kind of death . . . or . . . sleep . . . and in that sleep he travels somewhere else to another, larger Sacred Circle . . . leaving his body behind here. You somehow get into his head and go with him. Other priests 'think' in a circle round him . . . but you do not know what they are thinking. Is that right so far?"

"Yes."

"What happened then?"

"I do not know. I was suddenly in my own body again and you seized me and pushed me down in the grass."

Karne was silently cursing himself for having moved when he did. It was his fault she had jerked back. He sat, thinking hard, his hand automatically stroking Kyra's hair. He could see from her eyes that she had a very bad headache. She had become very important to him and must be looked after. The germ of an idea began to grow in his mind but he had sense enough to see that Kyra had had enough strain and worry for the day and would not

27

take kindly to his latest scheme, which was even more dangerous and daring than the last. How he wished he did not have to work through Kyra all the time. If only he had these powers himself! He wondered if she could teach him, but he knew she did not really know how they worked, nor even how to control them herself, although it seemed to him they were certainly growing. What she had done this day was so much more complicated than what she had ever been capable of before.

"Kyra," he said gently, "how do you do it?"

She looked at him questioningly.

"I mean . . . can you explain . . . what do you *do* to get into someone's head?"

"Nothing," she said sadly. "It just happens."

"But surely you notice something? . . ."

"No," she said firmly, "it just happens."

And she would say no more. He decided to leave it for the day and led her home. Their mother watched them coming slowly along the path and was ready with a sharp and voluble stream of abuse for their laziness in leaving her to do all their chores for a whole afternoon. They would not be drawn on where they had been and eventually she gave up trying to find out and settled for doubling their evening duties as punishment.

Karne, seeing that Kyra was near to dropping with fatigue, took over some of her tasks and let her crawl into her warm straw bed early.

Although he was tired too when he came to lie down he could not sleep for a long time. There was much to think about. A shaft of moonlight came through the doorway and fell upon Kyra as she lay sleeping, one pale arm outside the fur rug, lying beside her on the stamped clay floor, her face hollowed with shadow but curiously beautiful and peaceful.

"She is growing up," he thought. "It will not be long before she will be given in marriage." And he began to feel the urgency of what he wanted to do with her pressing upon him. But he knew that if he rushed her too much, worked her too hard, he could get nothing from her. It was like watching a plant grow, nothing would hurry it beyond its natural pace, though watering and care would help a little.

The Experiment

THE NEXT DAY Kyra would not talk of the matters of the previous afternoon. She avoided him and worked very hard and very close to her mother. He decided not to push her but to work on the background to his new plan by himself. When Ji and Okan called him to work on the boat he said he had more important things to attend to and that they could have the boat for fishing sometimes if they were prepared to spend time on it by themselves. They were overjoyed and rushed off to it at once.

He sought out one of the Elders of the Community, Faro, and set about questioning him as much as he dared. He wanted to know all there was to know about the Sacred Circle and the priest, and how often the priest visited the Circle. He really wanted to know when it would be safe for him and Kyra at the Circle. He also wanted to know if Faro could throw any light on the mystery Kyra had sensed surrounding the arrival of the new priest.

No one knew when he would arrive, Faro told him, but

he was expected soon. They all hoped Maal would not die before the new priest appeared.

"He does not seem ill," Karne said as casually as he could.

"That is because he is a brave man and knows how to hide it," Faro said. "Thorn says he is very ill and very near to death."

"How does the new priest know when it is the time to come?"

"The gods tell him."

"Where does he come from?"

"From the Temple of the Sun in the South."

"What is this Temple of the Sun? Is it for men or for gods?"

"It is for both. It is a place so holy that families of importance come from all over the world to worship and to bury their dead within sight of its Sacred Circle. But it is used for training as well and initiates from this land and from beyond the seas come to learn the mysteries from its powerful priesthood."

"It sounds a place of great wonder. How I would love to go there!"

"No one of our community has ever been there except the Lord Maal," Faro said. "He was trained there. He has told me of it."

"What did he tell you? What is it like?" Karne's voice was eager.

"There are many temples to our gods in our land but none so grand as The Temple of the Sun upon that southern plain. It is not just one Circle, but several. One is so filled with magic that it controls the sun and moon."

"How can that be? The Sun and Moon are gods! No man, however holy, can command obedience from them!"

Karne's face registered his amazement and old Faro was delighted at the attention he was getting.

"Ah, but in this holy place, the Stones are taller than you have ever seen and there is a god-like priest who commands the moon to disappear, even when it is full in the sky, blazing in all its glory, he commands it and it *disappears*!"

By the end of this sentence Faro's voice had risen from the low, hushed note of awe to a crescendo of triumph. He was enjoying impressing Karne.

The boy was truly shaken. These were wonders indeed.

"And from this place our new priest will come?" he asked, impressed.

"Not the very same. There is another Great Circle, part of the same Temple, but a day's hard walking from it. A Circle so great that we cannot conceive of it. I believe it has a wall of earth surrounding it that took a thousand men a thousand days to build."

"A wall of earth surrounding it?" Karne almost shouted, remembering Kyra's description of her experience in Maal's sleep-mind. "And many Standing Stones, much bigger than the ones we have?"

"Yes," Faro said, surprised.

"And many priests, not only one like ours?"

"Yes, many priests and many acolytes, initiates and students of all degrees."

Karne was sure this was the place. He was wildly excited and had great difficulty in stopping himself dancing about and hugging the bony old man.

"Has Maal ever been back there," he said, trying to restrain himself, "I mean . . . since he left as a young priest to come here?"

"It is a journey of many, many moons. Seasons of planting and of reaping would go by and still one would not arrive there."

"I know. I know it is a long way. But has he ever said he has been back there?"

"He has not left this village since he arrived here when I was young," Faro said with conviction.

Karne tried another tack.

"From whom does he receive his messages?" he asked, trying to sound casual.

"From the gods, of course," old Faro said impatiently, as though any fool would know that.

32

Karne thought about it for a while and was shrewd enough to know that he would not find out anything more from Faro. Faro, although a long-established Elder, did not know all there was to know.

Karne decided to speak directly to Maal.

During the next few days Karne watched for an opportunity to speak with the old priest every moment of his waking time. He volunteered to dig a certain field strip that had not been dug for years and consequently was particularly difficult, because it overlooked Maal's house. He broke many a sturdy digging stick and antler pick and worked until his back was aching. His father was amazed, but said nothing.

"Perhaps my prayers have been answered," he thought, "and Karne will settle to being a good farmer yet."

The boy's determined effort gave him some rewards. He learnt something of the priest's movements. Sunrise, sunset and midday seemed particularly holy times. Maal was often at the Sacred Circle then. He had heard from Faro, and indeed he knew from his own experience, certain rituals had to happen at night, but the times of these he could not figure out without the star knowledge possessed by the priest. He decided against the night for his plan. The priest's movements were too unpredictable then and the darkness, faced alone, too full of danger. There were nights when even the moon did not shine and on those nights the wolves and the spirits of darkness prowled freely.

On the third day of work on the field there was a time when Karne might have approached Maal directly. He could see the old man standing between the wooden entrance columns of his house, looking over the land to the far line of the sea. Karne fancied that he looked once or twice in his direction, and he could feel the old priest's gaze almost like a touch upon his skin, almost like an invitation.

The second time this happened Karne put his digging stick down and prepared to run the distance between

33

them, his heart pounding strangely, because what he was about to do was contrary to rule and custom in their community. But even as he took the first step the priest took a step back into the shadows, and Karne was unnerved. It would mean he would have to approach in full view of the old man, but Maal himself would not be visible to him. Karne hesitated, but he still might have dared to go ahead had he not seen Thorn approaching the house from the direction of the village. It must have been the sight of him that made Maal retreat so suddenly into the shadows.

Karne abandoned his plan, picked up his stick again and dug so viciously with it that he snapped it in half. He flung the pieces down with irritation, turned on his heel and strode back to his father's house.

"Kyra!" he said in a commanding tone that surprised even himself. "Come!"

He led her away from the place where she was scouring some earthenware bowls with sand and ash.

"What is it?"

She had to run to keep up with his striding pace.

"There is something I want you to do for me," he said with such determination that there seemed to be no question but that she would obey him.

"Not spying on the priest again!" she cried.

"No, not spying on the priest again."

She was relieved, but not for long.

"Karne, where are we going?" She realized suddenly they were making for the Sacred Circle again and approaching it from the side away from the village so that they could not be seen. "We are not going to the Sacred Circle?"

"Yes, we are. And this time you are going inside!"

Kyra stopped immediately, horrified.

"Karne!" she gasped. "You *cannot* mean it!"

"Yes, I do."

She turned to run, but he was too quick and too strong for her. He held her arm so tightly that she cried out with the pain.

"Karne, you are hurting me!"

34

He released his grip slightly, but did not let her go.

"Now listen, I have worked it all out. There will be nothing to fear."

"Then why do you not do it yourself?"

"Because I do not have the powers you have."

"I have no powers!" she cried miserably.

"You have. We both know you have. Think for a moment and stop crying like a baby. Would the gods have given you these powers, almost those of a priest, if they did not intend you to use them for their benefit?"

She was silent, knowing unhappily that he was somehow going to trap her into doing something she *knew* she should not do. He had always had this power over her. She loved him and she hated him at the same time and somehow he *always* won.

"You said yourself when you were listening to the Message about the new priest that you felt there was something wrong. No new priest is coming. The Elders believe he is coming. The community believe that he is coming. Maal even believes that he is coming. But you know he is not. This is important. You must find out what is going on. You are needed. You are our only hope of finding the truth."

"But I may have been wrong!"

"I hope you were. But we must make *sure*."

"But Maal's powers are great. He would not be misled or mistaken."

"How do we know that? He is an old sick man. We saw how his flesh hung loosely upon his bones, how pale his face, how he stumbled after the long night of Messages. His powers may not be as strong as they used to be. He may need our help."

"This is blasphemy!"

"No. Believe me, we do it for the gods' sake, for Maal's sake. I have seen him look at you. He *needs* you."

Kyra was silent. It was true he had looked at her in a way that was no ordinary way of looking. It was true that he was old and probably ill, otherwise there surely would be no talk of a new priest for their village. It was also true that she had the strangest feeling that she could not *see* a new priest coming. But how could she know if this was imagination or not? When she was having these strange "feelings" she was sure she was not imagining them, but once they were past she was not so sure.

Karne could see that she was hesitating, and he released her arm very gently. She rubbed it absent-mindedly where his grip had reddened her skin, but her attention was far away.

"But it is forbidden to enter the Circle if one is not an initiate of the priesthood or an Elder," she said at last, but her voice had no more serious protest in it.

Karne smiled, relieved, knowing that he had almost won.

"No one has forbidden us. It is just an old custom. I admit it would be wrong to go to a sacred place to play or fool about, but to find the truth to help one's people . . . that must surely be allowed!"

Kyra allowed herself to be led to the very rim of the Circle—and there she stopped.

"No," she said, "I cannot."

"You saw what Maal did that day. Do the same . . . see if it works. *Try*."

She seemed to be pulled from every direction now. She was standing close to the tall Stones and she could almost believe she felt them pulling her towards them. She was in many ways as curious as Karne to explore her capacities and find out more about the Mysteries, but she had a stronger respect for law and custom than her brother and feared the consequences of meddling with forbidden things.

His voice was soothing and his arguments convincing.

"Would it really harm," she thought, "to try?"

Still hesitating, she put her hand upon the nearest Stone, tentatively, compelled by curiosity. The Stone itself was taller than the tallest man she had ever seen. As her hand touched it her eyes were drawn to study it. The surface seemed cold and hard at first, like ordinary stone, and then began strangely to "hum" through her fingers, as

36

though it were forming a deep relationship with her which she would find hard to break. It had seemed grey from a distance, but when she looked at it closely it was a mass of crystals pressing together, black, white, silver and grey, their myriad surfaces glinting light in different intensities, from different angles, and through them all, running from earth to sky, from sky to earth, long intricate passages of crystal, ribs and paths and channels of crystal of dazzling whiteness. Her finger traced one of the lines upwards and she had the strangest feeling for a moment as though she herself was within the stone and somehow flowing upwards.

She withdrew her hand hastily and took a step back. Karne was close behind her and very gently, but very firmly, propelled her forward. Her shoulder rubbed against the Stone as she passed into the Circle and she noticed that her flesh tingled slightly. She fancied for a moment that the Stone could feel her presence as clearly as she could feel the presence of the Stone. But she did not think about this for long bcause she became aware that she, Kyra, was within the Sacred Circle and committed now beyond recall.

She was trembling and her heart was pounding with the enormity of the sacrilege she was committing, but somehow she was held within the Circle and could not have left even if she had tried.

Karne was outside, watching her anxiously, afraid now too that he had gone too far, but she was not aware of him. It seemed to her she was alone in all the world and no one could help her.

And then she remembered dimly Maal's movements on the day they had watched him and slowly, tentatively, she went to the first Stone and placed her forehead close against it as she had seen him do. She closed her eyes and waited, not knowing what to expect. She had chosen to start with the one she had already touched. Somehow she felt there was already a rapport there between them that would be less frightening than with the others. At first her own body was reacting so violently with fear she could

37

feel nothing but the racing of her blood and the pounding of her heart. But gradually the Stone seemed to take over and she quietened down, restful peace began to seep through her and as she went from Stone to Stone repeating the ritual, she grew calmer and calmer, till when she reached the final Stone she was in such a state of peace she had no recollection of her former doubts and fears and leaned as she had seen her master do as though it were the most natural thing in the world and she had done it often. She lay, relaxed and still, her arms stretched to their limits, but not straining. At first she felt nothing but peace and well-being, almost as though she were falling asleep on a grassy bank in the sunshine.

Karne watching had noticed the change in her and was frozen to the spot with interest. From being a frightened little girl, his sister had become a dignified and elegant woman, treading the ritual round of Stones like an initiate. He could see the calm confidence with which she laid herself in the last posture and was full of hope that the experiment would succeed. He noticed how still she became, how pale, but he reminded himself of the priest and refused to worry about her condition.

He sat on the grass outside the Circle and waited patiently for her to "return". He enjoyed the sun, the song of birds, the sea glinting and winking far away to the east. From time to time he looked back at his sister. She had not moved. The same still pallor was upon her. He longed to know what was "happening", but there was no way he could until she told him.

Suddenly he was shocked to see her jerk "awake" with tremendous force, her face distorted with fear. She half tumbled, half scrambled off the leaning Stone and almost fell out of the Sacred Circle into his arms. She was sobbing and clinging to him, at the same time beating him with her fists. He did not know whether to hold her off at arm's length, or hold her tight and comfort her.

"Why did you not *help* me!" she screamed. "You just *left* me there!"

"What? What!" He tried to ward off her blows. "How could I help?"

She sobbed and sobbed and he could get no sense out of her. But she stopped hitting him and he drew her down beside him on the grass and held her in his arms and tried to calm her.

"I want to go away from this place," she said, the little girl again. He decided not to say anything, but to help her to her feet and lead her away. When they were well away from the Circle and out of sight of it they sat down side by side and he tried to make her tell him what had happened.

"You just seemed to lie there. You looked peaceful enough. I did not know you were in any kind of trouble."

"It was horrible," she said, shuddering. "I thought I was dying."

"But Maal looked as though he was dying, but he was not," Karne said. "Did you not think of that?"

"I could not think of *anything*! It was so horrible!"

"What happened? Tell me about it."

"At first it felt all right," she said, sniffing slightly, "as though I was just falling asleep. But I did not fall asleep. I sort of *died*!"

"How do you mean?"

"Well, one moment I was lying there just the same as usual and the next moment my *body* was lying there but somehow *I* was not in it."

He raised his eyebrows.

"Were you in the place you saw when you were with Maal?"

"*No*. I was still here, in this Circle! I could see you as clearly as anything looking at the sea and some birds and not paying any attention to me, and I could see my body as clear as I could see you . . . only I was looking at it from *outside* and it looked dead. I tried to move my legs and arms but nothing would move. I tried to scream out to you but no sound would come. I even tried to open my eyes thinking that would make me wake up. But my eyelids would not move! And anyway I was not asleep. I really was awake, but I was not *in* my body."

"Are you sure you did not go anywhere else?" Karne asked, visibly disappointed.

"No!" she screamed. "You do not care about me at all! You just want your stupid questions answered. If I could not have returned to my body I would have *died*!"

"How did you get back?" Karne asked with interest.

"I do not know. I just tried and tried to get back in and suddenly there was a snap and I was *in* and everything was normal again except that I am never, *never* going to try that again!"

"I am sure it is a beginning," Karne said thoughtfully. "I mean . . . we could not expect you to do too much the first time . . ."

"It is not a *beginning*," she said vehemently, "it is an *end*!" And with that she stood up and marched off.

Karne remained sitting for a long time thinking about it all.

The Midsummer Festival

NOT LONG AFTER this the Chief Elder, Thorn, ordered the construction of Maal's burial mound. Maal asked for it to be sited on the line of earth power that ran invisible but straight as a spear throw from the Sacred Circle, along the processional route, through Maal's house, beyond and through an older burial mound, to the horizon where a notch had been cut in the skyline to lead the eye to sunset on Midsummer's Day.

Karne was among those deputed to gather stones of the right shape and size to line the tomb and the path leading to it. The actual construction was left to men who had the skill of building, the boys gathered the stones and piled them near the site. They worked in pairs and chatted cheerfully as they worked, not really thinking much about the purpose of their work.

Midsummer's Day was near approaching and there was much talk of the ceremonies and festivities that accompanied it. Dawn was always something special. Everyone

41

brought flowers to the Circle and Maal prayed and made obeisance to the Sun. There was singing and music and the whole day was holiday and pleasure. A great deal of barley ale was drunk, and there was dancing from the oldest to the youngest. By the evening they were all greatly tired and when the sun came to set directly into the notch on the hill it was a very solemn moment. The evening ceremony was a quiet one, and afterwards they wandered contentedly home to rest.

This year there was the added poignancy that it was Maal's last midsummer ceremony. Kyra went far into the forests in the south the afternoon before to gather some special white lilies she had set her heart upon. The forests were always considered dangerous places by the villagers because of the wild boars and other beasts and they did not venture there alone if they could help it. But Kyra was determined and she slipped away without anyone seeing her.

From the bright hillsides near her home it was as though she had entered a cave of dark and sinister green. It was much denser than the light woods she had known before and she could not help a moment of hesitation and fear. But the lilies hunters had once brought to the village from deep within the forest called to her and she plunged into the shadows trying to shut her mind to the dangers. Sometimes she heard the leaves rustling and twigs crackling as though creatures were lurking and moving in the undergrowth. She kept her attention sharp and moved quickly, making sure to note unusual things so that she would be able to find her way out again. After a long time searching she decided, tired, discouraged, filthy and scratched, to abandon the search. Hearing the whisper of water running she pulled aside some heavy and dangerously thorned branches to find a tiny stream picking its way carefully over moss covered stones to fall and disappear into a cleft in the rock. Drinking thankfully from it she could hear that it continued underground and longed to follow the intricate passage of its course, wondering what secret and beautiful delights of crystal and moss frond she would uncover. As she lifted her head from the water she met face to face the delicate, glowing whiteness of the very lilies she had been seeking. Breathlessly she stared at them, half afraid they were a vision and would disappear. But a very practical bee appeared and busied itself with one of them and that gave her courage to believe in their reality. She picked some, careful to leave enough behind for them to fruit and seed and reproduce themselves. The ends of the stems of those she had picked she wrapped in damp mossy earth to keep them fresh, and then she set off to find her way out of the forest again.

When she returned home just before nightfall, exhausted and very much muddied and scratched by thorns, but clutching triumphantly in her hands the lilies of her choice, her family realized where she had been and she was treated to a severe lecture on the dangers of the forest. But when she had finished her harangue, her mother hugged her close, greatly relieved that she was safe, and bathed her scratches herself as though she was a little child again, muttering many a tender phrase and name.

Karne brought rushes from the marsh in full flower and as tall as himself. Most of the rest of the family just picked the wild flowers from the hills and fields around. Even the baby had a little crown of daisies tied to its bald head. Karne could see it with its chubby hand trying to pull it off as they walked together as a family in the dim light just before dawn towards the Standing Stones.

Maal was there already. It is probable that he had been there all night. He was standing now in the dead center of the Circle facing east, his arms raised, his full ceremonial robes giving him a stature he did not normally possess.

One by one they arranged their offerings of flowers around the outside of the Sacred Circle. Kyra climbed to her special Stone, the one she had first touched, the one with the ribs of crystal pointing to the sky, bowed slightly and put her lilies at the foot of it. As she raised her eyes she met those of the priest looking directly into hers. She stood very still, feeling his mind closing in on hers. He was trying to tell her something, but the "noise" of all the other minds around was getting in the way. He was appealing to her, asking for her help, searching her for some way out, as though he were in some kind of trap.

She stood amazed. This could not be! She must be misinterpreting. She strained to catch something more specific but she could not. As more and more the general hubbub of the minds around intervened and pulled them apart she thought she caught the word "Thorn" several times and then something that sounded like "take care", and strangely she had a mental image of the sunset through the notch in the hills, but this time there seemed to be something in it . . . something dark. She could not make it out.

Someone pulled her back. She was too close to the Sacred Circle. It was against the custom for ordinary people to go so near to the Tall Stones.

"I see you put your lilies next to your Stone," Karne whispered to her as she joined him. Her face was troubled and she did not reply.

"What is the matter?"

She shook her head.

"It will not be long now," her mother said and they all began to turn towards the East. By the time the first running point of blazing gold appeared above the distant liquid line, the whole community was aware of it. A kind of gasp that seemed to come from one throat, but came from all in unison, greeted the god of Fire and Life. Maal lifted up his voice and the most beautiful hymn in the world, the hymn affirming life and the renewal of life forever, burst and rose upon the clean, clear air of the land. The gasp the people had given was the first note of the hymn and the last note was the people's too. Their voices rose above the priest's and seemed to fill the land from horizon to horizon. Tears came to Kyra's eyes. It was the most moving ceremony of the year and somehow this year it meant more to her than it ever had before. Somehow she was part of life's mysteries, life's renewal, life's magic.

Life would never again be for her a humdrum and meaningless daily routine of waking, chores, eating and sleeping. There was something more to it. Something she did not yet fully understand but which she knew would unfold to her as she grew, revealing with every unfolding something new and magnificent.

When the hymn was over and the sun fully risen one might say the secular festivities began. The women had prepared a special festival breakfast, the communal eating of which took up most of the morning. Karne's task was to help move the smooth, hot cooking stones from the fire into the hollowed log filled with water in which a special broth was boiling and back again to the fire when they had started to cool. He liked the way the water bubbled and boiled around the hot stones. But it was a tiring task and he was not sorry when he was relieved by his brothers.

After the meal there were the competitions, the log chopping, the pole climbing, the spear throwing, the steer catching, the dancing, the singing, the reciting of heroic poems handed down from their forefathers and extended by themselves.

The priest was not part of all this and Kyra did not see him again until he arrived for the sunset ceremony when everyone was more or less over-fed and worn out.

Karne was drunk on rough ale and impossible to talk to. He kept following one of the girls around, the one called Mia, the village flirt. She giggled at everything he said and Kyra felt sick that her brother looked at her with such eyes when there were girls like Fern present, tall and beautiful, thoughtful and dignified.

At the end of the afternoon the Elders gathered first and stood in front of their particular Stones very impressively. The tardy and somewhat dishevelled villagers gradually gathered themselves together for the last big event of the day, the sunset.

Maal approached with dignity.

The sky had become somewhat overcast without anyone paying it much attention. Now, however, there was some speculation that they would not be able to see the sunset in the special place because of the ominous black clouds that were gathering in the West. In fact the approaching storm lent drama and splendour to the scene. The clouds were broken enough for the dazzling light of the dying sun to illumine them in strange and royal ways. Purple and crimson were the predominant colours, where gold and silver and mother-of-pearl had been the gentler colours of the dawn.

Where the sky was not black and sullen with the weight of brooding storm, it was rent with blazing flame and flagged in purple and red. Directly above the notch on the hill there were no clouds at all, but a weird and sickly green.

The villagers grew very quiet as they turned to look at the West. While the morning sun had lifted up their hearts to joy and hope, the evening one was causing depression and despair. Kyra could not see Maal's face, but she was thinking of the experience of the morning and was watching for the sunset with some anxiety. The warning she had felt she sensed from Maal had something to do with the sunset. Perhaps it was the storm. Perhaps the storm would do great damage to their crops and houses. A rumble of distant thunder disturbed the air that had become so thick and silent. The sun sank blood red into the hole in the hill. Maal's voice, deeper than usual, droned the incantations of the evening, and for a moment as the great orb touched the hill they saw silhouetted against its fiery furnace a small but distinct black figure.

Kyra remembered the vision of the morning in a flash. Strange. Strange. A man standing in the sun!

How she longed to talk to Karne. This once when she would have liked to discuss matters with him he was incapable of it. She looked for him despairingly and he was standing as she had thought he would be with his arm round Mia, who was simpering and not even looking at the sunset.

How could it be!

She looked back to the hill but the figure had gone. The sun itself was sinking fast.

After it was over everyone started talking at once. It seemed most people had seen the figure, but some refused to believe that it had been there. Others believed, took it as an omen, and were afraid.

Thorn, the Chief Elder, lifted his impressive arms for silence and when he had obtained it, spoke in a loud and awesome voice.

"The man you saw walking in the furnace of the sun is the priest for whom you wait."

A stunned silence followed his words.

Kyra looked beyond Thorn at Maal. He seemed to have shrunk in size. Thorn had spoken in his place, with his authority. No one seemed to notice it but Kyra. She remembered the half-formed warnings of the morning . . . "take care" . . . and "Thorn" . . . and the vision of the black mark in the setting sun.

There were things she needed to understand.

The Arrival of Wardyke

THE COMING of the new priest brought a great deal of excitement to the small community.

Midsummer's night had been, as the sunset foreshadowed, a night of violence and storm. After the dramatic disclosure by Thorn that it was indeed their new priest who stood upon the hill, a deputation of villagers was sent to welcome him and guide him safely through the night to his new home. The father of Karne and Kyra was one of those chosen and the two young people stood beside their mother watching the flickering torches as the small group set off into the rapidly spreading darkness. As they reached certain high points on the track they lit beacons and the Sacred Circle itself was ringed with flame till it looked to Kyra like the flickering spectre of the Sun god itself.

Usually when darkness came to the land and the sea the people were safely in their homes, but this night, wild as it was, saw the whole community still upon the hills. At first the numerous fires upon the earth made up for the lack of stars and moon but as the wind rose that was the harbinger of the storm the flames were whipped every way, pulled and torn by the demons of the night, till some of them could hold their own no more and were extinguished. The villagers were afraid, but hesitated to leave.

Maal stood still within the Circle as though in trance. They could see his figure with its giant shadow intermittently as either the flames or the growing frequency of the lightning illuminated it.

Thorn and the other Elders stood at the entrance to the Circle and exhorted them to put more wood upon the fires.

Karne, sober now, worked energetically, Kyra at his side.

The women and smaller children were sent back to the huts and Kyra could see them as a sudden sheet of lightning lit the valley, scattering like leaves before the wind, wailing a high-pitched wail of fear.

She herself was very much afraid, but was determined not to give way to it. As long as Maal is there, she thought, he is in control. Concentrated in his body, through the Circle, through the inexplicable forces she had sensed in the Standing Stones, was a power that held chaos at bay. Around them, moving darkness was ripping at the trees, tearing the very roots from the soil, shaking and pulling and whirling, trying to reduce their ordered community to a scattering of useless fragments. But the centre held, the Circle held. *Somehow* they were held together. They were stronger than the demons of the air.

Was the power, the magic, that held them still working against the forces of disorder and disintegration, in the Stones themselves, in the shape of the Circle itself (the divine and perfect shape), or was it in the man within the Circle holding them together with the powers within himself, the powers of which she had only recently become aware?

She found herself smiling, in spite of the situation, thinking that she was becoming as curious about things, as questioning about the hidden mysteries, as Karne himself. Her brother would be proud of her.

49

Even as she thought of him he looked up from his work at her.

"Come on," he said, "stop standing about and give me a hand with this log!"

She bent to the work willingly. Moving logs was certainly easier than trying to answer questions.

They expected rain any moment, but strangely rain did not come. The main weight of the storm seemed to fall elsewhere and the wind, the weird flashing of lightning over the hills and the growling of the thunder in the neighbouring valleys showed that the night demons were satisfied with the role of warning and frightening for the moment.

As the storm moved off to the south, their fires grew stronger and the Stone Circle stood up clear against the immense blackness of the sky. Their hearts began to lift and there was talk amongst them about the coming changes. All were curious about the new priest. Maal had been with them so long it was almost impossible to imagine how it would be with a different priest.

"Of course the rituals will be the same," someone said.

"Will there be new Elders chosen?"

Kyra pricked up her ears at this. She had never realized it before this day, but she had never really liked Thorn. It would be no bad thing if new Elders were chosen.

"No," someone replied. "Elders are chosen for life." Kyra's heart sank. "Only death or disgrace releases them from their duties."

"Besides, who would we choose? Those already chosen are the best men we have."

"Ay," murmured someone else, "Thorn knows the ways of this village better than the priest does."

"That is blasphemy," came a voice from the shadows.

"It may be blasphemy," one of Kyra's uncles said with a laugh, "but it also happens to be true!"

"Ay!"

There seemed to be general agreement on this.

50

Kyra thought about what she had heard and she thought about Thorn. As long as she could remember he had ruled the village. Everything that had been done had been on his command. It is true he always spoke as though he was only delivering a message from Maal, but what proof had they that Maal's messages were being delivered honestly? She was shocked at herself for daring to think such a thought and looked round hastily, worried that someone might have caught it from her mind. But she need not have worried. Her kind of talent was very rare indeed.

What did she know of Maal? He was an old man, very much revered and honoured. So much so that no one dared speak to him, except Thorn and the Elders. She had seen him walking about the place from time to time. When he passed, the villagers bowed and kept silent. No one spoke to him. As far as she knew there was no law that said they could not speak to him, it was just a matter of respect and diffidence. Even when he came to their homes when there was illness, Thorn came with him and Thorn did most of the talking. But it was Maal who put his long gentle fingers on the ailing person and it was Maal who did the healing.

Kyra had seen such a healing once. A friend of her mother's was in great pain. Her husband brought Maal to her and the priest stood quietly by her for a while and then placed his hands upon her, bowed his head and closed his eyes.

The woman looked up for the first time as though she were aware of someone else in the world. She looked into his eyes and Kyra would never forget the dawning trust and peace that spread over her face. After he left she stood up and went about her chores.

Kyra remembered thinking that of all the powers in the world, the power of healing was the one she wanted most.

It was almost sunrise before the new priest arrived. Kyra and Karne were with the group of villagers still tending the fires and so were present when he and the deputation that had been sent to meet him arrived. From time to time they had taken it in turn to doze off so they were not too weary. Kyra was still asleep, curled up in a small hollow of grass, Karne's fur jerkin tucked round her, when the shout went up that greeted his arrival. She leapt up immediately, somewhat dazed, momentarily having forgotten where she was and what was going on. She was in time to see the new priest, immensely tall and broad, striding up the processional way alone, long cloak flowing, head held high, eyes blazingly fixed upon Maal still standing in the dead centre of their Sacred Circle. Above and behind him, as though his presence had disturbed them and his power was calling them from the secret places of the earth, an immense flock of crows was beating across the sky. Kyra looked up in alarm and in the half light of dawn, the crows, the flowing cloak, the hugeness of the man, all served to make her shiver. Karne put his arm around her.

"Cold, little sister?" he whispered gently. But even he could sense something did not *feel* right and he was cold too. They stood very close together trying to take warmth from one another.

"Is he not *huge*?" Kyra whispered.

"More like a warrior than a priest," Karne replied.

The man had reached the Circle and Maal stood like a Standing Stone himself challenging him with his eyes. The man paused as though for a moment he had encountered an invisible barrier. Kyra and Karne hardly breathed, they were watching with such fascination. They no longer dared even to whisper. Karne increased the pressure of his arm on his sister's waist and she nodded. Yes, she *had* noticed. Yes, she *was* trying to find out what was going on.

Thorn now stepped forward beside the man and together they stood confronting Maal.

Kyra put her hands to her head, pain searing through it.

"No!" she cried within herself, "no, I cannot!"

Maal was calling her to stand beside him, to add her strength to his. But she was afraid. Afraid she was not

52

really hearing the call but imagining it, afraid of what she could sense but could not understand, afraid of getting involved in something beyond her capacities. Even afraid she might make a fool of herself.

"What is it?" Karne's brotherly voice broke through the roaring of her inner voices. He shook her slightly.

"Kyra! Are you all right?"

Her face was filled with fear and pain. Her arms were over her head as though she was fending off something.

"Oh Karne," the tension broke with tears and she clung to him. "Oh Karne . . . I cannot . . . he cannot expect me to . . . he cannot . . . I would not know what to do . . . I am not ready . . ."

"What is it? Tell me!"

He tried to lift her face and look into her eyes but they were obscured by tears and she could say nothing but "I cannot" and try to hide her face. He held her close, bewildered, but knowing that she needed comfort. He turned his head to see if anything in the scene before them would give him a clue to her behaviour. Much had changed since he had last looked.

"Kyra," he gasped, "look!"

The new priest was within the Circle now, in the centre, facing East, his arms raised to the ocean where the sun would soon be rising. Thorn and the Elders with heads bowed were in their ritual places by the Stones. Maal had disappeared.

"Kyra!"

Kyra looked and saw.

She spun round and looked back along the processional way, tears forgotten now. The figure of Maal, ignored by all his community, small, steps somewhat unsteady, was making its way towards the pile of stones that had been gathered for his burial mound.

She began to run.

When she reached him he was sitting on one of the larger stones, contemplating the pile, looking no longer like a priest, mighty in magic and mystery, but like a very tired, old man who had decided to give up trying.

53

Out of breath she arrived and stood a little distance from him, watching. He did not seem to notice her but went on staring at the pile of rocks, his head turned from her. They stayed so, in that configuration, for some time.

Then he said, very distinctly and calmly, without turning his head, without apparently having seen her approach, "Come, my child," and he indicated another stone beside the one that he was on. "Sit awhile."

She approached like a shy fawn, step by step, watching him, ready to take off at any sign of anything untoward. He did not turn his head towards her until she was seated near him and then he looked at her with great gentleness and tenderness. As her eyes met his she opened her mouth and tried to say all the things that were hurting in her heart. The regrets, the fears, the apologies.

He held up his hand and stopped her before one word could leave her lips.

"I know, my child," he said quietly, "you were not ready. I should not have asked you."

So she had not imagined his voice calling to her!

She dropped her head and sat very quietly, gradually becoming more relaxed and peaceful in his presence.

It seemed to her now, as the first rays of the sun crept across the landscape and rested upon his white hair, that she had known him always. This was no strange god-like creature, remote from her everyday life, this was someone she *knew*.

She looked up with the realization and met his eyes again.

They were as old as the hills . . .

But so were hers!

The Questioning

THE NEW PRIEST took over vigorously and from the time of his arrival not much was seen of Maal in public places.

The younger man strode about in the village and in the fields beyond, surveying the narrow strips of cultivated grain the villagers worked, the cattle they owned, the wood and straw houses they had constructed. He was interested in finding out all he could about their ways. And wherever he went Thorn followed him, explaining things.

Wardyke (for that was his name) nodded imperiously at the people he passed but did not speak to them. Wherever he went, whomever he met bowed the head and knee to him and did not dare to look into his eyes. It was well known that if you looked directly into the eyes of a priest-magician he could see your inmost thoughts and had power over you.

The villagers were delighted with the novelty of change and there was talk of little else in the evenings when the families gathered from their work to enjoy the evening meal. Karne and Kyra's family were no exception.

"He will be a good priest," Karne's father said.

"We had need of a change," Karne's eldest brother Thon spoke boldly, aware that he was offering a tacit criticism of Maal and that this normally would be construed as blasphemy. He was aware also that the tide had imperceptibly turned against Maal and he would not now be called to account for it.

Kyra spoke up suddenly.

"Why?"

Everyone looked at her.

"I mean . . . why do we have need of a change? Maal has always served us well."

"He is very old, dear," her mother said soothingly, sensing a quarrel building up.

"It is not just his age," Thon said, "he was incompetent as well."

"I do not agree," said Kyra fiercely.

"What about the drought last year? We lost most of our grain."

"And the storm this Spring," her father interjected.

"He did his best! The gods to not *always* give what the priest asks. We do not know the ways of the gods. There may have been a reason why the harvest should fail last year."

"What reason?" Thon jeered.

"Perhaps . . ." Kyra thought desperately for a possible reason, but it was Karne who unexpectedly gave her one. He had been listening very carefully to the talk while he was eating.

"If the grain had not failed," he said thoughtfully, "we would never have learned that those plants in Fern's garden were so good to eat."

"And if we had not had that storm in the Spring," Kyra cried triumphantly, "we would not have had those giant trees blown down in the forest to use for building."

"Nor the animals to eat that were driven out of the forest by the storm practically on to our spears," Karne added.

"Nor the houses blown down . . ." Thon said sourly.

56

"Well, the houses that we rebuilt are much better than the old ones ..." Kyra was still defiant.

"Nor the water-logged earth that spoiled our first planting ..." Thon persisted.

"We planted again ... There was no real harm done ... and besides, Bera and Finn would not have fallen in love and married if they had not been trapped together for so long during the storm ..."

"But that is not the *point*," Karne's father intervened here. "The point is that a competent priest would not have *let* those things happen!"

"Maal is a competent priest," Kyra insisted. "There are just some things that have to happen, priest or no priest. There are reasons for everything. It is just that we cannot always *see* them."

"But the priest should see them and it is his task to explain things he cannot avert!" Thon said.

"No, I do not agree with that," Karne's mother interrupted.

"What do you not agree with?" Her husband looked at her sharply.

"I think the priest should see the reasons even if we cannot, but I do not think he has any duty to explain them to us."

"I wish there was more explanation of things," Karne said regretfully. "There are so many things I want to understand."

"It is not your *place* to understand," his father said. "Your place is to work for your family and worship the gods. It is enough that Maal, and now Wardyke, understand things. I must say I feel Wardyke will be good for the village."

"Maal used to come amongst us more," Karne's mother said musingly. "I remember when my children were born he came to bless them and talked quite a bit to me."

"What did he say?" Karne asked eagerly.

"Oh, I cannot remember ... it is such a long time ago. He hardly said a word the last time he came."

"Please try and remember," begged Kyra.

"Something about new life being precious, coming from the past, going to the future . . . everything linked in some way . . . tied . . . so everything . . . even my scrawny little baby howling its head off . . . is of vital importance to the Whole. I did not listen much, I must admit, I was feeling so embarrassed that he was in our humble house and everything was in such a mess."

"Oh mother!" cried Kyra impatiently.

"Did he say much when I was born?" Karne asked.

His mother thought for a while.

"He stood looking at you for a long time and then made the blessing sign. Then he said, 'This child has the strength to be a leader among men. Pray that before he leads he may be well led.' "

"And I? What did he say when I was born?" Kyra asked anxiously.

"I remember when you were born," Thon said. "I was hungry and I thought Maal would never leave."

"Yes, that is when he did most of the talking about everything being important and everything being dynamically (you see I remembered that word!), dynamically part of everything else. He went on and on . . ."

"What did I do?" Kyra was passionately interested in every detail.

"You just howled and howled as though this was the most miserable experience of your life. You were such a sickly, mewling creature I was not at all sure you were going to live. Maal said you were. And you did!"

"You see he is not so incompetent after all!" Kyra said, pleased.

"Oh, in those days," her father said, "we had no complaints. But lately he seems to have withdrawn himself more and more from the people. He stays in his house most of the time or walks in the hills by himself."

"He performs all the rituals well," Kyra said quickly in Maal's defence.

"True. But he used to do more."

"He used to speak comfort to us on days that were not

ritual days," her mother said. "But now he never seems to know when we need him."

"He came when Nidav was killed by the boar."

"Big things he still knows about. But before he used to know about the little things as well. He just seemed to know and care . . . about everything."

"Well," said Kyra defiantly, "I will be interested to see if Wardyke knows and cares about the little things!"

"Why are you so against the new priest?" Kyra's mother asked worriedly.

"I am not against him. It is just that I like Maal. There is something about him I trust."

"But surely you trust Wardyke? He was chosen by the gods and specially trained for our community."

"Yes, that may be true . . ." Kyra's voice carried no conviction.

"Enough of this talk!" The head of the household remembered his position. "Next we will be criticizing the gods!"

Kyra's mother threw up her hands in horror at such a thought.

"Then we are surely finished!" she said.

The next day Kyra took Karne aside and told him all that had transpired between Maal and herself on Midsummer's Day and the following dawn.

"What happened then?" he asked with curiosity. She had stopped talking when she had told him how she had felt Maal and she were as old as each other and that she had known him before.

"I do not know," she said sadly.

"What do you mean?"

"I just sat there . . . feeling those things . . . and I could not think of any words to say them in . . . and he just sat there not speaking . . . so after a time . . ."

"Yes?"

"I just walked away."

Karne looked annoyed and disappointed.

"You would!" he said bitterly.

59

"Do not be angry, Karne," she said miserably. "I have no one but you to tell these things to . . . no one but you to help me . . . and besides . . ." and here her voice took an upward turn with a hint of resentment in it, "besides . . . it was you who got me involved in the first place!"

"Nonsense!" He denied it vigorously as he felt a twinge of guilt. "You were involved by just being *born* . . ."

She sighed deeply.

There was silence between them for a while as they both tried to work the situation through in their own way.

Kyra was thinking how much she would like to speak to Maal and ask him outright the answers to all the questions that were now bothering her as much as Karne.

"I think our next move," Karne spoke slowly and with deliberation, "is to try and see Maal privately, without Thorn around, and talk to him, ask him outright the things we want to know."

"Oh Karne, do you think we can?" Kyra was relieved he was making the decisions.

"Yes, that is what we will do," Karne continued his line of thought, almost as though Kyra was not there. "I should have done this years ago . . . it was just that he seemed so difficult to approach . . ."

"I know. I think mother is right. He has withdrawn himself the last few years more than I remember when I was small."

"I tried to talk to him a little while ago . . . the time when Thorn announced that a new priest would be arriving and you said you felt that there was something wrong . . ."

"What happened?"

"I was just about to go to his house . . ."

"Karne!" Kyra was shaken at the daring of this.

". . . When I saw Thorn on the path."

"And then?"

"And then . . . nothing. I thought I had better leave."

"I wonder about Thorn . . . there is something about him . . ." Kyra's voice was puzzled.

60

"He seems to have organized everything . . . the new priest . . . everything . . ."

"And he talks about Maal's death as though it is prearranged!"

"I noticed that," Karne said thoughtfully.

"And Wardyke frightens me," Kyra said with a shiver, her mind running on.

"I think," Karne said slowly, "I would have accepted Wardyke quite happily if it had not been for the strange things you have been feeling. He seems right enough as a priest. I mean, he looks as I imagine a priest to look. I cannot sense anything wrong with him. Everyone else seems to like him."

"There is *something*, Karne, I am sure of it," Kyra said worriedly. "Or rather, sometimes I am sure of it. At other times, I do not know. Oh Karne . . . I am so confused!"

Karne put his arm around her shoulders.

"All right, little sister, calm down. We will go and see Maal about it."

"Now?"

She looked up, alarmed.

"Why not? While we are in the mood."

"I do not think we should . . ." She had lost all her conviction and courage.

"I think we should," said Karne firmly.

"But what are we going to do?"

Kyra ran along beside her striding brother, still flustered with anxiety about the whole project.

"We cannot just go in to his house and demand to speak with him!"

"Luckily that will not be necessary," Karne said.

She looked questioning.

"I saw him set off for the hills when we left home. If we hurry we may be able to come upon him as though by accident."

Kyra was relieved. This was certainly easier than braving the mysteries of the dark interior of his house, but she had her doubts that they would come upon him "by accident".

The day was hot and pleasant, the birds busy about their songs, the villagers peacefully pursuing their age-old customs in the valley, content that they were well protected from all harmful spirits by the ministrations of their new and mangificently tall guardian-priest.

The hills to the north of their village were rocky and wild, but there was quite a walk before one even reached them. Karne began to wish that they had brought some refreshment with them. He stopped when he found a little brackish stream running through the heather and had a drink, and then he plunged his whole head into it to cool himself and shook the water from his hair like a dog. After her drink Kyra sat on the bank with her sandalled feet dangling in the water, her eyes on the hills, thinking . . .

Once they started climbing they were soon above the spring line and there was no more water to be found, but the views around them were almost as refreshing as drink to Kyra.

Karne was just about to say that they must be prepared for a long hard day as they had no way of knowing exactly where the old priest had gone to find his solitude, when he noticed that Kyra was walking purposefully as though she knew exactly where she was going. Having faith in her strange powers, although not understanding them, he fell back so that he was walking behind her, following her lead.

At first she cut straight across the rough heather and their legs were sorely torn by the tough little branches. At one time she even disappeared to her shoulders in a sudden hole, the heather having hidden it from her sight, but Karne, after laughing at her discomfiture, soon had her out and on her way again. After that experience she went slower and picked her way more carefully, but she showed no sign of being uncertain of the direction to take.

She found a track and followed its meanderings for a long way. In the distance, further to the north, a lake was gleaming like a jewelled clasp in the folds of a soft blue cloak.

About noon they found Maal sitting on a granite boulder gazing into the distance. He turned to them as they arrived but showed no surprise that they should be there.

The two young people flung themselves down at his feet, exhausted and somewhat out of breath. No words were spoken, but even Karne could feel they were not unwelcome.

The silence went on for so long that Karne began to wonder if the other two were communicating in some way without words. He looked hard at both of them, but he could not notice anything. They were both sitting, relaxed and peaceful, gazing at the beauty of the ever receding lines of hills and valleys that stretched away through every shade of blue to the northern horizon.

He decided it was up to him to take the initiative.

He stood up.

"We have come," he said firmly, "to ask you many questions."

Maal looked at him with his piercing eyes, but they were not unfriendly. Karne remembered how he had been warned when he was a small boy never to look directly into a priest's eyes. He was half afraid, but his own determination to find out all that he wanted to know sustained him in his purpose.

"What is it that you wish to know?" Maal asked quietly.

Karne hesitated. Where to begin? There was so much he wanted to know.

"To phrase the right questions is as difficult as to provide the right answers." Maal smiled quietly as he spoke.

He was right. Karne had never realized it before. Somehow he had never had difficulty asking questions in the past, but that might have been because they were not so important or, if they were, that there was not much chance of their being answered.

He knew now the old priest would answer his questions and the answers might change the course of his life. He must be careful what he asked.

In that moment, as he stood upon the hill, with the rocks and the wild plants around him, the lake now a shining eye staring blankly at the sky, he knew the answer to at least one of his questions. He knew why it was that the community was content to let the priest carry the burden of knowledge, the Mystery of Mysteries, by himself. They were afraid that, if they knew what he knew, more would be required of them than was required by the comfortable round of daily chores, the friendly chat, the warming hearth fire. They were deliberately preventing their own development, afraid of what the next step would demand of them. By facing the priest, asking to enter his Secret Knowledge, he, Karne, was taking a step from which there would be no going back. The way to deeper and deeper understanding was through deeper and deeper commitment.

As these thoughts came crowding upon him he felt shaken and breathless, almost as though they had entered his mind by physical force. He took a deep breath and looked first at Kyra and then at Maal.

They were both sitting quietly looking at him, and it was as though they were together and he was a stranger.

"What shall I do?" he asked helplessly, as though he had spoken his other thoughts aloud and they knew what they were.

"It has to be your decision," Maal said.

Karne turned away from them and strode about on the rough hill top, trying to sort out in his mind this new development. All the time he was doing this they sat very still. It was almost as though they were part of the hill, the rock, the growing things, the air. And he, the intruder, was stirring things up, bringing change and discord.

At last he stopped and faced Maal, his decision made. He wanted to know. No matter what happened.

And as he made this decision all the sense of being torn apart by discord ceased. He joined them in their calm acceptance of what must be.

Maal lifted his hand and made a gesture for Karne to sit. Karne sat.

"Your first question?" Maal asked with a smile.

"Who is Wardyke," Karne said immediately, "and why are we afraid of him?"

"Two questions," Maal said mildly.

"They *are* connected," Kyra spoke up for Karne.

Maal smiled again, sadly this time.

"Yes, they are connected," he said, and was silent so long Karne was beginning to think he would not answer. Kyra and he looked at each other, uncertain what to do, wondering if they should repeat the question. But they need not have worried. The old priest was preparing to speak at last.

"I do not know who Wardyke is, but I know he is not the priest who was chosen and trained for you."

Kyra took a sharp breath at this. This confirmed her impressions.

"You mean he is not from the Temple of the Sun?"

"He has been there. He knows much of the mysteries that are taught there, but he does not carry with him the final mark of the priest."

"What is that?" Kyra asked quickly.

Maal looked at her closely.

"You will know that mark one day."

"Why not today?" Karne's curiosity had made him bold, but Maal was not to be drawn on matters he had decided were not yet for them to know.

"Did you know that a new priest was coming before Thorn announced it?" Kyra asked.

"Yes, I have known for some time. It is the way."

"Is it because you are getting old?" Kyra tried to soften the harshness of the question by the gentleness of her voice and expression.

Maal bowed his head in affirmation.

"Thorn says you are ill?"

"I am tired and I must move on. There is other work that I must do."

"Another community?" Karne asked.

"No."

"I thought you said . . ."

"I did not."

"But . . . but surely that is what you meant?"

"You cannot know what I meant until you know a great deal more than you do now." Maal's voice was sharp. Karne was momentarily silenced.

Kyra spoke up.

"Please," she said, "I know we should not be questioning you like this. But you *did* call for my help . . . and I need to know . . ."

Maal's face softened. He looked affectionately at her.

"You are right, my child. I owe you much and will owe you more before the sun is back to its full height. But I cannot tell you now everything I have taken many years to learn."

"Tell us at least more about Wardyke and how we can help."

Maal was silent again at this, thinking hard.

"I think," he said at last, "the way you can help me most is for Kyra to go once more into the Sacred Circle . . ."

At this Kyra flushed slightly. So he *had* known of their trespass!

". . . and," he continued, "take a message for me to the Lords of the Sun."

"But how . . .?" Kyra was bewildered and frightened. "How can I?"

"And who are the Lords of the Sun?" Karne asked breathlessly.

"Across the world, in places beyond even your imaginings . . ."

"Beyond the sea?" Karne interrupted.

"Yes, even beyond the sea and beyond the lands on the other side of the sea . . . there are people believing as we do in the Sacred Mysteries, and amongst them some have been chosen as Lords of the Sun. Their training is long and arduous, but they have great powers and can see

66

much that is closed to even the most highly trained priest."

"But surely," Karne said, noticing Kyra's terrified face. "*You* should be in touch with them. How can Kyra possibly . . . ?"

"Wardyke knows this is what I want to do. He will not let me near the Sacred Circle."

Maal spoke with conviction.

It was true. They had noticed and remarked that Maal had not been near the Sacred Circle since Wardyke had arrived.

"But . . . it is not guarded. Perhaps you could get in some time when Wardyke is not there."

Maal smiled and shook his head.

"It is not so easy, my children. Wardyke is a powerful magician and has cast an invisible ring of force around the Stones so that they will not admit me."

Kyra gasped.

"But what about me?"

"Wardyke does not realize you could be a threat to him. There is no ring of force cast to keep *you* out."

Kyra looked miserable. It became clearer and clearer that somehow a great deal was expected of her and she did not feel at all confident that she could fulfill Maal's expectations.

"But . . ." Karne realized her predicament. "Even if she does manage to pass unnoticed into the Circle . . ."

"As she did before," Maal said with a sudden twinkling smile.

"As she did before," Karne admitted. ". . . But last time she tried to travel in the mind as you had done she could not manage it and nearly died."

Maal nodded.

"I know," he said. "I would not ask if there were another way."

"Besides," said Karne with sudden inspiration, "if Wardyke is a magician, so are you! It is part of being a priest."

"Yes!" cried Kyra joyfully, thinking she saw a way out.

Maal shook his head sadly.

"I have been neglecting the magic aspects of my priesthood for many years now, and could not compete with Wardyke."

"But why?" Kyra cried accusingly.

"Because, my child, I found something more important."

What could be more important than magic! Karne would have given his right arm to be able to practice magic effectively.

"I used to think, as you do, that the practice of magic was of great importance and gave me great power. One day I tried to use my magic on a traveller from a far-off land, he was a merchant bringing flints from the south, a simple man I thought. We met on these very hills and fell into conversation. He challenged me as priest to perform magic for him. Being foolish I chose to accept the challenge and said I could ring him with an invisible wall of force through which he could not step. It was very similar magic to the one Wardyke now has wrought on me. I know I should not have used my priesthood knowledge for an idle trick, but he was mocking our religion and the ancient mysteries and I wanted to prove him wrong. I performed the rites perfectly and confidently expected him to be trapped within the ring. But he was not. He walked out of it with a smile and said, and this I will never forget, 'Your magic is worked around my body. You forget I am spirit and am everywhere'.

"I sat till it was dark upon these hills and thought about it.

"He was right, and what he had said I had always known.

"Indeed, this I had been taught in the Temple of the Sun, but somehow it had become overlaid by all the ritual and the magic tricks so that they had become the most important part of my religion to me. It was as though I had been given a great and precious Truth wrapped in layers of dry straw, and I had come to believe the straw was the Truth.

"Much of what he had said in criticism of our religion began to make sense to me. I resolved to throw away the straw and find the inner gift of Truth.

"But in doing this I made yet another mistake.

"I was so continually searching into the depths of my own Being to find 'the spirit that is everywhere', that is more powerful than magic, and that nothing can cage if it has the will to be free, that I sought solitude, I resented the intrusion of people, of duties, of anything that distracted me from my purpose. Before, I had neglected the inner life by concentrating on the outer; now I neglected the outer by concentrating too much on the inner. To me the whole of material existence became unimportant. Only spirit mattered.

"But this is not as it should be. Spirit and matter are part of the same Whole: different manifestations of the same God. The same Source. Each develops because of the other, not in spite of the other. We are not material form for no reason, as we are not spirit for no reason. We must use both. We must learn from both.

"I see this now, but it too late."

"What do you mean—too late?" Kyra said. She had strained to understand what he had been saying. It was not easy, but she thought she grasped some of it. The rest she stored in her mind to think about later.

"I have had my chance as your priest and I have failed."

They both opened their mouths to protest but he raised his hand to silence them. It was strange to think a priest could make mistakes like any common man.

"If I had my time again, knowing what I know now, I would be a better priest to your community. No. Say nothing. Time, an ambitious Elder and an unscrupulous impostor-priest have forced me to see where I was wrong. I left a gap which Wardyke could fill. I should have taught this community to rely on the living truth and the individual power of their own Eternal Selves so that *no one* could come and take them over as Wardyke has done.

"But my time in this life is used up. I can pursue the matter further only in another life."

"You mean you are going to die?" Kyra asked in a hushed voice.

"You may call it dying if you wish."

There was silence between them for a while.

"And you cannot use magic any more?"

"I cannot and I will not."

"But if it would help . . . ?"

"It would only help the immediate future—if at all. We must not defeat Wardyke with magic, it is too temporary a measure. We must defeat him by growing in ourselves till we are greater in inner strength than he. Till his magic circles will have no effect upon us, as they did not upon that flint merchant."

"But it has taken you *years* and you still have not managed it!" Kyra said wonderingly. "What chance have we?"

"Every chance. You have not made the mistakes I have made. You come fresh and strong to the task. I will help you and necessity will give you wings."

"But if we cannot . . ."

"You forget we plan to call upon the Lords of the Sun."

Karne decided that it was time for practicalities.

"What is the first move we should make?" he asked.

"I may be able to pass within the Circle without his seeing me," Kyra remembered her terrifying tasks, "but how do I reach the Lords of the Sun?"

"I will have to teach you many things. It will not be easy, and it will not be safe, particularly for someone who has had no training in the Temple of the Sun."

Kyra looked even more miserable, and even Karne was beginning to think the whole thing was becoming too difficult.

"Would it not be possible . . ." Kyra started tentatively and then stopped.

70

"Would what not be possible, my child?"

"I mean . . . how do we know Wardyke is really bad? Does it matter very much that he has not the final mark of the priest upon him?"

"The final mark is put upon a priest when he has passed the most stringent moral tests. Without that mark it is possible the priest has all the powers of priesthood, but there is no guarantee he will use them for the good of the people.

"If Wardyke has been refused the final mark, that means the High Priest of the Temple of the Sun thought he was capable of the misuse of his powers, and that means that your people are in danger."

"The very fact that he put up that ring of force to keep you out of the Circle is a bad sign," Karne said.

"Certainly it is. I think we should start Kyra's training as soon as possible. She has much to learn."

She looked so wretched and so small, he put his hand on her shoulder and through his fingers she felt the warm flowing of his own confidence in her, his love and need of her.

She bowed her head. So be it.

At least she would try.

The Training of Kyra

AS THE WEEKS WENT BY Karne and Kyra became more and more deeply involved in the new knowledge they were gaining from the priest. Maal arranged to meet them secretly at certain times in the hills, where they had met before, but one day he suggested they meet at the home of a friend of his, remote from the village and yet not as remote as the hills. Karne and Kyra had been finding it difficult to slip away unnoticed for quite the length of time required for visiting the northern hills. They were surprised when he mentioned a friend and thought perhaps he meant another priest or maybe even one of the Elders who was not totally loyal to Wardyke and Thorn. But they discovered it was Fern, a girl they had known slightly for years, a year older than Karne, living some way from the village in a beautiful leafy glade. On ceremonial days she came quietly to the village but on the whole she kept herself separate from the community. The richness of the plant growth around her homestead was well known and in times of drought the villagers had fed on food grown by her.

It was her father who had introduced the seed that gave the community the best wheat crop they had ever had and now it had become common practice to grow it year after year. Travellers from other communities had been astonished at the prolific yield and had bartered various goods for some of the seed.

Fern's parents were dead now and she lived alone, still keeping the land lush and green around her.

Some of the villagers worried about her.

"It is not good for a young girl to be always so alone," Karne's mother often said.

And some thought her strange.

"She talks to the spirits," Thon said. "Thera saw her the other day talking to that tree next to old Faro's strip."

"There is no harm in talking to the spirits," Kyra said. "We do it every time we pray."

"But such talking, such prayer, is at the right time and the right place. We use the words of our fathers, at the times our fathers have chosen . . . the priest is our channel."

Karne said nothing but he thought a greal deal. It seemed to him in the last year he had become increasingly impatient with the round of prayers they had to chant each day. No matter how he concentrated on the ritual he could feel nothing flowing back from it. He had no sense of the spirits he was talking to hearing him in any way or even being aware that he was there and trying to communicate. He had not dared admit even to himself that at times he wondered if the spirit world existed at all. He thought about Fern and wondered if she had found a way to communicate that was better than the one that they were using.

Maal first took them to Fern on a day when rain had fallen, but the sun had followed soon afterwards. Everything was fresh and smelling good. In Fern's garden raindrops were trapped on leaves and shone with sudden splendour as they passed. Kyra found herself gazing at one caught and poised on the tip of a tall grass spear, its weight slightly pulling the leaf towards the earth. She felt herself being absorbed into its luminosity and somehow becoming a form of light which shone upon the whole Universe ...

"Kyra," Karne shattered the precious experience and brought her back to the limitations of being contained within a human frame, "did you ever see such flowers?"

Kyra looked and marvelled. Every flower she had ever seen growing in the fields or in the forests was growing in Fern's garden, but somehow larger, richer, more magnificent. And flowers she had never seen were there in great profusion too. The colours, from the deepest crimson to the palest cream and white, midnight blue and mountain shadow purple, wove together in an intricate and dazzling pattern of delight, all set in rich and varied green.

Fern led them to a grassy bank and a fallen log and they sat surrounded by the garden. It was so beautiful and peaceful it was a while before they could bring themselves to talk and in the silence Kyra could almost fancy she heard the secret, intricate processes of growth going on all around them, roots pushing strongly but infinitely slowly through the rich black earth, branches lengthening, leaves unfurling, buds opening. Bushes of every kind of green surrounded them, some laden with berries. Fern saw Karne looking at them and asked if he were hungry.

His expression was answer enough.

Fern smiled and then to Karne's amazement stood very still in front of the bush with the most berries, not moving and not touching them. She seemed to be in a kind of silent communication with the plant world. After a moment or two she opened her eyes and picked the berries gently.

Karne's eyes met Kyra's.

When they had eaten their fill and all their mouths were stained with purple, they settled down to talk.

"How is it that your plants grow so well?" Kyra asked. "I have never seen such profusion of growth."

No one Kyra had ever met cultivated plants for beauty or for pleasure alone. The villagers grew crops in the strips that were allotted to them outside the village, but never had she seen a dwelling house surrounded by flowers.

Fern was shy and seemed uncertain what to answer.

"Fern has special powers, Kyra," Maal spoke for her, "not unlike yours. She is in tune with the earth, senses its inner needs and works with the flow of life within it."

"You seemed to be talking to that bush . . . I mean . . . in your head . . ."

"I was asking for the berries," Fern said simply.

Maal noticed Karne's expression.

"All life is animated by spirit," he said. "We should treat all things with respect. Our relationship with the plant world should be a relationship between two life forms, each respecting the other, different as they may be."

Karne looked at the bush. He remembered with shame how often he had walked through a field with a stick, absent-mindedly knocking off the heads of flowers and grasses.

"The earth has forces flowing through it, lines of power through which renewal and regeneration come," Fern said gently. "I work with these, and the feelings of need I get from the plants themselves."

"My brother says you talked to that old tree next to Faro's plot. It used to look as though it were dying, but now I see it has new leaves."

"I know," Fern flushed slightly, "I did not mean to talk aloud. The words themselves mean nothing to the plants. It is the *feeling* inside one, whether one is genuinely concerned for its welfare or not, that matters. It is a kind of communion through loving. Sometimes I use words just to help myself concentrate. But the plant cannot hear them, of course—unless perhaps it responds to the tone of them . . ."

75

"You mean whether your voice sounds angry or loving?"

"Yes. I suppose that could have an effect. Perhaps the resonance . . . But it is really the feeling that matters."

Karne was still curious about the renewal of Faro's tree.

"But how did you make Faro's tree grow again?"

"It was not 'Faro's tree'," Fern said firmly. "No man can own a tree. A tree is a free spirit, like man."

"Sorry. But anyway . . . how did you make the tree grow again?"

"I did not make it grow," Fern said patiently. "It grew, like man, when the life force, the spirit flow if you like, was not impeded any more by fear and anger."

"The tree 'feared'!" Karne was bewildered.

"You could say that. Faro had cut many of its roots and branches, brutally and without warning, to extend his growing strip. If a tree has to be cut there are ways of doing it, with preparation and with the flow of nature, that does not harm the living creature or make it angry or afraid."

"Where does this flow come from?" Kyra asked with interest.

Maal held up his arms and looked around him. He indicated everywhere, everything.

Kyra remembered the feeling of wholeness, of identity with the Universe she had experienced recently.

"In a sense," Maal said, "it does not come from anywhere or go anywhere. It is a flow that is within us and within everything else which makes us all part of the same Whole. The flow is within the Whole and so consequently within us."

"As though we are all in a closed circle with the flow going round and round within the circle?" Karne asked.

"Something like that."

"Is that why our temple is a circle? A sort of symbol of the Great Circle in which everything is contained?"

"Something like that," Maal said again. "Our little stone Circle concentrates power by trapping a bit of it within itself and then as it follows round and round within the circle it gains strength . . ."

"But that in a sense is impeding its free flow through everything and you said that was bad."

"Ah," Maal sighed. "It is all so complex and we have so little time. But I will try and explain. To capture the force within the Circle and to use it for your own purposes should not be done lightly. That is why only the priest is allowed within the Circle. Only he has the training and the strength to use the power the Circle has generated creatively. An unwary and untrained person might be destroyed by the concentration of power."

Kyra looked horrified. She had not forgotten she was expected to go within the Circle and use its powers.

Fern saw her expression and put her arm around her and kissed her gently on the forehead. She had been informed by Maal of the situation as it stood and was prepared to help them in any way she could. She was sensitive to the earth and all its life forms but she could not leave her body and travel in the spirit, which is what Kyra must do to reach the Lords of the Sun.

There was silence for a moment as they all looked at Kyra and thought about her ordeal.

"Come," Maal said, taking her hand, "we will go away from Karne and Fern and practice what you must do."

He led her deeper into the leafy wood and found a small clearing ringed with fronds of fern and feathery white flowers. The rocks lying scattered around were beautiful with lichen and moss. Sunlight flickered and scittered through the leaves of the trees high above them, their trunks tall and straight, forming a circle of living columns around them, a wooden circle of power.

Kyra lay down in the centre, her head to the east, her body aligned along the path of the sun. She looked straight up to the roof of interlocking branches above her and noticed the intricate patterning of leaves, subtly changing moment by moment as light breeze stirred among them but did not penetrate to where she lay in stillness on the earth. Maal sat beside her and waited for the frightened hammering of her heart to quieten down. She would not be able to travel far without the concentration of power from the Sacred Stones, but at least she could learn something of the technique.

He had questioned her again and again about every detail of her last experience and he was convinced that the most cogent reason for her failure was that she was afraid. He talked to her now quietly, gently calming her fears, trying to get her to relax, limb by limb. At last he could sense every bit of her body was lying limp.

"Feel as though your body is heavy . . . sinking into the earth . . . sinking into the earth . . ." His voice was soft, repetitive, hypnotic.

"Sinking . . ."

He let her lie feeling this for a while. Then he as quietly fed her other suggestions.

"Now feel as though your body is expanding . . . feel it stretching . . . your legs are growing longer . . . your arms . . . you are swelling . . . growing . . . becoming lighter and lighter . . . you are filling with air . . . you are floating . . . floating . . ."

She had her eyes shut and she could feel everything he suggested she should feel. His voice came as though in a dream from a long, long way away.

The solidity of her body was no longer there. She could make it become whatever she chose. But somehow she was still "inside" it. She was not travelling.

"You are separate from your body . . ." Maal's voice droned on and on. "Separate . . . You, Kyra, are not your body . . . your body is nothing but a dress you can put on or take off . . . put on or take off . . . a dress you can put on or take off . . ."

She could feel herself slipping, floating, separating . . .

Strange, now she was with the leaves, the brilliance of their flickering was hurting her. Far below her she could see two figures, an old man and a young girl. They looked familiar, but she was too comfortable, too relaxed to bother to work it out. She just kept drifting . . .

78

She could see so much more now, the rich profusion of Fern's garden, Fern and Karne sitting very close side by side on the log, deep in conversation. She could see beyond them, beyond Fern's little house, to the path that led to the village. Momentarily she seemed to drift off to sleep and lose her bearings and when she became conscious again she was not in the clearing with Maal, but beside the heap of stones that had been gathered for Maal's burial mound. She looked around her in some confusion, wondering how she came to be there, and then she noticed that she was not alone. Wardyke and Thorn were standing quite near, talking.

"He cannot have it here," Wardyke was saying. "We will put it over beside the clump of trees." He pointed.

"But . . ." thought Kyra, "but . . ." She knew there was something wrong with this but she could not think clearly enough to decide what it was. She still felt half dazed and could not understand how she came to be there.

"Do you still want a mound built?" Thorn was asking.

"Oh, yes," said Wardyke, "we will give him a mound but it will not do him any good over there."

That was it! She knew what was wrong.

Before she could stop herself she cried out.

"But that is not where he wants it. It is not on the alignment!"

Her voice seemed loud to her and she was not standing far from the two men, but neither of them seemed to hear her. Wardyke half turned his head and listened as though something had disturbed him, but Thorn was looking right at her and yet did not see her.

He did not see her!

As she realized this a shock wave of fear passed through her. She felt a terrible jerking and heard a snapping sound and suddenly she was back in the clearing with Maal, shaking with fear, very much the ordinary little Kyra. As she came back she had cried out and Karne and Fern came running to see what the matter was. Maal had his arm around her and she was crying.

79

"I had such a horrible dream," she sobbed, "I heard Wardyke and Thorn plotting to move your burial mound away from the place you have chosen and then when I called out to them they did not hear me or see me!"

Maal looked very interested.

"Where did they say they were going to put it?"

"By that clump of trees to the left, right across the field, nowhere near the alignment you wanted with the midsummer sunset mark and the Sacred Circle."

"Never mind your dream," Karne said impatiently, "what about the travelling? Did you do any?"

"I do not know," she said miserably. "I think I went to sleep."

"I think not," Maal said quietly.

"You mean . . .?" Kyra opened her eyes wide.

"I mean . . . I think you made your first journey. Now tell me everything you felt and saw."

They returned to the log as Kyra was anxious to get away from the clearing where she had had such a strange experience. Under Maal's skilful questioning she told them every detail. They were all very excited and even Kyra could not help feeling a kind of nervous elation and pride at her achievement.

"You see," Maal said, patting her on the head, "it was not so bad after all."

"I cannot believe it really happened!"

"Will you believe it if Thorn and Wardyke really do move the grave to the very place you described?" Karne asked.

"Of course. But surely it will not be so?"

"We shall see," Maal said thoughtfully.

"But if it is so," Fern said, "that will be bad for you surely?"

"In one way, yes. In another way, no. It will mean we are making progress with Kyra and we are that much nearer to being able to contact the Lords of the Sun."

"Why is it so important where you have your burial

mound?" Karne asked. "What did they mean by it not 'doing you any good' beside the trees?"

"It is all connected with the channels through which the earth powers flow," Fern said. "Where Maal chooses to place himself at the moment of death is very important."

"I want my dying to be a conscious and deliberate act," Maal said.

Karne and Kyra looked horrified. Fern seemed to understand.

"I have chosen this way," Maal said calmly.

"I do not understand!" Kyra cried. "Are you going to kill yourself?"

"Not quite. When I know I am about to die I am going to compose myself for death, use it as I have been trained to do, to influence the direction of my journey through the spirit worlds, maybe even the time and place of my rebirth on this earth."

Karne and Kyra were looking astonished. They had been told in ritual words many times that this life was only one of many, but until this moment neither of them had really thought about it.

"You mean . . .?"

"So you see it is important that he should meet his death while he is on the line of maximum life force," Fern interrupted eagerly, "so that he can have all the help he can in the difficult task of transference from one level to another."

"Wardyke knows this," Maal said, and there was a trace of bitterness in his voice, "and that is why he wants to move me *off* the line of maximum power."

Kyra gasped.

"We must not let him do it! We must stop him!" Karne cried angrily.

Maal raised his hand.

"Not so hasty, my friend. You are dealing with a very powerful magician."

Karne was silenced for a moment and then muttered "There must be a way!"

81

"There will be a way," said Maal confidently, "but we will not find it when our minds are all muddied and disturbed by anger."

"If we sit still and let our minds flow naturally," Fern said, "the solution to the problem will probably just float up from deep inside ourselves. I have noticed that. There seems to be another 'Me' somewhere deeply inside that I hardly ever notice, but when I do it seems to make more sense of things than the outside 'me'. I think it is this one that communicates with the plant world."

"Well, I am no good at sitting still," Karne said impatiently. "Things come to *me* when I am active!"

"That may be your way," Maal said, "but it is not ours. Bear with us while we try to find our hidden Selves. You yourself might be surprised if you were to join with us in this."

Silence fell between them and almost immediately the other three began to look remote and calm. Karne could *not* still his mind. The more he tried the more his angry thoughts churned and turned within him.

At last he could bear it no longer and burst out with the suggestion that the only way out of the situation was to kill Wardyke.

Kyra was horrified.

"If you killed Wardyke you would be just as bad as he is," she said indignantly.

"One must try to re-route . . . not to destroy," Maal said patiently.

"But killing him would be re-routing him!" Karne called out triumphantly. "I would re-route him straight out of this life in to the next!"

Maal could not help laughing, but Kyra and Fern were even more indignant. The old priest would have preferred to change the subject, but he had to say something more to soothe the girls and prevent Karne rushing off and carrying out his hot-headed threat.

"We are all part of the same pattern", he said. "We are dependent on each other in subtle and complicated ways and no man dare decide the fate of any other man. The mysteries of life and death are beyond our understanding and are meddled with only at our peril. By our interference we may bring about greater harm than that which we had hoped to cure. There will be ways of stopping Wardyke that do not run this risk."

"I wish we could think of something," Kyra said sadly.

"We will," said Maal with conviction.

It was time for them to separate.

Maal went first as it was important that no one saw them together.

As they watched his slightly stooping figure disappear around the curve of the hill, Kyra said,

"We are not even sure if any of this is going to happen. I may have dreamed the whole thing."

"I am certain it is going to happen," said Karne. "Of that I have no doubt!"

Kyra sighed.

Her brother had always had more faith in her powers than she had herself.

The Retreat

DURING THE NEXT FEW DAYS nothing was said in the village about the changed site of Maal's tomb and even Karne was beginning to think Kyra's experience might have been a dream.

They saw Wardyke once or twice but Maal had warned them to avoid him if possible and certainly not to meet his eyes. Their plan would only work if Wardyke's suspicions were not in any way aroused. Karne helped in the fields as usual and also spent some time gathering stones for Maal's burial chamber.

It was on the fifth day after Kyra's experience that Faro came to the place where they were piling the rocks and asked the boys to move them towards the clump of trees. He pointed out exactly where he wanted them.

"Why is that?" Karne asked, trying to keep his voice as unemotional as possible.

"I do not know," Faro said, "Thorn told me to tell you. It must be a better place for some reason."

Karne could not wait to tell Kyra.

The other boys grumbled bitterly at the extra work involved, but Karne worked silently and as he worked he began to think of a plan. Fern's wood was on the line of alignment from the Sacred Circle to the midsummer sunset notch. What if they dug another burial place in the woods behind her house, keeping it hidden and secret, and Maal buried himself in that instead of the official one?

He rushed home and dragged Kyra out to their meeting place near the boat. As they walked he poured out his scheme.

At first she was confused, but when she caught the gist of what he was saying her feelings were mixed. She was pleased that she had proof that she had started to "travel", but she was also afraid of the implications. How soon would Maal consider she was ready to enter the Circle? Surely it would be a long time before she was prepared enough for that. She had no real control yet over where she went or what she did. She remembered with a shudder that awful jerk with which she had returned to her body.

"What do you think of it?" Karne asked her eagerly.

"I am frightened, Karne. What if I cannot get back?"

"What on earth are you talking about?" He was genuinely surprised. He thought she had been listening to every word of his excellent plan.

"From the Lords of the Sun."

"Oh, *them*!" he said impatiently. "That is another problem. What do you think of my idea about the burial mound?"

He had to explain the whole thing again. She thought it was a good idea, but raised a few useful objections. The burial of a priest was always a ceremonial affair and the whole community would be there to see him go. There was no way Wardyke would let them use their own tomb.

"Of course not! He must not even know about it!"

"How are you going to manage it then?"

"I am not sure. There are things I need to know from Maal."

"What things?"

"How long does he stay alive after the tomb is closed? If he can stay alive long enough for the crowds to leave and for us to dig him up again, it will be quite a simple matter to transfer him from the one tomb to the other. He need not start his special life transference process until we get him safely into his proper place on the alignment of power."

Kyra thought of something else to worry about.

"I hope he does not die before we have another priest in Wardyke's place!"

"I think that is why he is driving you so hard with the training. He knows he cannot leave until he has seen that we are safe."

Kyra realized it was selfish of her to put up so much resistance to the training.

"We will see him tomorrow," she said decisively. "You can take the message to Maal now and I will go home and keep mother from sending someone out to find us."

Maal liked Karne's scheme and when they were once again with Fern they spent a great deal of time searching out the right place in the woods to dig the new burial chamber. He thought there would just be time enough for the move from the one tomb to the other to take place if everything went smoothly and quickly. As a priest of the Sun he was trained to control all his bodily functions himself, including breathing and blood circulation. He could so control his body that he could lie in trance without access to air or food for a long time, apparently dead.

"Almost like a seed that lies in the ground over winter and then springs back to life when the warm weather comes?" Fern asked.

"Something like that," Maal said. "But I could not compete with the seed."

"What time of day will they have the burial?" Karne wanted to know.

"At sunset, so the darkness that follows swiftly upon it will be a convenience to us," Maal answered. "You must have the route well marked out so that you do not stumble or get lost. It would attract too much attention to carry torches."

"Try to have the ceremony on a moonlit night and we will place white marker stones to show us the way."

"You may not be the only ones to follow them to their source!"

"But we need something!"

"Rely on your own natural skills. Train your eyes. Familiarize your memory with the shapes of trees and rocks."

"We must go over the route several times at night," Karne said thoughtfully.

Kyra was worrying again.

"It is not going to be easy to slip away from home at night."

"No part of it will be easy, I am afraid," said Maal and this reminded him that the most important and most difficult part of all was the part Kyra had to play.

"Come, child, we must have another lesson," and he led her away.

While they were busy Karne and Fern took two sticks of equal length as sighting rods and set about trying to work out an accurate alignment from the Circle to the notch. It was not as easy as they had first thought, because the trees often obscured their view, but they solved the problem at last by Karne climbing the tallest tree and Fern climbing the hill outside the wood.

Karne came down from the tree just as Fern arrived back from her work on the hill, and by swinging quickly from branch to branch he managed to land on her with a wild and frightening cry. They fell in a heap together on the mossy, spongy ground, she laughing at the fright she had suffered and he laughing at the pleasure of having frightened her. After a while they stopped laughing and lay quietly side by side, her hair spread out around her on the dark fallen leaves, like fire. They could feel the wood watching them, caring for them, being gentle with them.

"You know," he said at last, sitting up, "it is a strange thing but there is almost a pathway, a gap in this wood opening up along the line of alignment."

She looked where he pointed and it was true. The trees seemed to form a natural avenue, interlocked above, but at trunk level clearly grouped to suggest a kind of living tunnel leading the eye through the wood to the Stone Circle on the hill to the east, and to the notch on the hill in the west.

"We need not have gone to all that trouble," Karne said, "the line was there all along."

Fern smiled. She had enjoyed the afternoon and was not sorry they had worked it out for themselves. Karne caught the expression and smiled broadly. Yes, he had enjoyed it too.

But while they were having a happy time poor Kyra was in trouble again. She had managed to "travel" after a few false starts, but this time she found herself in a strange and horrifying situation. She was aware of her body lying on a beautiful golden couch but she was surrounded by a group of terrifying and hideous figures. Each had the body of a man clad only in a loin cloth that shone like metal, and each had the head of an animal, grinning and jeering and leering at her. She tried to get up but found she could not move her body. She tried to scream, but no sound would come from her throat. She realized she was outside her body again and had no control over it. She screamed and screamed, struggled and fought. She could *feel* herself doing all this, but she could see her body still lying there soundless and inert as though it were dead.

The creatures began tugging at her body. She could see them doing it, but could not feel their touch. They raised her into a sitting position and pointed at something on the ground that they obviously wanted her to see. They were laughing in a ghastly way that sounded more animal than human, laughing and pointing and poking at her, anxious for her to see what they had for her. She got the impression it was some kind of present. She could see, though not with her own eyes, what appeared to be a rug. As she looked at it one of the creatures pulled at it so that it moved and what was on it became sickeningly clear to her.

The rug itself seemed not to be of skin like the ones she was accustomed to, but of woven cloth, coloured and patterned in a way she would not have thought possible. Rich crimsons and blues and golds, amazing patterning of animals and birds. But upon all this beauty lay the hideous, rotting carcass of her friend Maal.

As she recognized him she screamed and the creatures jumped about with delight.

"Oh God! Oh God!" she cried with all the force and concentration of her Inner Being, "God of Life and Light, save me!"

She could feel the words bursting in her head and even as she finished them there was a kind of explosion of light and the same snapping sound she had heard before.

She was back with the living Maal in the clearing in Fern's wood, the creatures of evil nowhere in sight.

She was ashen and shaking and it was a long time before Maal could get a clear picture out of her as to what had happened. When he had heard the tale his face was very grave.

"What does it mean?" she cried. "Oh Maal, what does it mean!"

He was silent, his expression sombre.

"Tell me," she insisted, frightened by the gloominess of his expression and his refusal to answer.

He shook his head.

She jumped up and seized him by his thin shoulders and shook him fiercely.

"I *must* know," she shouted, "tell me!"

He just kept shaking his head. Tears of frustration poured down her cheeks and she did not stop shaking his shoulders for an instant.

"Kyra!" shouted Karne and Fern, arriving to find what to them had been an idyllic, peaceful afternoon shattered by the fury and despair they saw before them.

Karne took hold of his hysterical sister and pulled her away from the old man. Fern put her arms about Maal and tried to comfort him, amazed that Kyra should have attacked him so.

When at last Kyra was silent, sitting pale and tear-stained within the circle of her brother's arms, and Maal had walked away from them into the wood to think a while and returned looking calmer and more composed, Karne and Fern were told briefly what had occurred. They were both shaken and puzzled by the experience. Although Kyra would dearly have liked to ask yet again the meaning of it all, Maal offered no explanation, and she was too weary to insist on one.

"I have decided," Maal said calmly. "The work is too dangerous for Kyra. We must abandon it."

"But," said Karne, ". . . Wardyke?"

"I know. But a priest would train for years before he would take the risks I am asking Kyra to take. We cannot do it in the time available. We must try and think of another way."

"Who were those creatures?" Fern asked anxiously.

Kyra sat still and quiet, showing no interest or emotion now, too worn out to care if he answered Fern's question or not.

He paused a long time, but the expression on his face showed them that he was trying to answer.

"What I have been doing with you is wrong," he said slowly at last.

Karne opened his mouth to deny it, but Maal stopped him with a gesture.

"Yes, wrong. The world you lived in before, the world the villagers see all around them is a comfortable world. It is not the only world they live in, but it is the only world they think they live in. It fits them like their own clothes and they are happy with it. Only certain of their faculties are developed so they see only certain things about the world. Because they are not aware of anything

90

further they are quite content that what they have is everything there is to have.

"But there *is* more to reality than meets the eye of the average person.

"There are ways of growing naturally like Fern here, or being trained like me, so that one becomes aware of some of the other levels to reality. The more one grows, the more one learns, the more complex and wonderful the world becomes, deeper and deeper levels, higher and higher levels open up to one!

"You have started this growth with me. You will never be content again as the villagers are, with an inadequate sense of reality.

"But there is a pace to learning, to growing, to unfolding. Fern can tell you that, from watching her plants grow and flower and fruit and fall. All should be done gradually. As one is ready so one moves. That way whatever one grows to be aware of, one is ready for. I have been pushing Kyra too far too fast. She has come upon things she is *not* ready for. They will destroy her mind."

The three young people were silent.

Karne and Fern were thinking deeply upon what Maal had said.

Kyra was asleep, her head fallen upon her brother's shoulder. As he looked down upon her face he was moved almost to tears himself at the paleness of it, the weariness and despair of it.

The Training Changes Direction

During the next few days Kyra moved about as though she were ill. She was extremely tired all the time, and very pale. Her mother fussed and kept her close about the house. Karne watched with some anxiety but could do nothing for her. She did not seem to want to talk and indeed, even if he had wanted to call her away to their talking place at the boat, there were two reasons, apart from Kyra's own reluctance, to prevent it: his mother's vigilance over his sister and the presence of his two brothers, Ji and Okan, almost constantly at the boat.

Karne watched them go off one day eagerly discussing the day's work plan and realized he was feeling like a grown man watching two children going off to play. The boat had been so important to him at one time, but that enthusiasm seemed a hundred moons ago now, when he was a child. He smiled to think that he had once thought he could only find the answers to all his questions about life and death and the gods by sailing away across the sea. He knew now that the answers to life's mysteries lay wherever one happened to be. It was only a matter of the acuteness of one's vision whether one could use them or not.

Although he was forced reluctantly to agree with Maal that they should not push Kyra any further than she was able to go, he was determined to continue learning from Maal himself.

Fern too had much to teach although he learnt from her more by watching and being with her than by discussing things with her. She was not so good at putting things into words as Maal, but the way she lived her life was a lesson in itself.

Sometimes he went to see her when the others were not there and always found her quietly, gently, going about her daily work tending the plants. She seemed to sense everything they needed and would never allow herself to be too tired or too harrassed to give it to them. She paced herself steadily through the day. Karne noticed that with admiration. There were never moments in her orderly life, as there were in his, of rush and bother as too much to be done became bunched up into too little time. He noticed that when she was tired or overworked and beginning to get tense, she would stop what she was doing immediately and sit cross legged and still, her head tipped slightly back and her eyes closed. When he found her like that the first time, there was such a stillness about her he thought she had somehow fallen asleep sitting up. But she was not asleep and after only a few moments of this kind of intense rest, this sinking into the still point at the centre of her nature, she was refreshed and would rise up gracefully to start work again.

"Are you not lonely always by yourself?" he asked her one day as they sat together.

"I am never by myself," she said, smiling, "and I am certainly never lonely."

He believed her. Around her her trees and bushes and plants were sweetly growing, long tendrils of creeper reached down from the trees to stroke her as she passed. He could *feel* the love and peace all around, the feeling of

93

companionship. She sat in the centre of a green world and light both radiated from her and to her. In some ways she looked as though she herself was of the plant world. The stillness with which she sat, the quiet gleam of her red-gold hair, her eyes the colour of dark wood flecked strangely with the gold of sunlight, her skin nut brown and her body slim, supple and lithe like a young sapling. Living alone she worked hard, doing all the chores normally shared out among a family. She needed no wood for cooking, as she ate only plant material and that fresh and uncooked, but for the winter she had to gather wood and break it into reasonably sized pieces for her small hearth. She took only branches that were already dead, and chopped them with a fine flint axe her father had left her. All summer she worked on the wood little by little, so that when the cold winds came howling down from the north she was well prepared. When her house needed mending she mended it. When the earth needed digging she dug it.

Karne sometimes felt she had the strength of a boy and yet the beauty of a woman's shape. He felt totally at peace with her as though her thoughts flowed in unison with his. He never sensed as he did with other people that he was cut off, isolated within his own skin, unable to communicate.

As time passed Kyra gradually became less pale. She seemed to have decided to regard the whole experience as a bad dream, but nevertheless she was determined not to put herself in the position of having another such a one. It was a great relief to her that she was no longer expected to "travel", and Karne found her almost irritating in the way she put the whole thing from her mind and in some way returned to childhood. She played with the younger children noisily and enthusiastically, avoiding him and refusing to visit Maal and Fern. Indeed she was so unlike herself he began to wonder if her mind had been affected already, as Maal said it might be if they continued with their experiments.

Chafing at the inactivity and lack of progress he decided as they could no longer rely on her for any help and they must be sure at least that Maal's secret chamber was ready for him when he needed it, Fern and he must proceed with the work on it by themselves. They started digging on a day after rain when the earth was fairly soft.

"We will have to gather stones to line the chamber and keep them hidden somehow," Karne said.

Luckily the woods were very deep and lush with undergrowth and it would not be difficult to keep things hidden.

Fern wove a kind of raft of vines and branches which could be lowered over the hole they were making so that it would totally disappear from view when they were not actually working on it. Not many people came to the woods as a rule, but one could not be certain they would not. Children sometimes came to gather berries for themselves and their families a little later in the year. The wild berries were still unripe although those in Fern's garden were already edible.

"Maal seems to be avoiding us," Karne remarked one day. "Have you noticed?"

"I am worried about him," Fern said. "He seems very low in spirit."

"He even looks older. I hope he will not need this chamber until we are ready."

"How is the work on the other tomb? You never mention it."

"The stones are all collected and the digging has started, but I am not involved in that. I did enough collecting the rocks. Half of them had to be brought from the hills. It was no easy task!"

"But should you not still be working there?" Fern asked.

"Why? I have enough to do here and in the fields."

"But," said Fern a trifle anxiously, "surely it is essential one of us should know exactly how it is constructed? Remember we have to fetch Maal out of there, probably in the dark."

"I had not thought of that," Karne was silent. He had

stopped work and was frowning as he thought about the problem.

"In fact, not only that, but I should find a way to make it easier for us to open it. We will never be able to move the great stone that seals the entrance. We will have to work in from the side or back somehow."

"Could you make a tunnel?"

Karne strode about restlessly. A tunnel would be the answer, but he was appalled at the amount of work involved, and all of it in secret. As it was he was beginning to ache with tiredness and in the morning when light came he could scarcely bring himself to rise and start the day.

"I cannot do it by myself," he said despairingly.

"I will help you," Fern said, "we will work at night. I am sure Kyra will help as well."

"Kyra!" he said bitterly.

He had told Fern about the way Kyra was behaving.

"You must not judge her too harshly, she is very young and has been under great strain."

"She is fourteen. That is not so young. She behaves like a small child."

"She is trying to protect herself. She is frightened."

"How will behaving like a child protect her?"

"People do not ask children to face danger and responsibility. If she can convince us she is too young to do the things we want her to, she will not have to do them. I think she is trying to convince herself as well, which is not easy."

"Why would she do that?"

"So that she will not feel guilty."

Karne sighed. Fern was right, of course. But nevertheless it was most irritating that Kyra was the only one of them who could be asked to "travel" and she was too afraid to do it.

"If it were I," he thought with fierce pride, "I would do it without a second thought! I would give anything to have a chance at it!"

96

Kyra agreed to help with the tunnel and indeed seemed to have recovered enough of her old spirit for her mother to leave her alone again. She would still not think about spirit travelling, but with Maal's tomb she was prepared to help. The one in the woods was almost ready and Fern insisted she could finish it off herself. Maal had instructed them in its construction and it was of a much humbler size than the official one. Because of Fern's knowledge of earth currents and channels they dug *with* the grain of the earth, and the digging was easy. It was almost as though the earth was helping them. Worms loosened the next layer of soil for them overnight and it was ready to dig in the morning.

But on the open hillside beside the clump of trees Maal's official tomb was not so easy to construct. It was on no natural channel of energy and the soil seemed heavy and lifeless to dig. Many men and boys were engaged all day in digging with antler picks and hollowed hardwood shovelling logs. The boys carried the soil away in leather buckets, putting it aside to be replaced as the mound over the stone chamber when the priest was laid to rest.

Thorn came occasionally to check on progress and once Wardyke came and told them angrily to work harder. It was as though he was impatient to see it finished.

Very early in the morning before anyone else was stirring Karne, Kyra and Fern would creep out of their homes and meet at the tomb. They were digging a tunnel and it was hard and painful work. They were lucky in that the clump of trees beside the mound hid the entrance.

Time went by. Maal returned to them and lifted their spirits when they were ready to collapse, answering their questions and teaching them many things. No more was said of "travelling" but much was said of growing in strength within themselves so that they would be strong

97

enough to overthrow Wardyke by themselves if it became necessary.

One day Karne had yet another good idea.

"If you had help," he said to Maal, "would you be able to break through the barrier at the Circle?"

Maal thought about it.

"Maybe," he said.

"Well then," cried Karne triumphantly, "all we have to do is give you some help to get through the barrier and *you* will be able to travel to the Lords of the Sun!"

Maal looked doubtful still, but Karne, Kyra and Fern looked jubilant. It certainly seemed to be solution to the problem.

But how best to give the help?

Kyra thought of something.

"You know that day," she said, "the day Wardyke arrived and I thought I heard you calling me to help but I did not know what to do?"

"Yes," Maal said.

"I had the feeling Wardyke was trying to drive you from the Circle but that he was not succeeding when he was by himself. It was only when Thorn joined him that he began to gain control."

"That is so. That is why I was calling to you. If you had joined your powers to mine, we might have been able to withstand them at that point."

Karne was fascinated.

"But could you do it now," he said, "I mean, the two of you together?"

"It is possible," Maal said slowly.

"That would be a way!" Fern cried.

"But you would do the travelling!" said Kyra anxiously, half questioning, half stating fact.

"Yes, I would do the travelling."

"But together you could probably pass through the barrier. Particularly as it is not designed for Kyra at all," Karne insisted.

Maal began to look really interested.

"This may be possible," he said with growing confidence.

Karne smiled with relief.

"That is decided then!" he said firmly. "When do we start?"

Maal laughed.

"Impatient as ever, Karne! It is not as easy as you think. Kyra and I have much work to do together before we can attempt it. We may get only one chance to reach the Circle and cannot afford to bungle it."

Kyra began to look anxious.

"I will not have to go within the Circle?" she asked, still worried.

"I will try to avoid it," Maal said soothingly.

"I am *not* going within the Circle!" Kyra was alarmed now and made this announcement with great force.

"Of course you will not," Karne said hastily. "Maal will do all the work. You will just have to help him through the barrier." And then to Maal he said, "You do *believe* you can do it together, do you not?"

"Our two wills together will make it possible," Maal said with great conviction.

Kyra looked somewhat pacified.

"All right," she muttered, "as long as I do not have to do the 'travelling' or go within the Circle."

"That is understood," Karne said firmly.

The First Challenge

WHILE MAAL was training Kyra to project her will and mind to join with his, and Karne and Fern were working secretly upon the tunnel, new settlers began to come to their valley.

At first one or two families arrived, were greeted with great warmth by the community and soon made to feel at home, but within weeks others came and what had once been a very closeknit and related group of homesteads became an untidy and sprawling collection of disparate elements. The strangers were everywhere, taking over land that since the ancient times had been common grazing land. They put up their homes which were no more than badly built shacks wherever they wished with no regard to the harmonious flow of village life.

The original villagers began to grumble.

"They seem to have no sense of the flow of the earth spirit," Fern said. "All the other sites for homes were chosen carefully by Maal or my father, so that they fitted into the rhythm of the land. But these people just put their houses anywhere, making everything ugly and disorderly. It is no wonder they look so restless and dissatisfied!"

The original villagers at last bestirred themselves to have a meeting at the Meeting Stone. It was a mystery to them why so many settlers had come at one time. Over the years families had arrived from other communities and settled in, but never more than one at a time.

These people seemed to move in hordes, and be rough and noisy. They carried themselves with such arrogance and confidence that the milder mannered villagers found it impossible to stand up to them. They arrived and moved in as though they had a right, and each villager in his turn refrained from saying anything because he thought it was his own ignorance that made him unaware of the reasons for their arrival. It seemed to have been arranged in some way. But no one could make out how, or by whom.

At the meeting some of the Elders were present but Wardyke and Thorn had been away for three days and no one knew where they were or when they would return. It was a measure of the desperation of the villagers that they had dared to call a meeting without the sanction of their two formidable leaders.

Faro was in charge and he was particularly angry as the Strangers had put up their untidy shacks close to his home and were encroaching on the land he had always thought was his. No one actually *owned* land in the community, they all knew the earth belonged to the gods and the earth spirits, but certain parts of it were by long-standing custom used by certain families. When a family cared properly for the land no one questioned their right to use it, but if a family, as had happened from time to time in the past, misused or neglected the land, it was taken by common consent from them and given to the community until such time as the offending family proved itself worthy again to be trusted with the care of it.

The Strangers were certainly misusing the land. Their

rubbish was never returned to the earth to fertilize the new crops as Fern's father had taught them, but left lying about in untidy, smelly heaps. They killed animals wantonly, ate only a little of each, and threw away the rest, again to rot within sight of the dwellings. The winter was not far off and the meat should have been cured and hung for the long cold months ahead when no grain grew in the frosty earth and most of the animals had moved south or gone to sleep. The Strangers seemed to be making no provision for the winter. This made the villagers uneasy. Where were they going to get their food in winter? Where their wood and furs? The villagers feared the Strangers were not above taking what they needed from their more circumspect neighbours, by force if necessary.

Some villagers had even seen the Strangers killing birds and everyone knew that birds who flew so close to the sun and the moon were sacred, friends of the spirit-gods and not to be harmed in any way.

It was time indeed to meet and talk about what could be done.

Many of them felt they should have waited till the return of Thorn and Wardyke, but many others were too impatient to wait. A new family of settlers had moved in that very day and were chopping down trees most wastefully at the edge of the south pasture.

"Strangers have always been welcomed in our community and before this time we have never regretted our hospitality," Karne's father said.

"They do not follow the ancient laws." Someone else spoke. "Not one has called a meeting of the Elders to ask permission to live within our community. They have taken land no one has agreed that they should have."

"They do not seem to have a leader. There is no one among them elected to speak for them."

"Thorn has been seen talking to them," a nervous little man spoke up. He had been one of those opposed to the calling of the meeting without Thorn's approval.

"But that is not the way," Karne's father said. "A full

meeting of the Elders should settle land rights. Not just the word of one Elder."

"Or a priest," someone else muttered bitterly.

It seemed to Karne not all the villagers were as pleased with Wardyke as they had at first been. It might be time for Maal's return.

"Should we not call for Maal's help here," he said suddenly and with boldness. It was not usual for the young to talk at meetings and Karne had never spoken before. Heads turned to look at him in surprise, but no objection to his speaking was raised. He was tall, nearly sixteen, and without their noticing had become a man. It was more what he had said that called for objection.

There were murmurs.

"Maal? What could that old man do!"

"He has not been near the Sacred Circle or the people since Wardyke came!"

"He waits only to die."

There was a faction who was still blinded by Wardyke, it seemed.

Karne flushed with anger at these remarks and prepared to answer them but, seeing the situation and knowing his son well, Karne's father spoke quickly.

"Maal's advice as one who has lived long in our village and served us well . . ." and here he looked fiercely at the maker of the last remark, "should certainly be sought. But he is no longer priest here and his word is no longer our law," and here he looked hard at his son.

"I mean only his advice, father," Karne said mildly, realizing in time the wisdom of tact. "He has had much experience and has travelled further than any of us. Perhaps he could tell us where these people come from."

"Send for him." The man who had muttered earlier against Wardyke's sole word being law spoke up now.

Karne was off before anyone could offer an objection, and Maal was fetched. In hurrying him back to the meeting, Karne noticed impatiently that Maal was slow and feeble in his movements.

"Hurry," he cried. "Wardyke is not there. You may have a chance to influence the people."

"I am not as young as you, boy," Maal complained, out of breath.

"Could you not go a little faster," Karne pleaded.

"I am going as fast as I can," puffed Maal. "I am sorely in need of a new body."

Karne tried to swallow his impatience. Maal's mind was so vigorous and young, he always forgot it was housed in such a decrepit body. Karne had noticed that since Kyra's last experience with spirit-travelling, Maal had grown feebler. He remembered her description of Maal's rotting corpse and wondered fleetingly again if it was prophetic.

When they arrived back at the meeting everything had changed. Wardyke and Thorn were back and were enraged to find the villagers had taken the initiative in anything without their permission.

Wardyke was standing on the flat rock that served them as a platform and his eyes were blazing with anger. The villagers were terrified. Even those who had murmured against the control of Thorn and Wardyke were cowed.

Seeing the situation instantly, Maal pushed Karne aside.

"Go, boy, do not be seen with me," he whispered with the sudden strength of command in his voice.

Karne obeyed and ducked into the crowd, appearing again within sight of Wardyke and Thorn, but far from Maal.

Wardyke's voice was like thunder as he berated them for "forming this unruly mob to cause trouble and disorder in the community".

"Who called this meeting?" he roared.

There was silence. No one dared answer.

"Who called it, I say!" he roared again, and his eyes lashed at them with fire. Not one person dared raise his head and look him in the eye. He lifted his arm, his hand bony and immense, pointing to the sky, his black cloak

104

falling from it in magnificent folds. He seemed about to cast a spell upon them when a voice spoke up and he turned his attention to it.

It was Maal and he was standing straight, an old man sustained by determination and desperation.

"The people of this village called it," he said boldly, looking Wardyke straight in the face.

"Oh you gods! I wish Kyra were here now!" Karne could have wept that she was not. Maal was alone, and Wardyke was roused against him.

All eyes were on Maal now and there were many who were grateful to him, and were amazed and impressed with his dignity and courage.

"You!" screamed Wardyke, and Karne knew he was no longer in control of himself, he was so angry. The boy feared for Maal's life but did not know what to do.

"Yes, I."

Maal strode with amazing strength towards the centre of the crowd. The people fell back till Maal was facing Wardyke directly. Wardyke was still upon the rock and so towered above Maal, but Maal's eyes were blazing and he did not for a moment relax the beam of his concentration on the younger man.

"These people did not meet here to cause trouble but to prevent it. Since the ancient days strangers have been welcomed in our community. They bring new life and new skills. Where our ways are different from theirs we learn from them and they from us. But there are some who have come in to our village who bring nothing but disruption and dismay. They desecrate the earth spirit, taking what is not any man's to take. You as priest should have been working amongst them, guiding them and teaching them our ways, easing the difference between us. But time has passed and nothing has been done . . ."

"Enough!" bellowed Wardyke, and if his voice had been loud before, it was now more like a clap of thunder than a human voice.

"These are *my* people! I will not have them criticized!"

"Your people? Does Wardyke own *people* now?"

105

And Maal's lips had a curl to them that Wardyke could not miss. He seemed to rise upon the air with rage. His long and deadly finger pointed straight at Maal.

"Die, old man!" he screamed.

There was a gasp from every throat. Every eye was upon the doomed old man. Karne expected a flash of lightning to come from the sky and devastate the land. Every muscle in his body was tensed against it.

Maal stumbled and almost fell. Karne could see him crumpling as though he were a pile of dust and then . . . and then . . . to another gasp from the community, he stood up straight again as though he had received new strength from somewhere, and, slowly and with great dignity, he turned and walked away.

Stupefied the villagers stared.

Maal had not died. Maal was walking away.

Karne broke from the circle and ran as hard as he had ever run, over the fields to Fern's wood. Kyra had gone to see Fern that afternoon and neither of them had been at the meeting. He *must* know if what he suspected had indeed happened.

He found the two girls in the house. Kyra was lying down looking very pale and Fern was stroking her head.

"What is the matter?" he cried out, bursting in upon them, sweating from the run.

Fern looked at him in surprise.

Kyra opened her eyes and sat up reaching out her arms for him.

"Oh Karne, I do not know, but it seemed to me Maal was in trouble and needed me. I tried to reach him as he taught me to . . . and I felt the most terrible pain shooting through my head as though . . . as though I had been hit by a battle axe . . ."

"Or a lightning bolt?" Karne asked.

"Yes, something like that. It was horrible."

"She kept screaming and holding her head," Fern said, "and then she became all calm and pale. I brought her in here because she said the light hurt her eyes."

106

"Poor Kyra," Karne said gently, stroking her. "But you have saved Maal's life."

"What?"

The girls were eager to hear what had been going on and listened in tense silence while he told the whole story.

Kyra was awed and frightened by her own part in the drama. She knew her powers were important, had indeed proved themselves without any doubt, but she was still uneasy about them.

"I do not know what I do or how I do it," she said miserably. "If only I knew what I was doing and could control it!"

"It will come," Fern said gently.

"Even without knowing what you are doing, you manage all right!" Karne said admiringly.

Kyra gave a deep sigh and looked doubtful.

When Karne and Kyra returned to the village early that evening there was no outward sign that anything was wrong. The tangy smell of the blue smoke of the cooking fires permeated the air. The boys were bringing the animals back to the stockades and they could hear their constant whistling as they walked behind them. Karne ran on ahead of Kyra knowing that his father's herd was his responsibility this particular evening. He was late bringing it in and his father was not pleased, but after the evening meal the family settled down and there was a chance to talk.

"What did Wardyke mean," Karne asked his father, "when he said 'these are my people'?"

"It turns out," his mother interrupted indignantly, "all these people come from the community where Wardyke used to be priest, and he invited them here!"

"But surely," Kyra said, "priests train for one particular community and stay with it for life?"

"I know," her mother said and her children could tell that the events of the day had left her agitated and anxious, "but Wardyke announced it as though it was perfectly normal. I suppose we are old fashioned and isolated

107

here and do not know what is going on in the rest of the country."

"He says," Karne's father spoke now and there was an edge of harshness in his voice, "he wants us to be 'great', to expand and multiply and take over more land from our neighbours."

"*I* think it will be good for us," Thon said, "we have been too small and set in our ways for too long. I for one will be glad to have more land, more people around to talk to, a few changes about the place."

"But the land we have supports us well. We have everything we need, food, shelter, warmth in winter . . ."

"A healthy and a loving family around us," Karne's mother interrupted.

"If we had more land we would have more problems. More work to be done, excess food to be stored . . ."

"We could barter for more things."

"What things? We have everything we need."

"You have no imagination!" Thon cried impatiently. "No ambition! I am sure there are a lot of things we could do with if we only set our minds to it."

"If we have to 'set our minds' to look for them, they cannot be very necessary or urgent."

"And surely," Kyra said, remembering something she had heard from Maal, "the good life is based on proportion and balance. We have a good balance of work to what we need at the moment. If we either had to work harder, or we invented more 'needs', the balance would be destroyed."

"She is right," her mother said, "more possessions only bring more harassment."

"We could do with a bigger house?" Thon muttered.

"What is wrong with this house?" Kyra's mother looked around proudly at her neatly built and beautifully maintained home. No space wasted, and no space too crowded. These little round houses built sturdily of tree trunks filled in with a mixture of firmly packed twigs and clay, the roof thatched with marsh reeds and covered with hides lashed firmly down against the wind, had been built this way for generations and she could see no reason for change. The family slept together and kept each other warm and safe. The circle that surrounded them was the circle of the Sun, the Moon, the Sacred Stones. It gave them security and peace. They had no need of change.

But Thon could not see it. Since Wardyke's arrival he had felt restless. A different kind of restlessness to Karne's. Karne wanted to *know*. Thon wanted to possess. In a sense the houses of the two priests summed up the difference in the two attitudes.

When Wardyke had first come to the village he had stayed in the guest house the villagers always kept empty but clean for the use of travelling strangers. It was a modest circular construction similar to the others in the village. But within days of his arrival he had set the community to doing two things: constructing Maal's tomb and building his own house.

It was accepted that he would not take over Maal's house as it was the custom to burn the previous home of a person who had died. The people felt very strongly that the home of a person was in a sense like a further skin that enclosed him, that was personal to him and should die with him. After years of living in a house it became impregnated with the occupant's personal feelings and if someone else were to come and live in it, he would be troubled with the memories and concerns of his predecessor.

The villagers did not have any excess possessions. Those they had were in constant use and in a sense extensions of themselves, usually made lovingly by themselves or by their relations. A man's axe, a woman's bone needle, were steeped in personal history by the time they came to die and these things were not taken from them but left for their own use in the next life in a place where they would expect to find them, the chamber of the burial. Sometimes pottery vessels that had belonged to them but were not of prime importance to them were smashed against the burial mound or, in some communities, against the Standing Stones of the Sacred Circle itself.

As each child grew up and took a mate they would leave the family home and build one of their own which they would inhabit until their death. If parents died leaving children, the house would still be burnt and the children would go to live with relatives. It was accepted. It was natural.

Wardyke made it known that he did not want a house like the villagers, or like Maal's. He frequently came to the site and drew pictures in the dust of what he wanted. But first he chose the trees with care from the great southern forest. Some of the men were uneasy about penetrating so deeply into the forest. It was heavy work breaking through the undergrowth and chopping down the giant trees Wardyke chose, and there was a danger of wild boars and wolves as well.

Wardyke's timber was hard won and two men suffered for the rest of their lives because of it. One lad of seventeen had his leg crushed by a falling tree and for the rest of his life dragged himself around in pain. Another man lost an eye to a sharp and deadly branch. After these accidents some of the men murmured that the timber was cursed in some way, the spirits of the forest did not want Wardyke to have it for his house. On hearing this Wardyke called all the community together at the edge of the forest and held a ceremony to cleanse it of any evil curse that might have been lurking there. He chose his time well and as he intoned the age-old words of exorcism clouds as black as night gathered above the tall trees, wind groaned in the high branches and the people shuddered with sudden cold. His long black robes spread out around him in the wind like the wings of a bird of prey and his eyes were the colour of lightning.

"I command," he bellowed into the gathering rage of the storm, "the thwarting spirits of the dark! Begone and leave the forest to my pleasure!"

As he finished the storm broke and the people were drenched in hard and hammering rain. The wind tore at the trees and they could hear within the forest the ripping, cracking roar of a giant tree uprooted and flung upon the ground.

Terrified they fled, their last sight the figure of Wardyke like the pointing figure of the storm aimed at the forest.

In the calm morning that followed this upheaval, many trees were found to be upon the ground. Wardyke claimed that they were his, given to him by the repentant forest.

His house was to be circular as the others were, but many times the size. Concentric rings of tall and beautifully smoothed tree trunks held the roof of wood and thatch aloft. In the very centre the house was unroofed so that light could penetrate, and Wardyke could walk if he so wished in sunlight within his own house. Channels were dug to lead rain water out if it should fall to excess and hangings of hide between the inner columns kept inclement weather from the inner chambers.

"What does he need so many chambers for?" Karne's father asked. "He lives alone."

"The meetings of the Elders are held in there now," Karne said, "in secret, where the people cannot argue with what is said."

Karne's father shook his head sadly.

"I do not care for such changes. The old way was the best."

This time Karne was inclined to agree with him.

Maal's home on the other hand was small and compact. Kyra stood within it for the first time the day after the confrontation at the Meeting Stone. Maal had not been seen since the moment of his dramatic stand against the magician and she was anxious about his health.

He did not respond when she stood at the entrance and called to him, and after a few moments of hesitation she stepped into the shadows of the interior. In contrast to the brilliant sunlight without, the inside of the house was very dark indeed. She paused a few moments and gradually the darkness appeared to lift and she could see quite clearly. As with their own homes there were columns of wood holding up the roof, but unlike their own, these were carved with amazing designs, mostly circles within circles within circles, a great many of which seemed to be built round the spindly figures of men, as though (but she was not sure of this) they were standing with their arms raised holding a series of arcs above their heads, the arcs almost completing themselves as circles behind and around them. Some designs looked more like trees, each branch of which supported one of these concentric multiple circles. Amazed, she gazed from one to the other and had almost forgotten the purpose of her visit, when she suddenly became aware of Maal sitting in the dead centre of the room observing her.

"My lord Maal!" she cried with a mixture of confusion and relief. "I was worried about you. Are you all right?"

"Yes," he said quietly, "thanks to you."

She flushed slightly.

"Was it really me?" she murmured, hanging her head in embarrassment. "I cannot believe it!"

"Yes, it really was you," and he raised himself to stand beside her, taking her arm lightly.

Not knowing what to say next her heart was so full, she looked around her at the surroundings and gestured at what she saw.

"It is all so beautiful," she said with awe. "I have never seen anything like it."

Maal smiled and there was some secret knowledge in his smile.

"I will show you greater wonders than these, my child."

At a loss to know quite what he meant Kyra returned to the carvings.

"Did you carve them yourself?"

"Yes."

"All of them?"

"Yes."

"What do they mean?"

112

"They mean a great deal and one day you will understand them all."

"I would like to understand them now if it is possible," she said as humbly as she could.

"Ah," he smiled, "you remind me of Karne now, wanting to understand everything, immediately. Have you not learned that understanding is a slow growth and comes only in stages and when you are ready?"

"I know . . . but . . . there is so little time . . ." She meant until Maal was to die but she was sorry she had said this as soon as the words left her mouth. She could not help feeling, and Karne agreed with her, that Wardyke would not rest now until he had destroyed Maal. It was endangering his own position to allow someone to escape whom he had cursed.

Maal knew what she meant and looked thoughtful.

"You are right. There is no time to waste. Come, sit with me and I will teach you things you need to know."

"About the carvings?"

"The meaning of the carvings is only a small part of a greater whole, some of which you already know."

"Are the different circles the different levels of reality one can discover around one . . . gradually as one's understanding and awareness develops?"

Maal smiled.

"You see, you do not need me to explain things to you."

"But . . ."

But he held up his hand and she knew she had to stop talking.

"As you said . . . there is not much time. Today we must try something that I would not have chosen to try till much later in your apprenticeship."

Kyra looked anxious. Maal noticed.

"Not dangerous so much as . . . difficult," he said reassuringly. "If you do not succeed no harm will come to you. But if you do, our work together will be that much easier."

She was comforted.

113

"What must I do?"

"First, sit."

She sat.

"Now relax and go quiet within yourself as I have taught you."

At first she had found this very difficult to do. Her mind seemed to be continually chattering on and on, going over things repeatedly, worrying at new things, even remaking old memories with slight alterations. She had caught herself at this several times and had been quite shocked at herself. Somehow by the time she had "remade" a memory in words in her head her own part in it always looked better than it had at the time of the actual happening. Maal had been trying to teach her to control her mind so that it did not run on and on like this. At first he had taught her to blot out the incessant gabble by replacing it with one image or word that was so insistently and repeatedly thought of by her there was no room for any other. Once she had mastered this, it was her task to do away with the blocking word itself and keep her mind poised and still ready for messages from her deeper self, her Real Self, which was in touch with the other levels of Reality.

Another trick he had suggested to her to help her achieve this was to choose a word and use it as a kind of magic flower from which a thousand petals of meaning and association could be plucked.

"This way," he said, "you think of the word and what it suggests to you, and then you think of the word again and what else it suggests to you. You repeat this again and again, coming back each time to the original word, until you find somehow the word is associated with everything. Everything is associated with everything else. We are parts of a Whole and nothing is separate. As this conviction grows on you you will feel yourself more and more receptive to the Whole. Your own separate identity will lose its hold, your protective wall of mind wordage will be down, and influences from outside and beyond yourself will be able to penetrate."

It was this method she chose to use this day.
And the word she chose was "Stone".

Stone . . . mountains . . . stone . . . cliffs . . . stone
. . . rocks in rivers . . . rivers of water working at the
rocks of stone . . . water breaking rocks of stone into
sand . . . stone sand . . . stone earth . . . roots in earth
sand . . . roots in stone earth . . . roots drawing nourish-
ment from stone earth . . . water containing grains of
stone . . . earth . . . crushed stone . . . nourishing plants
. . . plants containing stone . . . crushed stone . . . nourishing her and animals . . . stone . . . animals with
crushed stone from the plants nourishing her . . . she,
part stone . . . part earth . . . part universe . . .

She could feel her identity growing and growing until it
encompassed everything . . . she was part of the universe
and the universe was part of her . . . and as she became
aware of this she also became aware that she was no
longer Kyra in Maal's house, she was Maal but Maal was
a younger man and he was standing in the thick dust of a
parched country.

She looked at her feet and they were Maal's feet clad in
unfamiliar sandals made of hide thongs. She noticed they
were not covered in dust although they should have been.
It puzzled her that they were not covered in dust. It
puzzled her that she should think that they should be.

Behind her stretched a steep road curving down a
rocky hill into a dry valley. The sun was blazing on everything, brighter than she had ever known it, bleaching the
colour out of the landscape. Beside her was a gigantic
wall built of huge stones placed one upon the other, one
beside the other, each one a slightly different shape and
size and yet all fitted neatly and intricately together with
great skill so that there were no spaces at all between
them.

Before her was a gateway so large one would think it
was made for giants and above it two great beasts facing
each other were carved out of solid rock. She gasped,

straining to lean far enough back to see the height of it all. But even as she was doing this she could feel herself impelled forward to enter the gate. Guards were posted, wearing strange clothes and carrying tall and deadly looking spears, but they seemed not to notice her. She found herself walking past them and facing a kind of citadel or palace built of stone.

The road from the valley continued through the gate and spiralled up the hill, the huge walls curving with the curve of the road. She walked on unnoticed by the people who were going about their daily business. To the right and to the left she saw more of the pale dust-coloured stone. She could not believe men could do such wonderful things with stone and wondered that her own people did not build temples and palaces in this way.

The hill was steep but the high walls gave shade. She walked where she fancied, exploring doorways and courtyards, confident that she could not be seen. As she climbed higher the view of the distant landscape she occasionally caught was breathtaking. She could see a line of ocean so deep in the colour blue that if it had not sparkled so, she would have thought it was a field of flowers. The palace-citadel was built on a high and isolated hill. To the left there were rocky mountains, the colour of ripe wheat, devoid of grass or heather. But in every other direction for a long way there was nothing but arid plains, until on the far horizon a line of hills ran down to meet the unbelievable blue of the sea.

"Greetings," a voice said suddenly beside her—or was it in her own head the word formed?

She spun round. She was in a vast courtyard paved with cool stone dazzling white and so smooth that a moment before she had stooped down to stroke it but strangely had felt no sensation in her hand. She saw now that she was not alone. An old man clad in a robe of a deep violet colour was looking directly at her.

"Greetings," she said tentatively, for the first time in this strange place at a loss to know what to do next.

The man smiled and approached.

116

"You have come a long way and you are welcome," he said kindly.

"Thank you," she said, but it was Maal's voice she heard saying it. She still could not make out if they were speaking aloud or merely "thinking" the words.

"Could you," . . . she began and hesitated, but his expression seemed so friendly she decided to take the plunge.

"Could you tell me where I am?"

He smiled.

"You are in the Palace of the King," he said proudly.

"Oh," she said, and the flatness of her voice indicated that this meant nothing to her.

"Come," he said, and he gestured for her to follow.

He took her across the white sunlit courtyard into the dark interior of a chamber and there he fetched an object and held it up to the sunlight that came shafting through the entrance. He held it with both hands above his head as though it were some kind of sacred object. She looked up and her eyes were dazzled as the sunshine glanced off and spun from a cup of gold of such beauty that she could scarcely breathe as she gazed upon it. As her eyes grew more accustomed to staring into the concentrated light of its surface she noted that there was a design beaten upon it, a design of bulls. Two bulls charging each other. So powerful was the impression of vigorous life within their rippling golden muscles, she almost stepped back as though they could harm her. Her sense of scale, of what was moving and what was not, of what was within her and what was without, had long since disappeared. If she had ever thought to put a limit to what is real and what is not she would have abandoned the attempt now.

She knew this was all happening to her. She had a strong sense that it was real . . . and yet . . . and yet . . . it was like nothing she had ever experienced before. The cup was real. She was sure she could reach up and touch it, and yet at the same time . . . as she gazed at it it was no longer a cup but an experience of sun, of gold, of fear and thundering hooves and tossing horns . . . an experience of overwhelming power and light.

She met the eyes of the old man and in them she saw herself reflected.

But it was not an image of herself. It was Maal, and Maal as a young man as she had never seen him.

She shut her eyes and for the first time she felt afraid of the strangeness of it all.

"Kyra," a voice said gently.

She opened her eyes and Maal, the old man, was outside her, looking deep into her eyes with affectionate concern. Around him the dark carved wood of the columns of his house enclosed them in familiar comfort. She dropped her head upon her chest wearily.

She was tired . . . so tired . . .

"Sleep," he said gently, helping her to lie down. "You will feel better after sleep."

"So tired . . ." she murmured to herself.

She wanted to think about the experiences she had just been through but she was too tired.

"Another time . . ." she whispered as she drifted off into a blessed dreamless sleep.

When she awoke Maal was still with her. She sat up and looked round her hastily, worried that she might have slipped unwittingly into yet another strange place.

"It is all right," he said, "you are here in your own village where you feel most at home."

She remembered the experience in the strange palace.

"Tell me," he said quietly.

"Do you not know," she asked, "you were there."

"Tell me," he repeated gently.

She told him everything.

"What was it?" she asked when she had finished. "Why did I seem to be you?"

"You were not travelling in the way you did before when you saw Wardyke and Thorn. In a sense you were

118

not travelling at all. You were identifying with me and experiencing my memories."

"You mean all that happened to you once when you were a young man and you were remembering it in this room now, and I somehow was inside your mind remembering it as though it had happened to me?"

"Something like that," Maal said smiling.

Kyra was silent for a while thinking about the complexities of it.

"Did it *really* happen to you?"

"Yes."

"I mean, did you *really* go there . . . to that *very* place?"

"Yes."

"Why was it that only that one man could see me . . . I mean, you?"

Maal looked as though he did not know where to begin to explain it to her.

"You see . . ." he began hesitatingly, but she interrupted. She felt she must get it straight.

"You were *really* there?" she insisted.

Maal laughed and threw up his hands.

" 'Real'? 'Really'? what do the words mean?"

"You know what *I* mean by them," cried Kyra.

"What do you mean by them?" he said with a touch of gentle irony in his voice.

"I mean . . . quite simply . . . that you were there as I am here now."

"And how are you here now?" he asked quietly.

She was stunned.

"I am *here*!" she shouted indignantly.

He just looked at her and for a terrible moment she was not sure if she *was* there now or not. After all, the experience in the palace had felt just as real.

But he saw her distress and decided she had had enough insecurity for one day.

"I will explain," he said soothingly, "as best I can. I was not 'really' there in the sense I think you mean. My body that you can touch in this room at this moment was

119

not there. But the inner me, the spirit Me, was really there."

"You mean you 'travelled' in the way I did when I saw Wardyke and Thorn that day?"

"Yes."

"And the other people could not see you because you were in your spirit body, but the one old man could because he was a trained priest?"

"Yes."

"That was a real golden cup he held up for me to see?" she said wonderingly, her voice filled with awe.

"Yes."

"Somewhere in the world at this very moment that gold cup still exists?"

"Very probably."

"Oh Maal!" she cried, "I wish I could see it again. I wish I could hold it in my hand."

"Maybe you will one day. I know there is a long journey in your life."

"You mean a real journey . . . I mean in my body . . . not just spirit travelling?"

He smiled at the epithet "just". How she had already come to take one of the greatest wonders of the universe for granted. "But then," he thought, "so do we all," and he fingered the green and delicate shell of a sea urchin that he wore on a thong around his neck.

She flushed slightly, realizing what she had said.

"Yes," he said smiling, "a 'real' journey."

"Where to?"

"That I do not yet know."

"When will you know?"

"*You* will know when it is time."

"How will I know?"

"There will be an omen, a sign."

"How will I recognize it?"

"You will recognize it," he said with confidence.

She did not look so sure.

He wondered if he should tell her more about the nature of omens.

He wondered if he should tell her that omens are around us all the time. Everything is an omen if we choose to make it so. What makes an omen work is something in ourselves. We sense something from deep within us, on a level in which we are not used to being conscious, and we choose something from the "outside" world to project it on, to make it understandable for us. For instance, she would sense a need to take a journey, a readiness, a ripeness . . . and because she was not used to recognizing such deep instinctual drives she would see a giant bird flying or a wind blowing a tree in a particular way and she would believe it was an omen telling her to go. She would think the message was coming from outside herself.

If she saw the same bird flying, the same tree bending, when she was not ready to go, she would not see them as omens at all. It was another case of what was reality. The omens were real, but not in the sense the people believed them to be.

He looked at her and decided she was not ready to recognize omens as part of herself. She had too much that was new already to cope with. It would be more comfortable for her to believe as most people believed, that omens were messages from the gods telling one what to do. Making decisions for oneself was always difficult and it was a sign of maturity when one could take responsibility for decisions. Kyra was maturing rapidly, but she was still a long way from this point.

"Will it tell me where to go?" she asked anxiously.

"Yes," he said comfortingly, "it will tell you everything."

"But . . ."

"No," he said firmly, "I have answered enough questions for one day. You will know everything you need to know when it is time to know it. Go home now, child. Relax. Everything is working out well."

"I did everything right today?" she asked, anxious for confirmation.

"You did." He patted her gently on the shoulder. "But

121

now it is time to be Kyra again, the daughter in a family."

She slipped out of the priest's house and ran home, overjoyed to be greeted by the noisy barking of Faro's dog and the crying of her baby sister wanting to be fed.

The Visit

While Kyra was having these experiences with Maal, and Karne was at work on Maal's tomb, Fern was disturbed in her green world by an unexpected and unwelcome visit from Wardyke. She was digging a small patch of earth not far from the clearing Maal and Kyra were wont to use for Kyra's "travelling" lessons and she was singing as she worked. The sun was warm on her back and a friendly robin was perched on a clod of earth nearby, glad to see her disturbing the earth worms. Every time she stopped digging for a moment to rest he would swoop in, tug out a worm and fly off to deliver it to his hungry family. Other birds were singing in the trees and the scent of summer honeysuckle was heavy in the air.

She first sensed something was wrong when she paused in her own song and noticed that the birds had gone quiet. The robin who should have been back from his mission to his family had not returned and there was a distinct feeling of waiting and tension in the air. She straightened up her back and kept quiet, trying to work out what could be wrong. She noticed she was no longer in sunlight and yet sunlight was everywhere else. The shadow of a man had fallen over her and she could feel the chill of it on her bare arms. She spun round to find Wardyke standing a few paces from her, his arms folded and his face brooding as he stared at her. As far as she could remember he had never been there before although she had heard that he had visited every one else within the first few weeks of his arrival in their community. She had been glad she lived so far away from the village, so hidden by the shoulder of a hill and the cloak of the wood. She had seen him when she went to the village and had taken the measure of him very quickly. What she had learned of him from Maal had not surprised her but had only confirmed what she already suspected.

She stood now as straight as she could, looking him in the eye boldly, unlike the other villagers, feeling around her the plant and bird world as poised on anxiety as she was. His eyes were black and fathomless, his granite face in shadow. She could not tell what he was thinking, but she could feel malevolence in the air.

"You are welcome, Lord Priest," she said at last with quiet dignity. No one would have been able to tell her inner disquiet from the steadiness of her voice. "Did you wish to talk with me or is it refreshment you seek on such a warm afternoon? You have strayed far from the village."

He continued to gaze in silence for a moment and then seemed to relax slightly under the influence of her calm voice.

"Refreshment would be good," he said, "I hear the waters of your spring are sweeter than those from any other in the district."

She bowed slightly. The water was good and fresh to drink at all times and on certain days of the year she knew it had healing properties. She herself drank from it daily and was never ill.

"If you will follow me I will show you where it is, my lord," she said politely and led him to the spring. It was

124

quite a way into the wood and she hated bringing him among her much loved trees. Somehow his presence felt wrong and she could sense the growing things resented it too. The spring from which a small and lively stream sprang started as a filagree fall of water over moss and stone in an alcove deep with fern. Even when she was not thirsty she spent many an hour in this shady place listening to the silver voice of the water over the rocks, and tracing with her eyes the satisfying and exquisite robes of moss and fern and lichen that clothed everything in the area.

In leading him to the water she was leading him away from the tomb they had built for Maal. It was finished and ready now and skilfully hidden, but Wardyke was no ordinary man and she did not want to risk his finding it. The spring would distract his attention and take him further away.

He stooped to drink at once, using the small hollowed stone cup that had always been beside the spring since the days of her grandfather.

She stood very straight and stiff beside him as he drank, wondering if he was sensitive to the influences and vibrations that came from people and things. If he was, he must surely be aware that there was not a living thing around him that was not fearing and resenting him.

If he was aware he showed no sign.

When he had drunk, he smiled. His eyes stayed shadowy but the rest of his face smiled at her.

"What I have heard is truly an understatement. It is the sweetest water I have ever tasted."

She bowed gravely again in acknowledgement, and then turned to lead the man away.

"No, stay," he said, raising his hand. "This is a most peaceful and delightful place. I would rest awhile here. The sun is hot on the long walk from the village."

She stood still, her head slightly bowed for a moment, and then moved as though to leave him.

"No," he said again, "stay."

She stopped, but did not look at him. Her whole being

was crying out with dismay that this alien, malevolent creature was sharing her peaceful grove.

"Sharing? No," she thought, "he is here and I am here, but we are sharing nothing."

In a sense, so different were the waves of feeling that came to each from the surroundings, they might well have been in totally different parts of the world. If each were to describe the place, an impartial judge might not recognize that it was the same scene being described.

"Are you not lonely, girl, living so far from the village?"

"No, my lord," she said in a low voice, thinking of the time Karne had asked her the same thing.

"Do you have many visitors?"

"No, my lord," she repeated.

"But you have one, many times," he said slyly, pacing about on the soft mossy ground restlessly, looking at her closely.

"My lord?" She looked up enquiringly and with some alarm.

"I have been told that the old priest has been seen coming here often."

So that was it! That was why he had come. She was even more afraid now and the fear from the living things around her seemed to increase as well.

"You do not answer? You know you cannot lie to me."

"I did not know, my lord," she said at last as calmly as she could, "that there was any reason a priest could not visit one of his community."

"Maal is no longer priest here," Wardyke said with sudden harshness, standing still.

"But he has been our priest for many years. He helped my mother when I was born. Has he done something, my lord," she asked with exaggerated innocence, "that is against the laws of the gods and so is banished from our company?"

Wardyke drew in his breath sharply and resumed his pacing.

"He has no longer the role of a priest. He should not practice still as one."

"He does not, my lord. He visits only as an old man, a friend."

"What do you speak of when he visits?" His voice was sharp and he was standing before her in an attitude of interrogation.

"Why, many things."

"What things?"

"Mostly about plants, my lord. My garden is well known in the village and my lord Maal is interested in the methods I use."

Wardyke studied her face, but could not see further than the smooth sun-ripened skin, the long lashes and brown, deep eyes, flecked with yellow. He noticed that she was very beautiful, young and firm and lithe, standing like a young doe ready to take off at the slightest scent of danger.

The harshness of his expressions faded and he walked round her, studying her with a new expression she liked even less. It was as though he had entirely forgotten what they had been saying.

"My lord!" She spoke with alarm.

He smiled, but continued to circle her, looking at every part of her. In spite of her dress of soft brown bark cloth she felt naked. She drew herself back, muscles tense, ready to dart away as soon as she could seize an opportunity. She had seen this look in men's eyes from time to time, indeed had encouraged it in Karne's . . . but this time . . .? This time it was not welcome.

"How old are you, girl?" he asked, still prowling, still stalking his prey.

"Seventeen," she replied but so low she had to repeat it as he thrust his face close to hers the better to hear what she said.

"Seventeen?" he said thoughtfully. "Why is it you are not wed?"

"I have not wished to be, my lord."

"Everyone should be wed, girl."

She was silent, her heart beating very loud.

"Only priests should not be wed."

"Why is that so, my lord?" Her voice was trembling slightly. She was not thinking of what she was saying. She was thinking only of how she could escape. She knew there was no one who could come to her rescue. The only possibility was that Karne might come visiting, but although she longed for this with the frightened part of her heart, she knew she would rather he did not. It would mean nothing but trouble for him and would probably mean they would never be able to be free of Wardyke. Maal would die and the Lords of the Sun would never know of their trouble.

"Priests must be free to serve the gods," Wardyke murmured, but it was obvious he too was not thinking about what he was saying. "Women are a distraction . . . they weaken one's resolution . . ."

"Then they are best left alone," Fern said, summoning up the courage to speak loudly, hoping that the sound of her voice would snap the web that he was weaving around them. But it was too late. Her voice broke the web, but it was the web that was holding him back. He suddenly seized her, flung her on the ground and, roughly and with great harshness, forced himself upon her.

When he was done he looked so dishevelled, off guard and tired, that it was easy to forget he was a priest-magician.

She pulled herself away from him easily now and rose swiftly to her feet. Her eyes were blazing.

"Wardyke," she said bitterly and there was no trace of fear in the way she said it, "you will be cursed for this day's work. When you taste water it will be bitter. When you taste sleep it will be full of dread!"

She turned and walked away with great dignity.

If she had paused to look back at him she would have seen him still half lying, half crouching where she had left him, his face dark and twisted, his eyes like charcoal.

The Night of the Rising Star

MAAL ARRANGED with Kyra in the days that followed that they would make their bid to contact the Lords of the Sun on the Night of the Rising Star. He claimed that during this night the powers of the Circle were at their greatest. At the rising of the star called Magus from the sea horizon, directly over the Stone of the Star, their particular Circle was in closer contact than at any other time with the forces of the unseen world. At a certain point in the night when the whole star pattern had wheeled silently over their dark fields and hills to lie in a particular configuration, Maal would best be able to manipulate his powers in conjunction with the powers of the spirit world and travel greater distances and with greater surety than at any other time.

"Is it a better time than even the Night of the Full Moon?" Kyra asked with interest.

"It is better," Maal said. "Different forces are at work. Deeper forces, more secret and hidden. The Moon's influence is strong but it is more on the surface of things.

Have you noticed how the sea answers to the Moon's call, the animals grow restless? Even people who are not particularly sensitive can feel the influence of the Moon."

"But if this Night is so important," Karne said, "Wardyke himself will surely be in the Sacred Circle?"

"That is so," Maal said calmly.

Kyra was surprised that he seemed to be showing so little concern for this problem.

"The whole village will be there for the ceremony of the Rising Star!" she cried.

"Not all night," Maal said.

"But surely for the important time, the actual rising?"

"The rising of the Magus star is but a signal. In itself it is nothing. The priest will be alone when the moment of the right configuration comes," Maal explained.

"But how are we going to manage if Wardyke is there?" pleaded Kyra, her forehead creased with worry.

Even Karne was beginning to feel the whole thing was impossible. But Maal was smiling a little secret smile.

"What is it," Karne demanded, "you are keeping something from us?"

"Yes, I am afraid so," said Maal cheerfully.

"That is not fair!" cried Kyra indignantly.

Maal laughed and then, seeing that she was genuinely upset, and knowing that he indeed was being unfair, he added, ". . . but Wardyke has the wrong configuration."

Kyra gasped.

"What do you mean?" Karne demanded.

"Is is the duty of the departing priest," Maal explained carefully, "of every Sacred Circle to pass on the secret of the configuration of the Night of the Rising Star to his successor. It is a secret knowledge kept very close within the priesthood of a particular community, as it is the key to great powers and, in the wrong hands, the key to great dangers."

"How do you mean?" Kyra said in alarm.

He put his hand soothingly on her arm.

"You know, my child, I have explained many times, nothing is good or evil in itself. It is the way it is used

130

that makes it good or evil. Wardyke and I have great powers that we have worked long years to obtain. They are the same powers. It is to what use we put them that decides whether they are good or evil. It is in *us,* in the inner drive we call the *will,* in the key to action we call *motive.*

"The powers of the spirit world could be called upon and, if the motive and the will of he who calls is strong enough for evil, the spirit action will be evil."

"You mean *you* could call up evil spirits to help you?" Kyra asked, not quite understanding. "Even if you are good?"

"*I* am not Good, nor Evil. I am Maal."

"But could you call up evil spirits?" Kyra insisted.

"It is not as simple as that. Spirits are not necessarily good or evil either!"

"It is so complicated," complained Kyra.

"That is why the ordinary person is usually content to pursue his own life, accepting a few simple precepts to follow and leaving the complexities for the priest or the Elders to bother about."

"I think that is wrong," Karne said firmly.

Maal looked at him with interest.

"I think we should think about these things. There should not be one life for the priest and another for the ordinary person. I feel the urge to know as strongly as any priest. I want to understand! I want to make choices and know what the possibilities are! I want to know myself so that I do not deceive myself by thinking I am doing a good deed when the motive for doing it makes it bad. I want to be responsible for myself! Even if I make mistakes, I would rather do that than be a kind of straw doll played with by someone else . . . even if the some-one else is a spirit!" he added defiantly, looking upwards at the bland blue sky.

Maal smiled and Kyra could see that he was pleased with what Karne said.

"I think," she said, "I agree, even though it seems so difficult at times. I would not like to go back to the time when I did not think about these things. It was so boring."

"You will not go back," Maal said to her, "nor," he added, turning to Karne, "will you even be the slightest bit like a straw doll!"

"If I were a priest," Kyra said, her eyes blazing with inspiration, "I would set about changing the old ways. Teach people the things you have been teaching us, let them expand and grow and flower!"

Maal smiled, partly in sympathy with her enthusiasm and agreement with her ideas, and partly also with amusement that she did not realize how difficult this would be to carry out. But he said nothing to discourage her. If what she spoke of could be brought about, it would be a great achievement.

"And what," he asked gently, "would you teach them about good and evil?"

"I would teach them . . ." she started, and then hesitated.

"Why do you hesitate?"

"I do not know if I want to 'teach'," she said, frowning, "it sounds a bit like the old ways where people were told what to think."

"If by 'teaching' you mean 'telling' then you are right not to teach," Maal agreed.

"I want them to think for themselves. Perhaps I should guide them a bit at first . . . point out things for them to watch out for . . . things I had noticed when I was struggling at first . . ."

"What would be the first thing that you would want to point out?"

"That everything is not always as it seems when you first look at it. That everything that happens has its roots in something else and the unseen roots are usually more important than that which you can actually see."

Karne and Kyra were thoughtful for a while.

"It is not easy to understand things . . ." Kyra said at last.

"It is not only the understanding that I find so difficult," Karne said ruefully, "it is the explaining."

Maal smiled.

"As long as you try to understand," he said, "try to explain, even if it is only to yourself. Always keep your mind open and ready for exploration, ready to consider any new ideas, any new explanations. The very act of trying helps you to grow. You will surprise yourself one day with how much your understanding has grown while you had thought you were making no progress."

At this point they had to break off as they heard someone coming. As Karne and Kyra slipped away. Kyra said, "He never did tell us what he meant by Wardyke having the wrong configuration."

"It is obvious," Karne said impatiently. "It was his duty to pass on the configuration to Wardyke and because he had his suspicions that Wardyke was not our rightful priest he took the precaution of giving him a false one, still keeping the real one a secret."

"So when our real priest comes . . . after we have consulted with the Lords of the Sun . . . he will be given the real one and then Maal can concentrate on dying."

"And this will mean that Wardyke will be in the Circle on the Night of the Rising Star but will have left it when the time comes for the real configuration of power. You and Maal can then slip in and . . ."

"Oh no!" Kyra stopped short and her voice was indignant. "Not *in*! You *promised* I would not have to go in the Circle . . ."

"A slip of the tongue, little sister," laughed Karne. "I meant, of course, Maal could slip into the Circle with your help."

"From outside," she insisted.

"From outside," he agreed.

Fern had not been with them during this discussion so at the first opportunity Karne went to visit her. Some days had passed since he had seen her last and, impatient to make up for this, he ran most of the way to her house.

133

He slowed down just before he reached the curve in the path from which her garden suddenly became visible, and because of this he came upon her quite silently as she was stooping over a flower. He stopped and watched her for a moment, thinking how graceful she looked, feeling a sort of warm glow of pleasure welling up from inside himself as though the sunshine was coming from within his very inmost being this lovely golden day.

But the peacefulness of the scene did not last for long. Fern must have sensed his presence because she suddenly straightened up and spun round, her face momentarily quite distorted with fear and dislike. He was startled. He had never seen such emotions on Fern's face before. She had always seemed so calm and poised on an inner centre of happiness.

"Fern!" he gasped, "What is the matter?"

As she recognized him she instantly turned her face away, her expression no longer the same, but still compounded of something Karne did not understand. She usually lit up with pleasure when she saw him. What had gone wrong?

"Fern?"

She turned back to him now, and this time she was composed.

"Why, Karne," she said, "I am sorry. You startled me."

He was still puzzled. He had never known her to be startled like this before.

"What is it?"

"Nothing."

He was close to her and trying to look into her eyes, but hers would not meet his. For the first time since he had known her there was the shadow of something held back between them.

"There *is* something."

"No."

He took her hands, but she still would not meet his eyes.

She tried to smile at him, to reassure him, but her smile

was not very convincing. She pulled her hands away and drew back.

"Come, Karne," she said brightly, "I want to show you something."

"You do not look well," he still persisted while he was following her down the little winding path that ran deeper into her garden, brushing aside trailing fronds of bracken as he walked. He had noticed that she was paler than usual, the healthy bloom of her cheek considerably reduced. There was also something about the garden, he could not make up his mind what it was but it somehow did not look as flourishing and vigorous as it normally did.

She noticed the frown in his blue eyes and took his arm. Her composure had returned. She smiled and kissed him lightly on his brown cheek and ran her fingers through his long, light hair.

"Come on," she said laughing, "are you going to be as gloomy as this all morning?"

He looked at her bright face and there were no longer shadows there. He began to feel he had imagined what he had seen a few moments before. He shrugged and smiled.

"That is better," she said, "and now I can show you something special."

She drew him to a place where that morning she had found a new flower growing, one she had never seen before. A tiny, spiky, defiant one, half hidden in the grass, but growing as though it meant to stay. She cupped her hands around it and their heads were very close together as they admired it.

"It looks as though it was trying to be a star," she laughed, "but it was too small so it had to settle for being a flower instead."

"I wonder where it came from?"

She shrugged and indicated the arching sky.

"The birds sometimes bring me presents. They fly to lands of which not even Maal has heard."

Karne laughed.

"That is hard to imagine. Maal has heard of everything."

"Not everything," she said suddenly, sadly, and again he fancied that he saw the shadow of secretiveness cross her face.

"In fact, I have brought a message from Maal," he said, and stood up.

She joined him and they walked awhile in the garden, Karne telling her about the night of the Rising Star and the timing of the attempt to reach the Lords of the Sun. She was greatly interested and added up in her mind the number of days left. Not many. She was glad.

As they walked she was tempted several times to tell Karne about Wardyke but she knew that if she did the boy would go crazy with rage and probably rush off to attack the man. Karne would not stand a chance against the giant magician, and she could not bear him to be hurt or killed.

None of them knew quite what to expect from the Lords of the Sun, but Karne, Kyra and Fern certainly expected the situation to be resolved immediately. If pressed, they might have admitted to expecting a sudden thunderbolt to remove Wardyke dramatically from office.

Maal knew it would not be quite like that, but he said nothing of what he expected.

During the next few days Kyra spent a great deal of time with Maal, learning everything she could, and so it was that neither of them noticed the many changes that were taking place in their community.

Wardyke had doubled the workers on Maal's tomb and it was very near completion. There was talk that the building of it was to be finished by the Night of the Rising Star and that it would be during that night, or very near to it, that Maal would be interred. Maal was not informed of this and was surprised when Karne, out of breath from running, told him of it.

Kyra was horrified.

"But how will we contact the Lords of the Sun if Maal is not with us?"

Maal looked grave and shook his head.

"Surely Wardyke has no right to set a time for your death?" Karne asked.

"No right at all," Maal said sadly and was silent, thinking hard.

At last he spoke.

"Was this an official announcement at the Meeting Stone?" he asked Karne.

"Oh no," Karne said, "it was just talk, just rumour. It may not happen at all, but I thought you ought to know that people were talking about it."

"What people?"

"Mostly Wardyke's Strangers. They have been working on the tomb with me and they are full of confidence that they know what is in his mind. There is something about a prophetic dream of Thorn's too."

"If it is only rumour I do not think we should concern ourselves too much."

"Maybe not . . ." Karne sounded doubtful, "but when I hear them talk like that it makes me angry!"

Maal smiled at last, the gravity lifting like a cloud from his kind face.

"You must learn to control that anger, lad, it will be the undoing of us yet!"

"Everything grows worse and worse . . . and I am doing nothing," Karne protested. "You and Kyra work every day, but all I do is wait! Even Fern," he grumbled, "seems to have secrets these days!"

Maal looked surprised. He had been so busy with Kyra he had not seen Fern for quite a time.

"What secrets?"

"How would I know," Karne replied irritably, shrugging his shoulders. "I cannot see into people's minds!"

Maal was thoughtful.

"I have neglected her," he said regretfully. There was so little time and so much to be done.

Kyra was about to say something, but Maal raised his

hand to keep her quiet. There was much he needed to think about. His expression became more and more withdrawn.

"Come," Kyra whispered to Karne, and took his hand. Quietly they started to move away.

When they were out of earshot, Kyra said, "I thought we ought to leave him. He looked as though he wanted to think things through by himself."

Karne nodded. He had sensed it too.

"Perhaps you could go and see Fern," he said. "You and Maal have been so busy in that house of his . . ." His voice almost carried a touch of resentment.

"I know," Kyra said, "but you have no idea how complicated everything is and how delicate the balance is between success and failure. Sometimes," she added miserably, "I get so desperate. I cannot believe I will do everything right, and if I do the slightest thing wrong we are finished!" She gave a deep sigh. "And now . . . what will happen if Wardyke puts Maal away before we can reach the Lord of the Sun?"

Karne shook his head, momentarily as despairing as Kyra. And then he pulled himself together.

"Somehow," he said, "we have to prevent that."

"But how?"

Karne shook his head.

"Somehow," he repeated, frowning with determination.

The following day Kyra slipped away to see Fern before she went to Maal.

She found her sitting by the spring, her knees drawn up and her head resting upon them, her whole posture one of despondency.

"Fern," cried Kyra with concern and knelt down beside her, her arm around her shoulder.

"Oh, Kyra," Fern said with relief and turned to bury her head upon her friend's shoulder.

"You are crying?" Kyra was amazed, feeling the warmth of the tears. Fern, who was always so calm and strong, was crying!

She did not ask what the matter was but held her and rocked slightly backwards and forwards as a mother does with a weeping child. Her cheek was upon Fern's bright hair and occasionally she kissed the top of her head.

Gradually as they sat together Kyra began to feel that strange feeling of knowing something she had no ordinary way of knowing.

"It is Wardyke!" she said suddenly with conviction. "Wardyke has been here?"

Fern nodded miserably.

The two girls were silent, sitting side by side. Kyra's arms had fallen from Fern's shoulders and they both gazed into the moving water of the busy little spring.

Kyra did not put it into words, but she knew exactly what had happened to Fern. She was surprised how calmly she was reacting. Although the knowledge had startled her at first, it seemed that almost immediately she had accepted it as something that had happened and in no way could be changed. There was no point in being shocked or moaning about it in any way. The situation existed and they must somehow cope with it.

"I have not told Karne," Fern said quietly. She was calm now too.

"I think you were right," Kyra agreed. Karne's reaction would have been violent and angry. She remembered Maal suggesting that it was just this quality in Karne that would be their undoing.

"He suspects something is wrong."

"I know," said Fern miserably. "I hate keeping anything from him, but this . . ."

"Yes, this . . . must be kept. At least till we have reached safety on the other side of the Night of the Rising Star."

Fern nodded sadly.

After a while the two girls parted, Fern to work on her garden with greater composure now that she had shared her burden, and Kyra to visit Maal. She felt as though she had imperceptibly aged since the day before. Some days were like that. One seemed to take a leap into further knowledge and understanding as though a lot more time had passed than could be measured by the passage of the sun across the sky.

In fact in this summer as a whole time seemed to have speeded up. She looked back on the long slow days of quiet routine she used to have with nostalgia. Everything had been so much easier then!

Maal had obviously been thinking a great deal about the problems facing them since they last met, and seemed to have worked out certain things in his mind. He seemed less disturbed.

He listed to Kyra's news about Fern quietly, his only reaction being a deepening line between his brows and a conviction that what he had decided to do was right.

"I am going to break a very ancient and very strict law," he said to Kyra, his face grave and tired.

Kyra looked alarmed.

"Is that wise?" she asked.

"I have no choice," he said heavily.

"I thought you said we always had choice?"

"I did," he said wearily, "and in a sense now, literally, of course I have choice. What I mean is . . . I have chosen this way because I think it is the only way in which we can be sure to stop Wardyke in the time we have available."

He paused.

"What is it? What law are you going to break?"

"The law that says the departing priest should tell no one the sacred configuration of Stars but the priest who takes his place."

"Who are you going to tell?" Kyra was intrigued.

"You," he said simply.

Kyra gasped.

"No!"

"You need to know," he said quietly and gently now, knowing that she would need persuasion.

"You mean? . . ."

"I mean that if anything happens to me . . ."

140

"But I cannot . . ." Her face was a study in alarm and dismay.

"You can," he said firmly.

"But . . ."

"Listen my child . . . listen to me . . ." He put his hand upon her arm. She was beginning to protest again, but was silenced by the soothing power of his touch. When he could see that she was calmer and prepared to listen he began to speak again.

"You mention choice. I have said we always have choice. Our ability to choose, to make decisions, is crucial to our development in all the different levels of existence through which we are journeying. When we reach the Source of Light and Consciousness, we will no longer see bits and pieces among which we have to choose, but will see the Whole as a magnificent pattern in which everything fits together in harmony. We will see it and we will Be it simultaneously. The agony of choice will at last be over."

Kyra sighed. It was a grand idea, but she was a long, long way from that kind of realization at this moment.

"I know . . ." he said softly, sympathetically, and sat quietly a few moments for her to absorb what he had said.

"But these choices we have to make," he continued at last, "are not always made with the surface and most obvious level of our Selves. The Kyra whom the villagers can see when she walks among them wants to make one decision, one choice, but the Kyra whom they cannot see, the one that is in touch with the deeper levels of Reality, knows the decision has to fall another way."

She knew he was right, but she tried still to fight against it.

"But I know on every possible level I cannot do what you ask of me!"

"That is not true," he said simply, and she was silent.

"If it were true," he continued, trying to give her more help, "you would not come to me for lessons . . . you would not ask the questions you have been asking, de-

141

velop the powers you have been developing. Over this summer you have been gradually getting ready for this moment . . . I had hoped you would have had longer . . . but no moment ever seems perfect to us . . . we can see so little of the Whole."

"But what if I am not ready . . .?"

"We will not know that until you have tried . . . but I would say the moment of crisis will make you ready."

Kyra buried her face in her hands. It seemed to her that inside her head was a great space full of darkness that was whirling and roaring.

"I cannot . . ." she cried, turning her head from side to side as though she was trying to escape some physical attack.

Maal put both hands upon her head.

"You can," he said. "You must!"

He held her head still, putting more and more pressure upon it until she cried out in pain. Then he withdrew his hands and they sat together in silence for a while.

Kyra at last lifted her face and it was pale and drawn, but resigned.

"What must I do?" she said quietly.

Maal moved away from her and fetched something from a shelf in one of the darkest places in his house. She watched him with interest as he returned to her holding something carefully in both hands. He motioned her to sit relaxed and he sat opposite her, putting what he carried between them. It was a small parcel wrapped in bark cloth. She looked at it with curiosity and stretched out a hand to take it.

"No," Maal said, putting his own hand over it to protect it from her. "Do not touch."

She could sense that a change had come over him. He was no longer the friendly, fatherly figure with whom she could talk so easily. He had become Lord Maal, the priest, and sat straight and tall, his face masked so that she could not read his eyes.

She was a little afraid and sat straight herself, feeling the solemnity of the moment most intensely.

142

When he saw that she had grasped the situation, he began to unwrap the parcel very carefully, using ritualistic movements, his lips murmuring something inaudible to her as he proceeded. Her heart began to beat faster and as he reached the last layer of bark cloth she was leaning forward breathlessly to see what lay between them.

It was a sphere of yellowish-grey stone, small but exquisitely carved, the patterning following the curvature of the surface in intricate spirals.

She stared at it fascinated.

Maal folded his hands. She noticed he had touched only the wrappings, the sphere itself he left strictly alone.

She looked up at him, her eyes questioning but not daring to say anything to break the impressive silence surrounding the stone sphere.

"Move your head from side to side," Maal said, speaking his priest's voice, "but keep your eyes on the sphere."

Kyra was puzzled but did as she was told. As she moved the light that fell on the stone from the doorway struck it from different angles. With sudden splendour the sphere seemed to send up shafts of green-blue light. Kyra gasped and retreated.

The stone lay still and dark again.

Maal drew her forward with a gesture and again as she moved the stone seemed to come alive with an inner luminosity. Each surface that had been carved reflected light in a different way. Reflected? No. Kyra was sure the light came from within the stone.

"How can that be?" she whispered to herself.

"Take the sphere," Maal said in a deep, quiet voice. "Hold it between your hands."

She hesitated.

"Hold it," he commanded.

Tentatively and hesitatingly she put her two trembling hands forward and cupped them around the magical stone. The light within it seemed to go out and it felt like ordinary cold stone.

"Close your eyes." Maal spoke still with firm authority.

She closed her eyes.

143

"Feel the pattern of the stone with your fingers."

Delicately she moved her finger tips over the cold surface. She felt the pattern.

"No. Do not open your eyes."

She was in a very dark darkness. It seemed darker within her head than it normally did when she closed her eyes. No images whatever came to her, not even those peculiar little wisps of shape that usually seemed to float upon the inside of her eyelids.

She could feel the icy ball of stone within the cup of her hands. Her fingers began to trace the spiral round and round the surface.

It seemed to have no end. Her finger tracing . . . the grove . . . the spiral . . . the sphere.

The spiral never left the sphere and yet never ended . . . as though the sphere and the spiral were eternal . . . She began to drift . . . to feel only the spiral groove going round and round the sphere until at last she lost consciousness of even her own finger in contact with it and was aware only of herself the spiral . . . herself the spiral . . .

In this state she was no longer aware of the darkness as darkness, but as the night sky, immensely vast and filled with countless stars. When she had looked at the sky at night on other occasions she had seen the myriad sparks of light dotted about apparently at random. Now she was aware of it as an intricate but definite pattern.

She *saw* it as a pattern, each star linked with each other star in a relationship that was unmistakable. It was as though fine gold lines, as fine as spider's web, were drawn between each spot of light to make an exquisite network, complex and yet ultimately simple.

But even as she grasped this the vision was altering slightly. The web was not flat but had depth as well. The stars she had thought were all the same distance from her appeared now to vary, some nearer, some further away. The golden threads linked them not only sideways, but backwards and forwards as well.

She felt herself moving nearer to them, somehow being

144

among them so that the network of fine gold lines was around her in every direction . . . stars were around her in every direction.

As the sensation of movement grew she realized that it was not only herself that was moving. The stars, the golden lines, the darkness itself . . . everything was moving and everything was changing in relationship to everything else in subtle ways at every moment, and yet the overall web of relationship was still there . . . the threads never broke . . . only adjusted, stretched and altered.

And still as she moved the vision developed further.

It seemed to her the points of light that were the stars were not only moving, but were growing. Or was it that she was approaching them?

They were no longer points of shapeless fire, but huge spheres rolling through the darkness, immense balls of concentrated power.

As they rolled the sound of them roared in her head until sounds and vision so overwhelmed her that she found herself screaming, a small insignificant creature, back on Maal's floor, trying to hold the full fearful magnificence of the Universe at bay.

She dropped the small sphere of stone and saw Maal move swiftly to catch it.

She flung herself down and beat her fists upon the hard floor.

"It is too much!" she cried despairingly. "I cannot bear it alone!"

Maal had quietly and quickly wrapped the small sphere in its coverings of bark cloth and had put it safely aside. He could now turn his attention to the hysterical girl.

"You will not be alone," he said, "Kyra! Kyra! No one is alone."

She sobbed.

"Was it not beautiful?" he said quietly when he could see that she had cried enough.

She nodded miserably.

"Are you not excited to be part of such a beauty?"

Tearfully she nodded again.

145

"Well then, accept it. Enjoy it."

She sat and thought about what she had just seen. Already the splendour was passed and she only had a shadowy memory of the experience, but even that was more beautiful and exciting than anything she had ever known before.

Enjoy it? Why not? She could no longer fight against it. As Maal had said, deep inside her the forces that were at work in her had already made a choice. She was only hurting herself by fighting against them all the time.

He saw the change in her and was glad.

"You may tell me the configuration now," she said calmly. "I am ready."

He smiled gently. The priest was gone. The man was back.

"You know it already," he said smiling at her.

She looked surprised, a line forming between her eyes.

"Was I supposed to get it from . . . ?" and she pointed at the stone sphere.

"You did," he said simply.

She shook her head slowly, trying to remember.

"I think I did not."

"Do not worry about it," Maal said, "you know it at the level that matters."

"But I can hardly remember . . . I remember a pattern . . . but I cannot remember exactly . . ."

"It will come to you when you need it," Maal said confidently.

She looked doubtful, but if he said so, perhaps it would be so.

"Promise me," he said seriously, "if it becomes impossible for me to go into the Circle on the night of the Rising Star, you will."

She sat very still, her heart beating painfully. How could she promise that!

"Promise!" he repeated, and he spoke with urgency and authority.

"I promise," she found herself saying in a very small, thin voice.

146

"Louder!" he commanded.

"I promise," she said, this time with a conviction that amazed her.

He relaxed.

"Good," he said, "now we can begin the lesson."

The Burials and the Promise

IT WAS three days later that Karne and Kyra woke to a feeling of oppressive malevolence in the air. The sky was obscured by heavy cloud which hung, grey and discouraging, neither falling as rain nor blowing away. Kyra particularly felt uneasy. She wondered what would happen if the sky was cloudy for the Night of the Rising Star. What use would knowing or not knowing the correct configuration be if none of them could even see the stars? It crossed her mind that perhaps there would be the ways of sensing it that she did not know about, but this line of thought was cut short by her brother Ji tugging at her arm and wanting her to follow him.

"What is it?" she said impatiently and irritably.

"We have finished the boat," Ji said excitedly. "Come and see!"

"Not now, Ji," she said, "I am busy."

"You do not look busy," he said, disappointed.

"One does not necessarily have to *look* busy to *be*

busy," she said grandly, and turned away. He stood contemplating her back forlornly.

"You never pay any attention to the family these days, Kyra," her mother said, witnessing the incident. "What is the matter?"

"Nothing." She wished they would leave her alone. She had things on her mind.

"I think there is something the matter," her mother persisted.

But luckily for Kyra Karne arrived at this moment and Ji pounced on him. Their noisy exchange of friendly blows diverted their mother's attention from Kyra and she could slip away.

She was sorry that she had been so short tempered with Ji and when he appeared again, somewhat dishevelled from the roll about with Karne, she asked to see the boat. Joyfully he led her to the secret place they knew so well, pulled back the cover of leaves and sticks, and revealed a tidy, well-constructed little boat, that looked as though it could withstand the onslaught of the waves quite well.

"It is good!" she cried in surprise. "I did not know that you and Okan were so skilful!"

"I did most of the work," Ji said proudly.

She ruffled his hair and laughed.

"You had better not let Okan hear you say that."

"I want to be a fisherman," Ji said, "We are going to try it out quite soon, will you come?"

"Oh, well . . ." she hesitated. "I do not think I have time, but I am sure Karne . . ."

"Karne is always too busy these days," Ji said sadly.

"I am sure Karne will . . . even if he is busy. After all, it is his boat."

"Will you ask him?"

"Ask him yourself."

"He always listens to you."

Kyra laughed.

"Not always."

"He does not seem to care about the boat now."

149

"Of course he does! It is just that he has other things he has to do now."

"What things?"

"Just . . . things."

"You and Karne are always going off by yourselves. He never takes us anywhere any more." Ji's voice sounded quite miserable.

Kyra put her arm around him, full of sympathy.

"Oh Ji," she said, "I am sorry."

She left Ji lovingly covering up his prized possession, and went in search of Karne.

She found him looking for her. His face was worried and gloomy.

"What is wrong?"

"I do not know," but he looked very anxious. "There is something about to happen. I can feel it. Maal's tomb was finished yesterday and all the Strangers are talking as though the burial is to be soon. I saw Wardyke going to Maal's house a little while ago. I have been looking for you everywhere! Where have you been?"

"I have been to see the boat. It is finished," Kyra said.

Normally Karne would have been interested in this piece of news, but today he was preoccupied.

"You must come with me," he said, turning towards Maal's house. "We must see what is going on."

"But," said Kyra, "it is important Wardyke does not notice our interest in Maal!"

"I know. That is why I want you to come. We will hide somewhere nearby and perhaps you can listen to their minds or something."

"I cannot do it just like that!" complained Kyra.

"Oh," he said impatiently, "there is no time to fuss about what you can do and what you cannot. Just *do* it!"

She started a resentful reply and then thought better of it. It was important that she did what she could to protect Maal, more important than whether she was irritated with Karne's attitude or not.

She followed him and they tucked themselves behind some bushes.

"Is Wardyke still inside?" she whispered.

He shrugged and shook his head.

"I have been away looking for you for ages. Can you not tell if he is inside or not?"

She stayed very still and concentrated, but nothing would come to her. She was still aware of the pricking of the grass against her leg, the sound of Karne breathing and moving from time to time beside her. She was still aware of herself crouching uncomfortably behind the bushes trying to get in touch with Maal. If she had learnt nothing else that summer she had learnt that her powers could not work until she had completely forgotten herself and somehow merged absolutely with something or someone else.

"It is no good," she whispered at last. "I am trying too hard. It will not come."

Karne gave an expression of disgust.

"I cannot help it," she complained bitterly.

"Try!"

"I *am* trying! That is the trouble. I need more time to relax first."

"We have no time!"

"I know! I know."

She looked ready to cry.

"Oh no!" he muttered, thumping his forehead with the palm of his hand in frustration.

At that moment a sound from the village called their attention away from Maal's house. It was the sound of the horn that was blown when a special meeting or ceremony was to take place. The sound of its weird hollow call went out across the valleys and the hills, disturbing even the animals in the forests and putting a flock of jet black birds to flight from the grain fields. They wheeled above the village, their wings adding a strange resonance to the sound of the horn, their dark, shadowy bodies in flight adding a touch of the ominous to the already oppressive air.

Some of the villagers had started wending their way to the Meeting Stone, while others were preparing to leave their fields and their work.

Karne and Kyra were in a quandary.

"What shall we do?" Kyra asked anxiously.

Karne hesitated.

"I think we ought to see if Maal is all right before we go," he said at last.

"Wardyke will be at the Meeting Stone. He has forbidden us to have a meeting without his presence. But I wish we knew if he was there already."

"There is nothing else to be done," said Karne, with sudden determination. "I will have to go to Maal's house."

"Why you? Perhaps I should go," Kyra said.

"No. You are the only one who can work with Maal to contact the Lords of the Sun. It is even more important that you escape suspicion than that I do."

This was true. She nodded, but she wished that neither of them had to go.

"Wait here and keep watch for me," Karne whispered and before Kyra could say anything more he was gone. He walked swiftly and boldly up to Maal's house as though it was the most natural thing in the world for him to be doing.

Kyra saw him pause at the door to call out and then she saw him go inside. She did not have long to wait before he came running out. He seemed shocked and distressed and came leaping over the uneven ground almost as though he were flying. He flung himself down beside her, out of breath.

"What is it?"

"Maal is gone," he gasped, "and all his things are smashed about and strewn everywhere. It looks as though there has been a struggle in there. It also looks as though whoever did it was looking for something among Maal's possessions."

"O Karne!" She was horrified. "That poor old man!"

Shock on Karne's face was giving way to anger. He stood up and his face was black with rage.

"Karne!" she cried. She leapt up and seized his' arm. "We must not do anything wrong now."

"I will tell you what I will do to Wardyke!" he snarled, shaking himself free.

"You must not, Karne! We dare not! We have a real responsibility now and Maal is relying on us."

Karne stood still, his face still thunderous.

"Karne!" she pleaded.

He looked at her with smouldering frustration.

"All right," he said. "I will hold back for now . . . but just wait . . ."

She had realized very quickly that for once she had to be in charge of the situation. An image of Maal's special stone sphere came most clearly and insistently to her. She knew he would not want that to be in the hands of Wardyke. Perhaps that was what he had been looking for.

She thought swiftly.

"You go to the Meeting, Karne," she said decisively, "keep control of yourself and do nothing to arouse suspicion. It is very important. Promise."

"I promise," he said unwillingly.

"See what is happening. I will go to Maal's house to see if I can rescue any of his most precious possessions. I will take them to Fern for safe keeping. She can bury them in the wood somewhere until we can give them back to Maal."

She was not prepared to admit even to herself that she might not see Maal alive again.

Karne nodded affirmation and was off to the village immediately.

No one saw Kyra slip into the old priest's house and she was not disturbed in her search. Karne was right. The place was a mess. His handsome drinking vessels and water jars were smashed to pieces on the floor. What clothes and rugs he had were ripped and flung around. The collection of delicate sea urchin shells he kept in or-

153

derly rows ranging from the smallest to the largest were powdered on the shelf on which they had stood as though a hard fist had smashed down upon them.

Her heart beating loudly, she felt in the dark corner from where she had seen Maal take the stone sphere and, miraculously, it was still there. She held it close to her heart in its bark wrappings, thankful she could rescue at least one of Maal's precious possessions.

She looked around, tears beginning to come to her eyes at the devastation of the room in which she had spent so many interesting hours. She would have stood there indefinitely if she had not suddenly "felt" the approach of someone.

She rushed to the door and looked out. Thorn was approaching. She had not heard him for he was too far away. She had "felt" his approach.

A lump of fear began to rise in her throat. She stood poised, uncertain what to do. Thorn was approaching rapidly, a burning branch in his hand. She looked round frantically for somewhere to hide, but the burning branch suggested he might be intending to burn the house and if she were inside she would certainly be burnt with it. She had seen this kind of house burn before. Wood and straw, twigs and furs, turn to flame fast.

Another thought came to her distraught mind. If he was burning the house, Maal must be dead!

Before the full implications of this could take effect, however, she saw Thorn pause on the path and turn to look back at the village. He was straining his neck to see the Meeting Stone as though he were looking for a signal.

Like a shadow Kyra slipped out of the house and ran for cover, clutching the small stone sphere close to her, some of the bark cloth wrappings working loose as she ran. Her fear sharpened her instincts and she found a route to Fern's house that was quicker and safer than any that she had ever taken before.

Meanwhile, at the Meeting Stone, nearly all the community were gathered. Karne was hovering on the outskirts, occasionally looking anxiously in the direction of Maal's house. Strangely the Elders were not on the platform in their usual formation but scattered amongst the villagers looking as puzzled and as ill at ease as their fellow men. Only Wardyke was on the platform and he was in his most magnificent cloak with a tall headdress of hard dark leather and tall black feathers to add even greater height to his stature. He was standing still as rock with his arms folded on his chest, only his smouldering eyes moving continually, scanning the faces of the cowed people below him.

Karne had the presence of mind to slip behind a taller man so that he would not be subjected to the deadly scrutiny. He knew Wardyke would not miss the hostility in his own eyes if he were to look into them. The others were trying to avoid his eyes as well, but somehow the beam of his attention forced their eyes up to meet his no matter how hard they tried to avoid it. If he saw the slightest flicker of anything but fear and awe in their expression, he concentrated longer upon them until at last they were forced to surrender their independence and cringe like the rest. Karne escaped only because he was aware in time of what was going on and kept well out of sight.

When everyone was gathered Wardyke lifted his left arm to point at the grey and lowering sky above Maal's house. It must have been a signal because almost immediately a low and sombre drumming started, and a column of smoke rose from the direction of the old priest's house. The villagers gasped, but had no time to talk to their neighbours about what was happening. The drumming was growing louder and as all heads turned from the smoke to the direction of the sound, six men, Wardyke's men, were seen approaching carrying a bier of branches on which the body of their old priest was lying.

A murmur of dismay started, but swiftly ceased as Wardyke's burning eye fell upon them. Behind them walked six drummers. Again, Wardyke's men.

Karne could have burst with the feelings that were racing through him, but he managed to keep control of himself. He had no doubt Wardyke had killed Maal and with the one act had frustrated their chances of reaching the Lords of the Sun and so rescuing the hapless villagers from his clutches, and at the same time frustrated Maal in his plan to influence his passage at the moment of death. All that they had been working for during the past few months was now wiped out. He thought of the sweat and the backache moving all those rocks, digging that tunnel. He thought of Kyra's troubles, trying to link her mind with Maal's.

It was strange she had felt nothing when Maal was killed. He had called to her when he was in trouble before. Why not this time?

The bier came nearer and nearer. The drumming grew louder and louder until he could feel the vibrations of it coming as it were from the thump, thump, thump of his own heart.

Maal was carried amongst the crowd of villagers, who drew back in respect as he passed. Karne could see him quite clearly for a few moments. His face was composed and white. The face of death. His body lying straight, hands folded on his breast. There was nothing to show that he had died violently.

For a moment a thought went spinning through Karne's heart. What if Maal was not dead after all? What if he had managed to cheat and was doing what priests were quite capable of doing, feigning death?

With the coming of this thought everything became possible again. They would keep the original plan! If Maal was truly dead it would not hurt to move him. If he was not, his passage through the many different planes of spirit could be made easier.

But against this hope he thought of the signs of violence he had seen in Maal's house and he knew that if Maal was to feign death he would have needed a long time to compose himself. It could not be done under conditions of harassment and stress.

Karne wondered about Kyra. There was no doubt that Maal's house was being burnt to the ground. Thorn must have set the tourch because Thorn joined the Meeting from the direction of Maal's house almost immediately after they had seen the smoke. He hoped Kyra was safely away with Fern. How he longed to be with them, but he dare not leave. He was in danger both of missing something that they needed to know, and of drawing attention to himself.

After the bier had been carried right round the community it was lifted on to the platform to lie at Wardyke's feet. Thorn made a move to step up and join him but, surprisingly, Wardyke gestured him down. Karne saw the look of puzzled fear that suddenly passed through Thorn's eyes. Karne felt a sense of satisfaction at that. It looked as though Wardyke had used Thorn to come to full power, but now no longer needed him.

Seven men from Wardyke's old community stepped up at this point and took their places behind Wardyke in the positions of the Sacred Stones, in the positions of the Elders of the Village.

A gasp went round the confused villagers and a few men stepped forward as though they were going to protest, but immediately there was a move from behind them and they realized they were entirely ringed by Wardyke's people, armed with axes and spears.

Without their realizing it the friendly, peaceful villagers had been taken over completely by a hostile group.

The rest of the Meeting passed like a nightmare. Wardyke spoke the words of burial over Maal and the villagers listened to the age-old terms of respect and comfort, realizing for the first time that they meant nothing in themselves. Only the feeling that was in the heart of he who spoke to them meant anything. And in Wardyke's heart was malevolence and greed.

After the words of burial he made a brief announcement that he had appointed seven new Elders for the Community, silenced any protest with a look of such ferocity that no one even dared to think dissent, and then gestured for the funeral procession to lead off to Maal's tomb.

The six men carrying the bier went first. The drummers next. The villagers followed them in a straggling untidy line and Wardyke's Strangers came behind as though to make sure no one strayed.

Wardyke himself came last of all and they had to wait for him at the tomb, listening to the sullen and disturbing pulse of the drums and their own thoughts struggling to find a way out of the situation.

Karne could see Maal from where he stood and he had to admit to himself that he looked very dead. His thoughts went round and round, trying to decide whether to risk transferring Maal's body to the other tomb and wondering if Wardyke would post a guard overnight. It was fortunate that they were having the burial ceremony so late in the afternoon for there would not be time to cover the burial chamber properly and complete the mound. The rest of the work would probably be done over the next few days, the whole community working in shifts.

There were no prayers said aloud while the villagers waited for Wardyke, only the insistent low throb of the drum, but Karne for one (and he did not think he was alone), was praying privately and silently. He had never wanted anything as much in his life as he wanted Maal to be alive at this moment. There were many of the villagers, even among those who had welcomed Wardyke and slighted Maal, who were not praying for Maal's spirit, for his help in the dark days to come.

Just before Wardyke's arrival Fern and Kyra joined the crowd unnoticed. Karne's first knowledge of their presence was when he felt a touch of his arm and Kyra's hand slipped into his. She stood close to him, her eyes dark with sorrow, seeking comfort in him. He kissed her forehead, thankful that she had come to no harm in the fire. On his other side he felt another touch. He looked around and Fern was beside him, her bare arm against his. His whole body responded to it in spite of his sorrow. Her face was as grave and as pale as Kyra's.

They had found a hiding place for the stone sphere and

had hurried back to the village in time to see the funeral procession winding along the path to the tomb Wardyke had chosen for Maal. They had paused to weep and to compose themselves. Now they were with Karne and the combined strength of their love for Maal and for each other was helping to sustain them.

Wardyke's arrival was announced with an impressive roll on the drums. The day, which had been dark from dawn, was growing darker every moment. The magician strode between the silent rows of mourners and took his place at the entrance to the tomb, facing the crowd, the dark cavity they had dug for Maal behind him so that he seemed to have two cloaks, one of black fur and one of icy shadow.

A chill passed through the watching villagers. Kyra could feel it creeping along her flesh and she shuddered slightly, pressing closer to her brother. He put his right arm around her and made to put his left around Fern, but she had withdrawn from him since Wardyke's arrival and was standing stiffly away from him. She shook her head sharply at his overture and insisted on standing clear. He looked at her closely, hurt and puzzled. Every muscle in her body was tense and taut. Kyra could see at once what was happening and drew Karne's attention back to Wardyke.

The drums rolled again and then cut dead. The silence was palpable. Wardyke used it to full effect and then, sensing the tension was at a breaking point, broke it himself with a high pitched and dreadful wailing sound that reminded the villagers of nights of fear in the forests surrounded by wolves.

Transfixed, they stared at their priest who at this moment seemed half-animal, half-god. He lifted his great arms slowly as he wailed until they were high above his head at the peak of the sound, and there he held them till the sound of the howl that came from him had penetrated the marrow of their bones.

No one could have moved. They were locked rigid in a kind of terrified fascination.

Kyra was paralysed like the rest, but what she saw was not quite what they saw.

In an arc behind Wardyke, but crowding him closely, were standing shadowy figures, and she knew with a deadly certainty that she had seen them before. Their bodies were those of men, brown and strong, clad only in metallic loin cloths. Their heads were the heads of animals and their eyes were the eyes of demons. At their feet (at Wardyke's feet), the body of Maal was lying and as she looked in horror at it it began to change from the calm, pale priest, lying as though asleep upon the bier, to an ugly, rotting corpse.

Inside her head she screamed.

"No!"

No sound came from her. No movement of her body betrayed her, but she knew at this moment a force was working from her to blast the evil influence of their power away from Maal.

Her eyes if anyone had looked were blazing with a kind of vivid light. Her love for Maal, her longing to protect him, gave her the strength. Her training gave her the skill.

Even as her will cried yet again "No!", the figures behind Wardyke seemed to cringe and waver, their eyes, no longer triumphant, seeking their enemy.

Standing among the crowd of villagers no ordinary mortal could have noticed Kyra was different from the others, but these creatures' eyes ranged everywhere and it was not long before they found the source of their discomfiture. As Kyra held with great strain the concentrated power of her will to protect Maal, the cringing creatures recognized her with demonic malevolence. She summoned up one last and desperate effort and in that moment the air around Wardyke seemed to vibrate in a way Kyra had seen it sometimes on a very hot day, and with the vibration the image of the creatures dissolved and disappeared.

Wardyke was alone again at the entrance to the tomb and, as Kyra's eyes fell upon him, she thought that he too had momentarily lost strength. His arms were lowered and the once livid blaze of his eyes was dimmed. She fancied he too was looking around, seeking an answer to something that puzzled him.

Aching with exhaustion from her experience she could face no more and took a step back so that she was hidden from his sight. Karne looked down at her questioningly. She looked ill. He held her tightly thinking that she might faint. She rested her head against him and shut her eyes. Oh, if only she could sleep!

It was fortunate for her and Karne that they were not the only ones to move at this time or they would certainly have been picked out by Wardyke. Kyra's power had temporarily broken the spell with which he held them, and everyone was shifting and murmuring uneasily in their places.

Suddenly realizing this, Wardyke postponed his search and set about regaining the attention he had lost. He nodded sharply at his drummers and within seconds the pounding of their insistent beat had wound the villagers to a fever pitch of anxiety again. From there he took them through a range of emotions ending with passive acceptance of whatever he wished.

Kyra was not listening, but Karne, who was, was impressed with the way he handled the crowd. He watched it all as though he were somehow outside the whole scene and when he realized this, and that he was not a slave to Wardyke's power as the rest appeared to be, he was surprised. He looked at Kyra resting against his shoulder also unmoved by Wardyke's will and Fern beside him still standing straight and independent, but he could feel the strength in her that was separate from the crowd.

"Why are we three the only ones not to fall under Wardyke's spell?" he thought. "Not all these villagers are fools."

His eye fell upon Maal, lying quietly almost forgotten on his bier. Wardyke was using the funeral for his own ends, for power weaving and establishing control. The ordinary human emotions of a burial had been forgotten. Karne studied Maal's face, sadness returning to him. It was still calm, composed, pale as stone. There was no way of telling how he had died, or indeed if he was dead at all.

The key to their power to withstand Wardyke lay partly with Maal, partly with themselves. Maal had helped them develop certain tendencies already within themselves. He, Karne, had asked questions the other villagers never asked before Maal knew him, Kyra had seen into people's heads before she had become Maal's pupil. Fern had talked with trees. Each of them were what they were, but Maal had helped them to grow. He had not tried to change them into something they were not or could not be, but had helped them develop along the lines they were already going. The rest, and here Karne looked around him at family and friends, were content to stay as they were, content to use over and over again the things they already knew, too afraid to take in new knowledge, new skills, in case their comfortable routine would be disturbed, their comfortable view of existence have to be revised. That way they were easy prey for people like Wardyke. They followed him blindly, until too late they realized he was leading them away from the very comfortable and familiar world they were trying to preserve.

Maal was right, Karne thought, the most important thing in life is to grow inwardly, to move always towards greater awareness, greater understanding, of all the different levels in which things are existing and happening simultaneously.

The villagers shut off whole areas of thought as taboo, limiting themselves, stunting themselves.

Karne remembered Kyra's description of her vision of the stars and the incredible web of constantly changing relationship between them and yet the overall pattern of relationship staying the same. Everything is moving, he thought, changing, ceasing to exist one moment and coming into existence in a different form the next. If one did not accept this but tried to keep everything rigid, damage

162

would certainly be done. One must move with the movement, flow with the flow, become new with each renewal . . . judge each person and each incident on its own merits, from its own unique standpoint . . . and yet see it in relationship to the whole.

Wardyke was evil because he was reducing the individuality of people and welding them into a single tool for his own use. This was very different from Maal who believed in the delicate balance of individual to whole, increasing each person's individuality while at the same time making them aware of their responsibility to the whole.

After Wardyke's peroration Maal's body was carried into the dark cavity of the tomb and the first stones were put in place to seal it overnight.

Darkness was moving in upon them and now the rest of the work was left until the morning.

As they turned to go the dank clouds that had hung above them all day began to leak and before they reached the village it had grown to a steady downpour. Wet, bedraggled and discouraged villagers tramped sadly back to their homes. Karne could hear a group of Strangers laughing as they passed on their way. They at least seemed pleased with the turn events had taken.

Fern was invited by Kyra's mother to spend the night with them and she accepted gratefully. She helped prepare the meal and fitted so well into their family circle that Karne found his mother looking at him and then saying loudly to Fern, "You know, you really ought not to stay so much alone in that valley of yours. You are always welcome here!"

Fern smiled and Karne looked embarrassed. He was longing to find out why she had withdrawn herself so sharply from him at the funeral but he knew that they had much to arrange about the transference of Maal, and his personal affairs would have to wait.

It was Kyra's weariness that gave them the opportunity for action earlier than expected. She was obviously so exhausted that her mother suggested they all retire to sleep earlier than usual. The day had been an unusually heavy one and no one was in a talking mood.

One by one the fires flickered out all around the village.

Karne lay a long time conscious of Fern not far from him, silent in the dark. Kyra was fast asleep and he was in a quandary as to what he should do about her. They needed her help. Two of them could scarcely handle the task that lay ahead and yet he realized that Kyra must have been through some particularly harrassing experience at the tomb to make her so unnaturally and excessively tired. He did not know how much he dared push her beyond her normal strength. To add to this the rain was pouring down outside heavily and steadily as though it would rain forever. The whole project, which had seemed so feasible when he had first thought of it, began to look impossible. He again wondered if the point of it was now lost. Maal was dead, killed by Wardyke. There was no way they could bring him back to life. He knew Maal had wanted to be buried on a particular line of invisible force within the earth and that he had wanted to be in conscious control of his death because he knew that the way he reacted to it, his self-control and his acceptance of his place in the design of the universe, would influence, as all that he had ever done would influence, the progress of his life beyond death. Each life is part of a long and varied process of learning, each thread of will and motive, love and hate, good and evil, has to be gradually refined until the Being is at his full potential which, Maal had told Karne, was far beyond our present imaginings.

Maal knew he had learnt a great deal from his mistakes in this life, but there was still a great deal he knew he had to change within himself before he was ready even to take a lowly part in the next level of spiritual existence whose Beings no longer needed to be reborn on earth in bodies, although they still worked with Earth Beings through the medium of spirit on the inner levels of the Self. With their help and his own effort he hoped to make a leap in progress, but there was a long way to go to reach the ultimate. Beyond the spiritual Beings who were helpers to mankind were other levels of Beings, each level with its own purpose to fulfil, its own work to do.

Having seen a vision of how things were, he was anxious to make what progress he could at the swiftest pace he could master.

Had Wardyke succeeded in slowing down this pace?

Maal had tried to describe Existence to them once but Karne's mind could not grasp the idea of everything being at once infinitely diverse and yet ultimately simple. Many, and yet One.

"It is as though millions of different entities, some so small that they cannot be seen, some so huge the earth would be small beside them, were each occupied with its own individual unfoldment, and yet everything it did at every moment of its existence affected something else, which in its turn was subtly altered because of this to affect something else, and this process was not only happening once to one Entity, but all the time to every Entity."

Here Maal paused looking at his three pupils, their faces a study in concentration and, in Karne's case, bewilderment.

"This you will say," smiling at Karne, "would make for complexity and confusion?"

Karne nodded dumbly.

"It does not," Maal said quietly. "Look around. Be silent, 'feel' the Universe. It is working with great efficiency. Out of all the disparate elements working at their own Being, the whole is held together harmoniously as a single unit."

"So what we do at any given time does not really matter . . . everything will even up in the end and it will all go on working harmoniously?" Karne said.

"Yes, and no," Maal answered. "Although the Universe as a whole, as a unit, *will* go on working harmoniously in spite of us, our own individual existence is affected vitally by what we are, and how we react to what happens to us.

"Good may come out of evil, and evil may come out of

good, in a way we cannot understand yet because we can see no further than the immediate and limited part of the whole in which we are at present, but what we do, what choices we make at any given time, affects us, our surroundings and our development crucially."

Karne lying in his fur rug on the night of Maal's funeral knew that he had a choice to make. His body cried out to stay warm and snug, protected from the cold needles of the rain and the exhausting and difficult, not to say dangerous, task that he knew he ought to be preparing for at that very moment. But he knew deep inside himself that he had committed himself to this action and could not shirk it. He did not understand the full implications of it, but Maal had wished it and he must honour that wish.

Even as Karne decided he must pull himself together Kyra suddenly awoke and sat upright. Fern must have been awake all the time because she arose immediately to join them. They crept out from amongst the sleeping family like shadows, the snoring of the father effectively covering any sound they might make.

Once outside they found the rain was petering out and the clouds were breaking up. Mercifully some rays of moonlight were beginning to penetrate the dark valley. Stumbling through the wet grass and clinging mud, Karne holding Fern's hand, they hurried, bare-footed and shivering, towards the dark bulk of the clump of trees beside Maal's tomb. Once clear of the houses they ventured to whisper to each other.

"I thought you were unwakable," Karne whispered to Kyra.

"It was a dream," she said.

"What?"

"That woke me."

She slipped and nearly fell. Karne and Fern steadied her and they hurried on.

"Tell us about the dream," Fern said when they had reached an easier, grassier place for walking.

"It was nothing much," Kyra said. "I seemed to be in a thick fog . . . moving but not seeing anything . . . and then I heard Maal calling me."

"Did you see him?"

"No. I just heard his voice and he sounded muffled and strange at first and I went on drifting in the fog not taking any notice. I still felt tired although I was asleep. And then suddenly he sounded quite sharp and commanding. You know how he does sometimes? And it was then that I snapped awake."

"Do you think," Fern's voice sounded eager, "it might be that he is still alive?"

"Maybe . . . ," Karne said, and their hearts lifted. They were more determined than ever to move Maal from the wrong tomb.

Karne did not know about the other two, but he had decided, if Maal was still alive, to persuade him to live on hidden in the woods near Fern at least until they had contacted the Lords of the Sun.

The night was a long, hard one. The tunnel they had dug was difficult to locate in the dark. Once found, the crudity with which it was constructed hampered them in every way. Bits of it had fallen in and had to be scooped out. They had sensibly left dry wood and straw and digging implements within the first few yards of it and they soon had a torch burning to give them light as they worked.

They worked in the tunnel by turns, one keeping watch at the entrance all the time. During Kyra's watch she was frightened almost into hysterics by the sudden screech of a night bird which took noisy flight just above her head. Fern had to spend valuable time comforting her before she was prepared to stay alone again. She was constantly looking over her shoulder for the half animal, half man, demon figures she had seen earlier. She could feel the presence of something hostile but she could see nothing.

She was glad when it was her turn to go inside, crawling in the earth like a worm, to be beside strong, dependable Karne who was always so unaware of mysterious presences that being near to him she could feel that they did not exist at all.

At last they broke through to the burial chamber itself and stood side by side looking at Maal by the flickering light of the torch. There was no sign of breath or pulse. Kyra clung to Karne's arm.

"He is dead," she whispered miserably.

Karne was silent. It certainly seemed like it.

"Go and fetch Fern," he said at last, "she is stronger than you are. We will take him to the wood as we planned. He would want that."

Kyra nodded and crawled back along the tunnel. Fern took her place in the chamber and she and Karne dragged the stretcher-like bier behind them to the entrance. It was heavy work and breathing was not easy in the dark and confined space. Panting and sweating, their bodies aching from the strain, they finally emerged from the earth. Kyra started the work of filling up the tunnel while they recovered.

The moon was fully out now but low in the sky, touching everything with an eerie beauty. Karne and Fern sat back to back, leaning on each other, too exhausted to talk, almost too exhausted to think. Each glad of each other's company but making no sign of it.

At last Karne was recovered enough for action.

"It will not be long before the moon sets, we must be in your woods by then or we will never find the way."

Fern nodded wearily.

As he removed his supporting back from hers and stood up, he turned and put his hands upon her shoulders, leant down and kissed the top of her head. This time she did not withdraw herself. He could just see the little wan smile at the corner of her lips as she turned her face up to his. Fleetingly he brushed his lips across hers and then turned to call Kyra. She crept out of the tunnel almost immediately but they could see she was agitated.

"I am not nearly finished," she complained, out of breath.

"Never mind. We have no time to finish now. We will cover it up again and come back tomorrow."

They dragged the heavy cover of leaves and branches and grass over the entrance and set off with Maal as best they could. The load was heavy, the ground uneven, the light inadequate, but somehow familiarity with the route and sheer determination sustained them. The last thing they saw as they entered the dark but friendly woods surrounding Fern's garden was the magnificent sight of a giant moon, the colour of blood, slowly sinking below the horizon. They put their load down for a few minutes and stared transfixed. When it was gone they resumed their journey. At Fern's house they dared to light a torch again and so found their way to the secret burial chamber with greater ease. Their main difficulties were now over. Within minutes Maal was safely laid to rest in the place he had chosen and the three stood beside him, the light of the torch revealing their muddy, haggard and dishevelled appearance beside his calm, composed and peaceful one.

What to do now?

They looked at each other. It would soon be dawn and they should be back with their family, but they were loth to leave Maal.

"Should we say some prayers?" Fern asked tentatively.

Karne nodded.

"That is a good idea."

But they hesitated. What prayers, and who should say them?

Fern and Karne looked at Kyra.

She caught their look and seemed alarmed.

"But I do not know the words of the burial ceremony," she said.

"That does not matter," Fern said. "Say what you feel."

"Pray for him, Kyra—any way you know," Karne said.

Kyra sat on her heels beside Maal. For a while she looked silently and with deep love at his gentle, strong face, then she shut her eyes and lowered her head. The two beside her could hear no words, but fancied they could feel the warmth of her love for Maal and the concentration with which she was thinking about him.

Inside her head no words were forming. The shutting of her eyes plunged her in a featureless, wordless darkness. She waited, quietly breathing, letting the darkness happen to her. Gradually, gradually she began to distinguish darker shapes within the darkness. She thought at first they were the figures of men, but later she realized they were the shapes of gigantic Standing Stones, different from their own in that they were taller, closer together, and joined at the top from one to the other by slabs of stone, curved to follow the shape of the circle.

She seemed to be in the centre of the Circle, looking out, and there were other Stones around her within the Circle. She could barely make out the shapes and sizes in the dark. There were no stars. No moon. She was not even sure that it was night. The darkness with its darker shapes was not like anything she had encountered before in her ordinary life. She let the experience happen and waited for whatever would come next. As nothing changed, her mind began to drift back to Maal and as the thought of him came to her an image of him appeared as a slightly lighter area in the darkness of the mysterious Stone Circle.

"Maal!"

It seemed to her she cried out and moved towards him, but something prevented her from going too near. The image of him grew slowly lighter and lighter until she could see him as though through a light mist. She could see that he was holding something in his hands and that he was trying to attract her attention to it, although he was not moving in any way. Her eyes kept going to the object in his hands, but the image was too blurred for her to make out what it was. She could see his eyes beginning to despair, his image beginning to fade. She was conscious that she had let him down by not recognizing what he was trying to show her. She began to feel anxiety.

"Maal!" she cried, "Come back! Give me another chance."

But the image had disappeared and all the dark shadows of the Standing Stones had gone with it. She was left with the featureless darkness she had experienced first.

She opened her eyes and found Karne and Fern looking anxiously at her.

"What is the matter?"

"What happened?"

She looked from one to the other and then to Maal, her face pained and bewildered.

"He was trying to tell me something . . . trying to show me something . . . and I could not make out what it was . . ."

She was trembling. Fern put her hand on her arm.

"I think he may be still alive," she said. "I *feel* it."

"So do I," Kyra said tearfully, "but I do not know what to do to help him and I can feel he needs my help."

Karne bent over Maal and listened to his chest. There was no sound. He hoped the girls were right, but he could feel no life in the old man.

"There is something he needs . . . the thing he was trying to show me!"

"Try and go back into the trance you were in," Karne suggested. "Perhaps this time . . ."

Kyra tried to compose herself, but she could not. She stayed where she was.

"It is nearly dawn," Karne said urgently. "We have not much time."

"I know," Kyra said miserably, "if only . . ."

"Perhaps it is that little stone sphere of his," Fern said suddenly.

Kyra gasped.

"Of course!"

The two girls clutched hands excitedly.

"Well," cried Karne impatiently, "where is it?"

"I will go and fetch it," Fern called, already on her way.

"I am sure it was that," Kyra said happily to Karne.

"Now that I think of it I cannot imagine why I did not think of it before."

"Try and make contact with him again. Now that we have come so far we do not want him to slip away thinking that the whole thing is hopeless."

Kyra knelt beside Maal and tried to make contact with him as he had taught her, but she found that she could not.

She opened her eyes again and looked at Karne.

"It is no good," she said. "I cannot."

Karne looked worried.

"I wish Fern would hurry," Kyra said anxiously.

"I am sure she is," Karne spoke in her defence quickly. "I do not know why you did not put the stone in here. It seems the obvious place."

"We did not think of it," Kyra said gloomily. "We did not really think Maal was dead. It all happened so quickly."

Fern arrived back at this point with the little parcel of bark cloth in her hand.

"It is getting light outside," she said, out of breath, "the birds are making a tremendous noise."

"Here," Karne took the parcel from her and handed it to Kyra. "Do whatever you think Maal wants you to do with it, but hurry. We will be in trouble if people start looking for us and it reaches Wardyke's ears that we are missing."

Kyra took the parcel and knelt down beside Maal. She tried to compose herself again. After a moment or two she looked around at Karne.

"Be quiet," she said sternly.

He looked indignant.

"I did not say anything."

"You are worrying and disturbing the air," she said, fixing him with an accusing eye.

He flung up his hands in disgust and muttered something under his breath.

"You see!" she said triumphantly.

"Just get *on* with it," he snapped impatiently.

Fern put her hand on his arm and drew him back a little way.

"Perhaps we should leave her," she said quietly. "I too am agitated and probably making it impossible to concentrate."

He nodded and they slipped out of the stale-smelling burial chamber into the glory of the dawn light in the wood flickering with green leaves and bird song. He took a long deep breath.

"I could do with some of your spring water," he said, and she led him there.

After they had drunk, they washed themselves and then wandered through the wood tasting the freshness of the air and the closeness of each other. The sorrowful and harassing experiences of the past night and day began to fade slightly, and only the aching of their limbs reminded them of the darker side of the reason for their being together at this early hour.

Inside the chamber Kyra unwrapped the little parcel as carefully as she had seen Maal do it, and when she reached the little sphere she placed it gently on Maal's chest, folding his hands over it to keep it in place.

Then she sat beside him very quietly, trying to offer herself to him to be used in any way he wished. She tried to imagine how it felt for him to be dead. This was not difficult as she had the experience in the Sacred Circle to remember. She began to feel it was herself lying on the bier unable to move her limbs, but this time she was not afraid. She lay there as still as stone, at first feeling nothing, and then gradually beginning to feel the weight of the little stone sphere on her chest. After the weight of it, the sensation associated with it was one of tingling. Then of warmth. The sphere seemed to be generating flow and warmth in her chest which was gradually spreading to the rest of her.

She fancied she heard (or was it "felt") a deep, low drum beat (or was it a heart beat?). She opened her eyes in surprise and found she was not on the bier at all but

173

was crouching beside Maal looking at him. She stared fascinated at his chest and could have sworn she saw the little sphere rise and fall, rise and fall, with the rhythm of what *must* be breathing.

She wanted to call the others, but did not dare break into the sequence of slow awakening. She did not want to do anything that would set back the process in any way.

There was no doubt in her mind now that Maal was not dead, and her heart was filled with joy.

She watched and waited. The process was painfully slow.

She took his finger and used it to trace the spiral pattern of the stone sphere as he had taught her to do. She thought this might help, and indeed it seemed to, as his eyelids started to flicker as though he were dreaming. She was just wondering if she dare call his name aloud when Fern and Karne broke into the chamber, fresh and bright from their walk in the woods.

They were amazed to see the breathing, but she held up her hand to keep them quiet. The three of them watched over him now, all in their own ways, calling his name inside their heads, *willing* him to wake up and be with them again.

"Maal!" Kyra dared to whisper the word, and as no ill effect seemed to follow, she said it again and again, louder and louder until it became a kind of chant which they all joined in. The flickering of his lids became more agitated, his breathing more definite, colour began to creep back to his cheeks, his fingers gripped the sphere of spirals without Kyra's help.

At last he opened his eyes and looked at them.

"Maal!" they cried joyfully.

Wardyke had not won after all!

Their first overwhelming excitement soon gave way to a more sober appraisal of the situation.

Maal was very weak, so weak he could not sit up and could barely talk. He had been through a great deal and although he was certainly alive now, it was ovbious to

174

them he was only just so. Karne began to realize he probably would not be well enough to go to the Sacred Circle on the Night of the Rising Star and undertake the difficulties of the journey to meet the Lords of the Sun.

"What can we do?" Kyra pleaded. "Tell us . . . how can we help you to get better?"

Maal turned his head a fraction to look at her, his eyes full of love.

He was trying to speak but his voice was so weak she had to lean very close to his mouth to hear what he was saying.

"There is no way I will get better with this old body," he whispered.

"Do not say that!" cried Kyra.

He shook his head very slightly and a smile flickered at the corners of his lips.

"One must accept it, my child. It is so."

"I do not *want* to accept it," she said with unusual fierceness. "I cannot live without you. I *need* you."

"You will have to live without me," he said gently but firmly, "but not forever. I promise you . . ." and here his voice faded to nothing and he closed his eyes as though he were slipping away again.

"Maal," she cried desperately, seizing him by the shoulders and trying to force him back to life by the sheer passion of her desire.

"What do you promise?" she almost shouted into his face.

His old, tired eyes flickered open again.

"I promise you . . ." he whispered and his voice was like a breeze rustling in dry grass ". . . that I will join you again some time, some place . . ."

Tears streamed down her face. She tried to stop herself sobbing so that she would not miss a word that he was saying.

". . . we have been together before . . . and we will be together again . . . many times . . ."

"How will I know you?"

"You will know . . . you will know."

175

"But how?"

"You will know when the time comes. Now you must leave me . . . I must prepare for the transfer of my spirit . . . it is not an easy matter . . ."

"But what about the Lords of the Sun?"

Karne thrust his question forward anxiously.

The old man turned his tired eyes to the boy.

"Kyra must do it herself."

Kyra drew in her breath sharply.

"And you," he said to Karne, "and you . . ." he turned to Fern, "must help her and protect her in every way you can. You must do it," he said directly to Kyra and his eyes were anxious. "It is very important. You have promised."

"And *you* have promised!" Kyra sobbed, "You have promised to come back to me."

He nodded almost imperceptibly and then his eyes closed.

They could not rouse him again.

Fern and Karne held back the weeping Kyra, afraid she might harm him, she was so desperately trying to wake him again.

"He is so old," Fern said gently to Kyra, "and he has been through so much. Let him go his way in peace now."

Kyra drew back and tried to control herself. She did not want in any way to harm Maal, but she felt very much alone and vulnerable without him.

"Come," Fern said, taking her arm. "You have done everything you can for him."

"I will leave the sphere with him. It might help him in some way," Kyra said, looking her last at the frail discarded shell of her friend, his thin hands locked around the spiral stone.

"Yes, do that," Fern said, and gave her a gentle tug.

The two girls went out first into the sunlight. Karne stayed behind to have one last look around to see that everything was safe and ready for the long centuries ahead. They had built this little chamber well, half dug into the

176

earth and lined with stone. During the day the girls would cover it with soil and then Fern would transfer growing plants to it so that soon it would look like nothing but a natural mound of trees, ferns and bushes, and would be unnoticeable.

He beat out the torch and followed the girls.

In the early morning sunlight they worked together to put the largest stones they had found to seal up the entrance.

It was arranged that Karne would run home and make up some story to cover their absence. Fern and Kyra would meanwhile have a few hours' sleep and then do their best to disguise the tomb.

When Karne could find an opportunity he would fill in the tunnel to Maal's official tomb. As no one suspected it was there he was not anticipating any trouble.

Kyra awoke from her sleep at noon to find Fern already at work on the mound.

"You look better," Fern said with a smile as she saw Kyra approaching. She did indeed. Fern would almost have said she looked happy as well as rested.

Kyra smiled cheerfully.

"Yes," she said, "I had a good dream."

"About Maal?"

"Yes."

"Is he all right?"

"I am sure he is."

"What did you dream?"

"I cannot remember exactly . . . but I know it was all good. Instead of the fog I had in the dream I had about him before . . . there was a great deal of light and beautiful luminous things . . . even the people were tall and shining . . ."

"Did you see him choosing a new life?"

"No. I do not think it happens quite like that."

"I cannot imagine how it happens."

"Nor can I," Kyra said thoughtfully, "but all the darkness and fog was gone. Of that I am sure. Everything

177

was light and beautiful. But it was as though I was looking at it reflected in something . . . I think it was a pool because something dropped and the whole image shimmered and broke up . . . sort of shattered into millions of sparkles of light . . . and then I woke up."

"Perhaps being still in a body you could not look directly at the scene, but only at a reflection of it. The direct brightness of it might be too much for you."

"Something like that," Kyra said, and then they both laughed at one of Maal's much used phrases.

"Come on," said Fern then, "we have a lot to do."

They worked hard together and the mound was finished and covered with growing plants before the sun set over the hills.

Kyra washed herself in Fern's little stream and walked home, her limbs weary, the shades of the night gathering around her.

The Triumph of Wardyke

WHEN KYRA WOKE to the dawn of the next day she knew that she would not sleep again until she had spoken with the Lords of the Sun. All day she thought about it as she went about her work and the more she thought about it the more anxious she became.

She had not been given specific instructions about what to do. Maal had said enigmatically that she would "know" when the time came, but even that was referring to working together. It was he who was supposed to find the Lords. Her task was to have been to help him through Wardyke's invisible barrier and boost his failing strength with what embryo power she had. Even the secret knowledge she was supposed to have about the correct configuration of the stars was a mystery to her. She could remember the beauty and the splendour of the vision, but no specific configuration. The impression she had gained in that moment of illumination was that there was no set and rigid pattern, but that everything was moving and changing all the time. The driving force of the Universe worked through a process of minute, delicate and orderly adjustments between each specific thing, great and small.

In the afternoon her family task was to grind the grain to make flour. She knelt beside the grinding stone, crushing the grains of wheat into the hollow of it with a sea-rounded pebble. As she worked she tried to bring together in her mind all the teachings of Maal, to see if from their accumulated bulk she could pluck what she needed for the night. She had learnt a great deal, but Maal had warned her that knowledge never really took root until one had occasion to use it.

As she worked and pondered, her baby sister sat in the dirt beside her and played with the pebbles she was not using. One by one they were picked up in the chubby little hands and chewed and slobbered over. Those that were too big to lift the baby leant down and gnawed at with toothless gums as Kyra had seen a dog gnaw at a bone.

Sometimes Kyra would have to break off what she was doing to thrust her finger into the baby's mouth to remove one of the smaller pebbles she was in danger of swallowing. It seemed to her no matter how hard she concentrated on the work of grinding, her mind was working busily on several other levels at the same time. One on the difficult task of creating order and system out of the bits and pieces of knowledge she had gained from Maal, another looking after the baby and noticing when it did anything that was potentially harmful to it, yet another noticing the village life around her, Faro and her father talking in lowered voices, women bringing washing back from the stream, children playing a game of hopping and jumping. It seemed a long time since she had played such a game and she felt the urge to drop everything she was doing and go and join them.

And through it all, separate from all these different threads of consciousness, she was aware of herself being aware of them.

"And Maal says we only notice a few of the threads

180

with our ordinary minds, there are many others within me at this very moment."

She knew she wanted more than anything else to train herself to be aware on all these different levels, of all these different states.

"How rich it would make life," she thought. "How much richer than it already is."

She stopped her work for a moment and bent down to pick up the baby. She held it high above her head and noticed with a smile that it was beginning to be really heavy. The little creature laughed delightedly as she dropped it to chest level and gave it a hug. It clung with its legs and arms around her, nuzzling its dirty little face against her neck, loving her.

She was just about to put it down again and resume her work with the grain, when she heard a shout and turned to see what was happening.

Her brother Thon was running, waving his arms and shouting. He seemed agitated and shocked. Villagers were looking up at him and some left what they were doing to follow him. He stopped when he reached Faro and her father and waving his arms and gesticulating he began to tell them something. A little group of villagers began to gather round the three men.

Kyra, still holding the baby, ran to join them. She could not make out quite what was happening because everyone was talking at once, but she gathered it was really horrifying.

"What is it?" she cried, nudging people, trying to get nearer the center of the group so that she could hear what Thon was saying.

At last one of the women, unable to make herself heard against the strident voices of the men, and anxious to communicate her horror with someone, turned to Kyra and told her the whole story.

Thon had found the body of Mia, battered to death amongst the trees just beyond the north pasture.

"We are going to fetch her now," the woman added and moved off with the others, led by Thon.

Kyra rushed back to her home and deposited the baby unceremoniously with her busy mother.

Breathlessly she ran to catch the others. Mia was a pretty girl, much sought after by the village boys, a little dull Kyra had always thought, but nevertheless she was fond of her.

What a terrible thing!

What was happening to their village?

There had been anger and hatred between people from time to time but no one in her memory, or indeed in the memory of her father and grandfather, had killed another except by accident. Now Maal was dead and probably Wardyke had killed him. Was he responsible for Mia's death as well?

A group of people had already gathered round the body of the girl when they arrived. Standing in a circle round her, silently staring. Kyra pushed forward to see, gasped and withdrew immediately. Whoever had done that to her was evil beyond anything Kyra had come across before. She stood back, her heart beating. The girl's clothes were ripped and soaked in blood. Where the bones were broken Kyra could see white splinters sticking out of the flesh.

She must find Karne. She was afraid for Fern, for herself, for all of them. The feelings she had had that Wardyke was evil and inspired evil in others were being confirmed with dreadful speed. The urgency of her mission to the Lords of the Sun was becoming greater at every moment.

Karne met her on the path leading back to the village from Maal's tomb.

"What is wrong?" he called as soon as he saw her face.

Words tumbled from her. His face went black with anger. She could see the muscles tensing along his arms and shoulders.

"No, Karne!" she cried in alarm.

"We *cannot* let this happen!" he shouted and left her, running like a deer across the rough terrain towards the village. When she arrived panting and out of breath, he had already joined a group of men all of whom were angry and ready for action. She heard his claim that Wardyke had killed Maal, and Wardyke must surely have killed the girl.

"Wardyke is no true priest. He is an impostor!"

"Karne! Karne!" she cried, trying to stop him. This was not the way. This way they would not stand a chance. This way Maal had warned them not to try.

But her voice was thin and womanish and did not carry across the storm of their anger.

As one unit they turned and strode towards Wardyke's house, seizing wood and stones as they went, determined to put an end to what they were beginning to feel more and more as a tyranny. The mood was ugly and there was the scent of more blood in the air.

Kyra ran behind, desperately trying to think of a way to stop the inevitable catastrophe.

As the angry marchers neared Wardyke's magnificent house they were joined by others, until almost the whole village was marching. As they marched they chanted, an impromptu chant of hate.

"War-dyke! War-dyke! War-dyke!"

Kyra's blood ran cold to hear the peaceful, friendly villagers so twisted and locked upon a knot of rage and blind hate. She knew there was no way they were going to win against Wardyke in this battle. In a sense they were becoming just what he wanted them to become, a senseless mob pulled by primitive feelings that he could manipulate as he wished, their god-given gift of reason and intelligence overthrown and helpless.

As they mounted the last ridge before his house they were brought to a sudden halt. He was standing before them, gigantic and imposing. He held up his hand and for a moment they were cowed, then one of their number, it might even have been Karne but Kyra could not be sure, shouted belligerently,

"Who killed Mia?"

The others took up the cry.

"Who killed Mia?"

"Who killed Maal?"

The shouting and the noise was deafening, some of the younger boys clattering sticks together to make a kind of terrifying drumming sound. But although they shouted and they were still angry they did not move forward. Wardyke's hand was up and it was as though there was an invisible barrier keeping them back.

He waited as though he were carved of rock. Only his eyes had life in them and they were like black fire, their flames licking the earth in front of the marchers, daring them to take a step forward.

Suddenly another noise joined the one the marchers were making and a quick imperceptible movement of Wardyke's hand and head subtly directed the marchers' attention to it.

To the left of them was another mob, mostly consisting of Wardyke's Strangers, and they too were shouting and angry and they were dragging the figure of a man in their midst.

Wardyke took advantage of the momentary pause of surprise amongst the hostile villagers to say in a voice of thunder, the deadly dagger of his bony finger pointing directly at the captive man.

"He is your enemy. He killed Mia!"

A sort of composite scream went up from the mob and within a second they had transferred all their hate from Wardyke to the captive.

Horrified Kyra saw them turn upon him and join with the Strangers in beating him with sticks and stones, until he was lying bleeding and broken in a heap on the ground.

Only then did the people pause and think about what they had done.

They did not even know who it was they had destroyed. If questioned they might have said they thought it was one of the Strangers because he was among the Strangers, but they had not used their minds. They had moved like one body of concentrated venom on the point of Wardyke's finger.

Kyra, trembling, looked for Karne. She found him back from the mob, alone on the path. He had realized what was happening in time and had not joined the mob in stoning the man, but his face was a study of stunned horror. He had played his part in rousing the rebellion. His words against Wardyke had seemed justified at the time. But now, when he could see where it had led, he knew Maal had been right to warn them against this course of action. They were deeper in the mesh of Wardyke's evil than they had ever been.

Someone cried out. The broken body of the man was lifted and recognized. It was one of *them,* one of the villagers, not a man at all, but a boy of sixteen, simple-minded but gentle. The villagers knew with a terrible certainty that he could not have killed Mia.

There was silence now as they realized what they had done. The Strangers had cunningly disappeared, leaving the stunned villagers to survey their handiwork.

Wardyke had disappeared as well.

They were alone on the hill with their pain and their guilt.

A woman started sobbing and this was the only sound as they picked up the mangled heap of bones and carried it home.

That night the bodies of the two young people, Mia and the boy, were laid side by side to await burial. The villagers lit fires around them and kept vigil all night.

Never had they needed guidance and help so much but there was no one to whom they could turn.

As the stars wheeled quietly across the sky many of them turned inwards for help, trying to think it all out for themselves, questioning themselves . . . looking at the bodies, the dark earth, the fires around them and the stars in the sky . . . puzzling about the relationship of each to each and the meaning of the whole.

The Lords of the Sun

WARDYKE WAS within the Sacred Circle when the bright and wandering star the villagers called Magus rose above the Stone of the Star. He stood in the centre and spoke the incantations to the gods that were expected of him. Around the Circle, making another circle, the seven new Elders walked with slow and measured tread, keeping a constant circular current going. Beyond them Wardyke's Strangers stood, and beyond them again some of the villagers who were not at that time keeping watch by the burial fires waited forlornly, still numbed by the events of the past few days.

Karne, Kyra and Fern were among these but well to the back, in the shadow, keeping carefully out of sight.

Kyra was very tense. Her fingers gripped those of her brother with an almost crippling force. Once or twice he tried to loosen her grip, but it was no use. She needed him and she was not letting go.

They could see Wardyke clearly as torches were placed between each Standing Stone. The combination of flickering fire and darkness and the fact that the Circle was higher than the watching villagers made him and his Elders seem like giants.

As the star rose it was the custom to sing and some with stringed instruments and reed flutes would play sweet music. But this night the watching crowd remained silent and the star rose only to the sound of Wardyke's voice. He lifted his arms and called on the gods to give him strength to carry out his work among the people of the Magus. He spoke of his prowess as a priest and how he had gathered together people of many communities to form a larger community which he would lead to be the greatest people on the earth.

"They will glorify the names of the gods and carry your power wherever they go.

"They will spread over the face of the earth making one people, led by one priest, Wardyke your servant. Wardyke your right hand.

"They will trample on your enemies and slay your foes.

"Your names will be revered and feared as they were in the ancient times."

His voice rose in a kind of ecstasy. It magnified against the rocks and reverberated among the people.

Fern drew closer to Karne and slipped her arm through his. Kyra bit her lip until it bled.

But suddenly the gods answered in a way no one had ever seen them answer before on the Night of the Rising Star.

The hand of Darkness seized a group of stars and flung them to the earth. With a sharp intake of breath the villagers saw the burning embers fall from the heavens in a shower of swift and vivid light. As suddenly as it happened, it was over.

Wardyke was temporarily silenced, shocked by the unexpectedness of the meteor shower, but before the villagers had recovered their breath he was in charge of himself again.

He bowed his head, and this was the only time since he

187

came to the village anyone had seen him bow, and said in a deep and apparently humble voice,

"We thank you, gods, for the sign of your favour. With this burning seal of light you have sealed forever with your approval the appointment of Wardyke as your natural spokesman upon the earth."

Bewildered, the villagers looked at each other. They had put a different interpretation on the sign of the falling stars. But who could say which was the one the gods intended?

Not long after this Wardyke dismissed them all and they silently dispersed, the villagers to watch beside their friends over the bodies of the two young people, some of the Strangers to their homes, and some to prowl the night watching that the villagers gave no more trouble to their lord and master, Wardyke.

Fern, Karne and Kyra remained behind some bushes, well hidden, watching Wardyke. The torches were burning low and they could not see as clearly as they had done, but they could still follow his movements. He walked the Circle as Maal had done the first time they watched him, touching his forehead to each stone. He then leaned against the leading stone, extending his immensely long arms on either side to touch the two uprights, shut his eyes and went into the kind of trance state that they had become familiar with since knowing Maal.

Kyra put her head in her hands and cringed as though she could feel great pain. Fern and Karne looked at each other worriedly over her head, but did not interfere. Kyra's role was not an easy one but it was necessary. They were finished with games and childhood now. On her shoulders rested the lives of many people.

Wardyke remained still for a long time and then suddenly strode out of the Circle. As he passed the brightest remaining torch they could see his expression quite clearly. It was angry and disappointed. He strode down the path and out of sight, the very sound of his footsteps giving away the impatience he was feeling.

188

When they were quite sure he was out of earshot Karne and Fern asked Kyra what had happened.

They were amazed to find her smiling triumphantly.

"I tried to play a trick on him," she said joyfully, "and it worked!"

"What did you do?" Karne asked, surprised at her daring.

"I thought the deaths of Maal and Mia and the boy, over and over again as vividly as I could manage. I was determined he should suffer at least a little for what he has done."

Karne was impressed.

"Do you think he saw the images you were trying to project upon him?"

"I am sure he did. You saw how he looked when he left the Circle. I do not think he managed to do any spirit travelling at all. Whenever he turned to try and leave the Circle an image of one of the people he has just murdered came before him, blocking his way."

"You took a terrible risk," Fern said anxiously. "What if he had suspected that it was your doing?"

"I had to be very careful not to project anything I did not want him to know."

"Do you think he has any idea how it happened?"

"I do not think so. He has never really noticed me and I am sure he has no idea anyone in the village has any special powers now that Maal is dead."

Kyra could not help feeling pleased with herself. Karne was delighted as well, but Fern was still uneasy. She knew Wardyke was no fool. He had spirit-travelled many times and would know this failure had some special explanation. With his skill it would not take him long to track down the reason.

"I am afraid for you, Kyra," she said.

Kyra wondered if she had been wrong to do what she had done.

"Perhaps it was a mistake, perhaps it was not," Karne said. "At any rate it is done, and it is now time for you to go into the Circle and find the Lords of the Sun."

Kyra swallowed hard. So it had come at last!

He took her hand and led her to the Circle, but before she went inside he put out the remaining torches one by one so that no one would see her. At first the darkness was so intense that they found it difficult to move about, but as their eyes grew accustomed to it the Stones loomed darkly against a less dark sky and they could orientate themselves.

Karne kissed Kyra on the cheek and hugged her close.

"Little sister, do not be afraid. We will be right here. If it looks as though things are going wrong we will rush in, Sacred Circle or no Sacred Circle, and rescue you."

"Promise?" she said in a very small voice.

"I promise."

Fern kissed her too and held her very close.

"If there were another way . . ." Kyra said in a low voice.

"If there were another way," Karne said softly, "Maal would have told us about it. He believed you could do it. For his sake, at least try."

Kyra nodded dumbly and broke away from their comforting and loving arms. She knew the urgency. She knew the necessity . . . it was just that she felt so very small and the Sacred Stones that loomed out of the darkness seemed so very large.

She passed through into the Circle itself and stood for a moment or two looking upwards at the sky. As she did so the giant Stones themselves seemed small and insignificant against the vast and arching dome of infinity above.

It seemed to her all scale and measure had altered instantly as she entered the Circle. She now was the pinpoint centre of the Universe, the millions upon millions of stars that rode the darkness above her were turning on the centre point of *her* Being. The earth itself beneath her feet no longer felt like grass and sand, but like a huge ball of living rock which turned slowly and inexorably with the stars. She rode the earth like a ship that sailed the sky. But even as she felt all this, the scale and image changed again. From being the minute point on which

190

vastness turned, she was vastness itself and all that was happening was happening within herself. All these stars moving were moving within her, the earth turning was turning within her. As she had looked up and out, she now looked in, and saw the same vision.

Somewhere in her mind she remembered she had something important to do and as much as she would have liked to stay and enjoy the constantly changing visionary experience, she knew she must fulfill her purpose there or many people would be lost.

It seemed to her she heard Karne's voice in her head reminding her.

Slowly she moved, trying to think what she must do first.

She remembered the configuration. She must be sure that was right if she was to travel as far as was needed to find the Lords of the Sun.

She noticed with one part of her mind that she was not so much afraid as she had expected to be. She felt she was moving in some strange dream. The reality around her was very different to the one to which she was accustomed as Karne's sister.

She looked up at the sky again, trying not to let the filigree of gold seduce her from her task. She tried to see the pattern in the stars she had seen when she had held Maal's stone sphere.

At first she saw nothing but brilliant and random lights. Then she thought to focus on the star Magus which was directly above the Stone of the Star at this time. As it became for her the brightest and most central point in the sky, the rest of the stars seemed to fall into place around it in a specific way. The configuration! It must be! It looked so right!

She felt strange as though there were currents of power running through her, circling round her. Slowly, as though already in a trance, she walked from stone to stone, touching each as she had done before with her forehead. This time with each touch she seemed to be becoming more and more in tune with the vibrations of power that were all around her, so that by the end she no longer felt them as vibrations outside herself but as part of her own inner rhythm.

When she came to close her eyes upon the final stone she was completely at one with the forces in the Sacred Circle and she slipped out of her body with no trouble at all.

Karne and Fern fancied they heard a faint humming coming from the Stones but could not be sure. They crouched in the darkness just outside, their arms around each other to keep fear at bay, watching Kyra's every move within the Circle. At first they were worried that she was taking too long and Karne wished impatiently that she would stop staring at the sky, but now that she had started the process of "travelling" he was content to wait as long as it would take.

How he longed to be with her! How he longed to see what she was seeing.

She found herself standing in the yellow dust of a road, a high wall built of stone of the same colour on her right, stretching a long way past her in both directions. She stepped back somewhat to get a better view of the height of the wall and saw upon it for the first time a disc of dazzling gold. It was pure and plain, no carvings, no attachments. The polished gold of the Sun. Against its surface the real sun, high in the sky, was reflected, the beam of its brilliant light touching the disc and bouncing back along a straight line to fall upon a building many measures away. Within the courtyard of the building a tower, on which another such disc was placed carefully at an angle, reflected the light yet again and beamed it further across the landscape where it was picked up and reflected on. Kyra could see that where she was standing must have been the highest point because she could see for a long way in every direction. Below her a landscape of great subtlety and harmony unfolded, low and gently rising hills were separated by water courses threading their way, beaded with willow trees. Buildings with strangely peaked roofs were upon the surface of the land so naturally placed that they looked as though they had grown from the earth. It seemed to her the whole was held together within the golden network of the sun's light reflected from disc to disc.

She looked for an entrance to the wall beside her, remembering the citadel she had visited as the young Maal, although she realized instinctively that this was not in the same country. As there seemed to be no entrance she turned her attention to the building nearest to her in the valley and decided to walk towards it. There was something compelling about the ray of light that beamed from the disc directly above her head to the disc on the tower of the building. She followed it and found there was a path leading directly to it.

As she approached she realized it was much larger than she had thought. The plan as seen from above was a series of squares and circles within each other.

The outer wall surrounded a square. Within the great square smaller squares of even shape and size surrounded a central courtyard. The squares themselves consisted of rooms built round small courtyards. The great central courtyard and each smaller one had the same design. Although they were constructed as squares, within them circular fountains and flowers of every kind of beauty were planted in circular beds so that, looking from above, there were circles within all the squares. The central tower itself was square, but the disc of the sun that was placed upon it was circular. Kyra remembered something Maal had told her that she had not quite grasped before.

"The circle is the symbol of the spirit. It contains within itself its own completeness which has no end. The square is the symbol of the earth, of body, of material things, made up of angles and relationships. The circle within the square is spirit manifest in body."

"This must be some kind of temple," Kyra thought. "Perhaps here I will find the Lords of the Sun."

She found to her surprise that one moment she was looking down upon the temple, contemplating the harmony and the symbolism of its overall design, and the next she was standing in the central courtyard, the water of a ring of fountains softly singing to her, the scent of a thousand varied flowers soothing her, the sun disc on the tower above her giving her the feeling that the people who had built the tower were accustomed to using knowledge gained from nature in an orderly and significant way.

"If only Fern could see this garden," she thought. It did not have the wild profusion of Fern's garden. It was much more formal and controlled. Beds of contrasting colours were placed to form a pattern within the whole, where Fern had flowers of every colour growing together instinctively forming a beautiful relationship. Kyra was impressed with the formal elegance of the design and moved by the feeling of peace and security it engendered, but if she were asked she would have to say she preferred the feeling she had in Fern's garden which was one of overwhelming joy and pleasure at the sheer fact of living and growing.

Someone had joined her in the courtyard. She spun round to see a man watching her. He was small and wizened with age, his skin folded in hundreds of wrinkles, his eyes, which were a strange and slanting shape, like black beads.

She found herself bowing to him with respect. He acknowledge the obeisance with a slight inclination of his own head. He did not seem particularly surprised to see her, though he was curious.

He walked towards her and then circled round her looking her over very carefully. She was suddenly aware that she must look as strange to him as he to her, a fourteen-year-old girl, slim, wiry, fair hair in a loose plait down her back, brown, rough woolen dress tied at the waist with a leather thong, sandals of leather with thongs crisscrossed over bare legs. He was clad in a soft flowing garment, of a cloth so fine and shining she could not

194

imagine how it could be woven. It hid his whole body so that when he walked he seemed to glide. Traced on his cloak was the shape of an animal in coloured threads, a kind of serpent, with legs and jaws breathing fire.

She stared fascinated and as she stared she began to understand things. She understood somehow that this was a "dragon", a symbol to these people of the unseen forces of the Universe that move throughout the sky and the earth revitalizing it with spirit. She understood somehow this idea was similar to that spoken of by Maal and Fern, the lines of power and force that flow through the earth and can be tapped and used by all living things.

These people seemed as a whole to take much more interest in this idea than her own did. She understood the man before her had a special kind of knowledge, a knowledge of these lines of power, and his task was to plot them for the people so that they could use them, build upon them, design their lives around them. She realized suddenly that the beauty and the harmony with which the man-made constructions she had seen from the top of the hill fitted so perfectly into the landscape was probably due to the skill of this man in plotting the flow currents of the dragon spirit. She realized also that the system of alignments in straight lines from one Sacred point to another used by her own people was crude compared to the subtle following of curving and constantly changing flow paths that these people had mastered. She wished Maal was still alive and she could discuss it with him.

She looked with even greater respect than she had at first at the small figure before her.

He was shorter than she was, yet had such presence she would not have dared cross him in any way.

She found herself asking him if he were one of the Lords of the Sun. This she did in her mind, forming images, not in words of her own race.

He in his turn spoke no words, but lifted his delicate hand and indicated that she should follow him.

She left the bright and beautiful garden, the colourful

195

butterflies, the bees and singing water, and entered the chill darkness of an enormous chamber. At first the contrast from the sunlight shining on so many light surfaces to the shadows of the room made it impossible for her to see anything at all but when her eyes grew accustomed to the change she could see a man of great bulk sitting cross-legged in front of a small brazier gazing into the embers with great concentration. The little man she was with indicated she should draw nearer. The huge man did not look up even though her sandal scuffed against something and made a noise.

"Perhaps he cannot see me," she thought.

But even as she thought it she knew the answer was that he was very well aware of her presence, but was not yet prepared to break off what he was doing. He went on staring into the small fire so long she became restless and began to look around.

Several large bronze vessels caught her eye, one in particular lit clearly by the light coming through the door from the courtyard. It was huge and cast with great skill, and designs that reminded her of the fiery serpent on the cloak of her new friend, but somehow more formalized, covered the surface, which was broken up into three main sections. The base on which the heavy vessel stood itself was decorated most beautifully, and the centre section, which was the largest and seemed to be a container casket of some sort, was decorated among other things with two piercing eyeballs.

"To keep off evil spirits," Kyra thought.

The lid was heavy and dependable, but also beautiful. She had never seen such bronze work in her whole life. What kind of people could these be to have such knowledge, such temples, such gardens, such fine and shining cloth, such skill with metal and enough gold to decorate the landscape with discs to represent the sun.

She felt eyes upon her and turned to see that both men were looking at her. When they were sure they had her attention they pulled something out of the fire with little bronze tongs. She stepped forward to see more clearly and found that they had what looked like pieces of bone on a dish of bronze in front of them. The bone was crisscrossed with delicate little cracks probably from the heat of the fire. Both men concentrated on them, bending low and ignoring her again. She wandered about the room, noticing the door into another smaller courtyard and finding it an exquisite miniature of the central one, but without the tower. All the flowers in this one were scarlet and their rich colour fairly took her breath away. She found more bronze vessels of many different sizes and shapes. One small jug in the shape of an owl she longed to take home with her to show to Fern and Karne.

The men were looking at her again so she returned to her place before the brazier, looking at them with a question in her mind. Neither spoke, but the huge man pointed with his fat finger to the little pieces of bone. He wanted her to look closely at them. She did so, puzzling what it was she was supposed to see. As she puzzled thoughts came into her head that were not her own. This was a kind of divination, she realized. They were asking the gods, who in some way were connected with their ancestors, to tell them if she was to be trusted or if she was an evil spirit.

At this she felt quite indignant. She? An evil spirit!

Her indignation cost her her concentration and the channel of their communication was temporarily lost. She intercepted an impatient look passing between the two men. She tried to be calm and concentrate again.

"What do your ancestors say?" she found herself asking aloud.

They frowned at her and she realized she had made a mistake to talk aloud. She tried to think the question.

The men seemed to understand. The fat one raised his great bulk from the floor and stood beside his colleague, and both looked at her with their strange slanting eyes, but no feeling of fear came to her. The look was kindly and welcoming. The ancestors must have given a favourable answer.

She was just beginning to frame another question of

her own when she realized she was no longer in the room. The whole scene, room, courtyard, temple, landscape, yellow road and wall of yellow stone, was gone.

She was in darkness and she was alone.

She was trembling uncontrollably as a kind of current thrust its path through her. She tried to keep from being afraid, knowing that fear was her worst enemy.

She tried to think the words "Lords of the Sun" over and over again with all her concentration. Maal had told her to do this if she were in difficulties. It would help them to home in on her, he had said. She was not sure that this is what she wanted, but she was enough in control to know that it was not what she wanted that mattered now.

As she waited in the darkness beating out the words "Lords of the Sun" over and over again, it seemed to her that the sound of the words became louder and louder until she fancied they were not in her head at all but were coming from outside, and although she could still distinguish them they were part of a greater gabble of words, most of which she did not understand. She felt she was no longer alone but in a crowd, a noisy, ebullient crowd shouting frantically for the victory of someone.

She heard the thundering noise of hooves coming towards her and she opened her eyes in terror. She was horrified to see an enormous and muscular bull approaching in a cloud of red dust, every ligament straining, steam coming from his nostrils, his eyes wild and bloodshot. She screamed and leapt back, but she need not have worried. He turned before he reached her and pounded off across a huge enclosure.

There were people all around her, people everywhere, dressed as she had never seen people dressed before. In amazement she saw women with breasts bare, flounced and flaring skirts of varied colours, bright ribbons in black hair coiled and towered upon the tops of their heads. Young men with brief skirts but otherwise bare and gleaming bodies, hair in strange curls, eyes accentuated with black paint. Old men in tunics. She stared and stared, knocked and pushed from side to side every now and again by excited people who were trying to see the sport of the bulls.

Behind one of the barricades was a raised dais and upon it such grand people sat that she was sure they must be Royalty. She had heard of Kings and Queens, Princes and Princesses, Chiefs and Chieftainesses, but never had she seen anything like them before. Round the Queen's neck was jewellery of such splendour, gold and amber, combined in strings so many and so thick they appeared almost solid, amber hanging from her ears and gold snakes coiling around her arms. She was the most beautiful woman Kyra had ever seen. The king beside her, although dark and magnificent, was outshone in every way. Behind them a palace of translucent stone rose, tier upon tier against the panorama of a distant mountain range.

Someone brushed past Kyra and caused her to turn. It was a young girl not much older than Fern, almost naked, so beautiful in a healthy animal way that Kyra drew in her breath with awe. The girl looked at her and Kyra realized she was the only one in the whole throng who could see her.

Amazed she stared into the girl's dark eyes. She too had paint around her lids to accentuate the almond shape. Her hair was bound tight with gold ribbon so that not a thread of it dared stray.

She seemed as surprised to see Kyra as Kyra was to see her.

"You want me?"

Kyra thought she heard the words but knew now they were only in her head.

"I do not know," Kyra replied carefully. "I am looking for the Lords of the Sun."

Acknowledgement and recognition flickered in the almond eyes but before she could phrase a reply a shout of such a pitch went up from the crowd all concentration was shattered and impossible. The girl moved like a young doe and leapt with the economy of an arrow to

199

stand poised and beautiful upon the barrier wall that divided the crowd from the bull.

Kyra rushed forward and before she knew what she was doing thrust her hand out to seize the girl and pull her back to safety, but before she could do this the crowd roared again, this time with adulation, and Kyra realized the girl was the subject of their attention.

She stood magnificently poised for an instant. Her arms were raised to accept the greetings of the crowd and then she leapt and was down on the red dust with the bull.

Horrified, Kyra stared.

Like whipcord the body of the girl twisted and leapt in the most amazing way. She was dancing to the bull, challenging it with the flickering fire of her movements. For a moment he stood bemused and then could stand no more.

He charged.

Kyra's heart nearly burst with anxiety for the girl.

But as he was upon her she seized his horns and with a graceful arcing flip she somersaulted across his back and was gone, dainty as a bird, across the other side.

The crowd went mad. Kyra thought her head would explode with the sound. Dust and noise and violence was everywhere.

Kyra shut her eyes and put her hands to her ears.

But as suddenly as it had come, it cut out.

"Oh no!" she cried, disappointed, and opened her eyes again. But it was too late. She was back in the ante-chamber of darkness waiting for the next part of her journey.

She was growing used to the strangeness of the things that were happening to her by now, but she could not help being a little anxious that she did not seem to be getting any nearer to the Lords of the Sun.

She started her silent but urgent chant again and this time when she opened her eyes she was in a colonnade of stone columns so huge that it seemed they would reach to the sky. She bent her head back and looked up the length of them. They were carved and spread at the top like trees and the sky was roofed out. Between them she could see further columns and beyond them dim chambers.

It seemed to her she was walking along the outer colonnade of a temple and from her left bright and burning light shafted in to fall between the columns in stripes on the stone flags of the floor. Dimness and coolness were to her right. Beyond her at the head of the colonnade more sunlight streamed in white heat on endless plains of white sand. This must be the desert country over the sea in the far south that Maal had told her about.

Having felt the force of the sun falling through the columns she decided to turn inwards and seek the cool depths of the Temple, but as she passed close to one of the columns she noticed that its surface was not smooth. It was marked its whole length with strange little markings and figures. As she gazed at it she was startled to come across several small representations of the figures of the half-human, half-animal demons she had seen before. She drew back in horror. Was this a temple to *them*?

She was just thinking she had better try and get away when a young man emerged from the darkness within the Temple and beckoned her.

She stared at him nervously, but was relieved to see he did not have the head of an animal. He was tall and well featured, shoulders broad, nose aquiline. The upper half of his body was bare except for a necklet of marvellous workmanship. His hair was thick and must have been mixed with something to make it stand so stiffly around his face. A band the same deep blue colour as his necklet, similarly decorated with a central eagle figure, was bound around his forehead. His feet were clad in gold sandals, the lower half of his body in folds of soft white cloth, bound with a girdle of gold.

She was attracted to him immediately and felt no more dread.

She followed him first through colonnades of columns, then through dim chambers and even dimmer passages. At last he brought her to a halt within an inner chamber lit by torches. She stared around her and felt her old

201

uneasiness come back as the same half-human, half-animal figures were depicted large upon the walls.

Ahead of her on a great plinth of black stone, a stone eagle stared back at her, a sun disc carved upon its forehead.

He noticed her fear and touched her arm comfortingly.

She looked at him and then looked questioningly at the dread figures around the walls. It was true she could not feel the malevolence from them she had felt before, but she could not forget the horror with which she had encountered them on other occasions.

He put his finger on her lips and another on her forehead.

His thoughts came clearly to her.

"These are our gods," he said.

"Your gods!"

He could feel the revulsion in her.

"Why do you fear them so?" he asked.

She thought about the other two occasions and he seemed to receive the image of it.

Gently he shook his head.

"I was wrong," he said, "these are not our gods. They are the images of our gods."

"How does that explain it?" she thought, still suspicious of the place.

He smiled.

"There is one God, and beneath him hierarchies of spirits we call gods, but God and spirit are impossible for human minds to understand. We are too undeveloped, too primitive," he added.

She hoped he did not add that last epithet after looking at her. She was beginning to feel more and more like a primitive country girl of no account faced with so much grandeur and skill. He caught her thought and smiled again. She noticed that there was no condescension in his look. He liked her and respected her in spite of her crude clothes and untrained mind.

"Having no words and images that are adequate to describe their intuitive feelings about God and the spirit world, people choose images from their own earthly experiences and use them somehow to 'parcel up' the feelings that they have."

She looked puzzled.

"Some people choose the Sun and call it God, some the Moon, some the king, some an animal or a bird. They know deep down when they begin that what they have chosen is only a symbol, a representation of what they really mean. But there are times when they forget that this is how it is and you will find people worshipping the image and not what it is supposed to represent.

"My people carve a statue of a man with a jackal's head and it is supposed to represent the spirit who guides the dead into the spirit world.

"To some who are far along the path to enlightenment the figure in stone is no more than a sign post that points in the direction where the truth about death and the crossing from the material to the spirit world may be found. It is the sign at the entrance to a whole group of understandings. It is no more than that. They look beyond the image to the Reality.

"But to someone not so far developed, incapable of grasping subtle and abstract concepts, it is accepted as the Reality itself. The worshipper stops short at the image, sees no further, may even see himself reflected back from it. The statue, the image itself, is believed to be a god.

"The jackal's head was chosen originally maybe because jackals are creatures of the night who seek out the dead. The human body was given to the jackal to add, symbolically, the human dimension. In one hand he carried a divine sceptre, denoting divine power, in the other the ankh, the symbol of life.

"It is clear that Death and Life are contained in this one image, with the power that transforms the one into the other.

"But when the symbol becomes downgraded into an image of a god that is taken literally, all kinds of misinterpretations of the symbolism can occur.

"A holy image that set out to bring comfort is turned

203

into its opposite and brings fear. The jackal head can suggest devouring nocturnal beasts preying on the dead."

"I understand," cried Kyra, "that makes sense."

"So you see the images of the gods can bring comfort and fear depending on the interpretation of the people who worship them, the same god-image can be good or evil depending on the worshipper, can bring death or life."

Kyra frowned, trying to grasp it all.

"Demon or kindly spirit, beast or human. Both interpretations are possible from the one image. It is we who draw the one, or the other, from deep within ourselves. That is how it is possible for men to kill and commit atrocities in the name of their god. They have forgotten the god behind the word and use the word with all its powerful connotations to excuse whatever it is they wish to do.

"The priest who sees the jackal-god as a powerful weapon to inspire fear and keep his people cowed has brought this from within himself.

"The priest who sees the jackal-god as a powerful but kindly guide and guardian brings this also from within himself.

"There are no gods of stone or fire or flesh, but there are unimaginable spirit influences from the Scource of All that we clothe for convenience in words, in images, in stone and paint.

"Those figures you saw as demons were figments of your own mind."

"But they were *there*—as surely as you are now."

The young man looked at her kindly.

"Evil influences you feared were there. *You* gave them the clothing of our gods."

"But I had never seen or heard of your gods before!"

He looked thoughtful at that.

"It is possible someone near you knew of our gods and used them in thought form to frighten you."

She thought about it and told him about Wardyke and Maal.

The young priest walked with her back through the Temple, passing sights of great strangeness. There was hardly a section of wall that was not covered with their weird signs and paintings. He listened quietly to all that she had to say and when they reached a quiet shady garden with a lily pond he motioned her to sit on a warm slab of stone.

"I think this Wardyke," he said at last, "has had dealings with some of our people."

His face was grave and sad.

"There is much that is wrong with our priesthood," he said. "Many have lost the insight and use the image-gods to extract blind obedience and riches from their people. Fear is a weapon they are very skilled at using."

Kyra knew she had found someone at last that she could ask about the Lords of the Sun.

He listened and nodded.

"You have not been wasting your time . . . each journey you have made has been an invitation to one of the Lords of the Sun."

"Who are they, these Lords?"

"I am one," he said, and she started back in amazement.

"Probably you met several others. They are not pure spirits, but people who are trained amongst the priesthood in the special tasks of communication over great distances, over the whole world."

She was shy of him now. She had thought he was some kind of trainee priest, much nearer her own level.

"Do not be afraid of me," he said quietly. "You have come a long way to find me and I will help you."

"What must I do?" she asked humbly.

"That I cannot tell you now. No, do not look so disappointed. You have found me and I will not desert you. But what Maal wanted you to do was to call a meeting of the Lords of the Sun in your country. That you must do and we will all be there. Together we will help you. Together our powers are greater."

"But how do I call a meeting?" she asked despairingly.

He looked at her with great affection. She seemed so small and vulnerable, far too young to have the burdens of her community upon her shoulders.

"*Will* it," he said simply.

She looked puzzled.

"Shut your eyes," he said patiently.

She shut her eyes.

"Now *will* that the Lords of the Sun will come together to help your community.

She squeezed her eyes tight shut and wished, as she had never wished for anything in her life, that her travels and her troubles would be over and that the Lords of the Sun would come together to help her and her people.

The good-looking priest was gone. The huge temple of red sand stone columns was gone, the little garden surrounded by a wall painted with a scene of wild ducks and reeds was gone.

She was alone again and she was afraid.

This time it *must* work. She could not go on much longer.

"Please!" she whispered, tears pricking at the back of her eyes. "Please!"

Music made her open her eyes and the scene before her staggered her imagination.

She knew that she was back in her own country, but a long way from her home. She was in the giant Sacred Circle that she had visited once before as a passenger in the mind of Maal.

It was early dawn. First light was creeping over the sky, some stars still shining in the rich blue air. A light and gossamer mist was drifting close to the ground, so that everything, even the gigantic blocks of Stone that stood around the circumference in their hundreds, seemed to be floating and moving.

As she had noticed before a high ridge of earth and grass surrounded the whole and blocked out the rest of the world. She had never seen outside this Circle and could not imagine how the community who used such a great place would live.

Within the great Circle of Standing Stones she was aware of circles within circles of people moving rhythmically to the music of drum and flute, stepping sideways slowly and with elegance, their arms raised so that the tips of their fingers brushed their neighbours' as they moved. On a certain beat they dipped their heads and bent their knee in a way that gave the whole ring movement a sinuous serpentine character. As each concentric circle was moving around the Stone Circle in a direction opposite to the one within and without itself, the currents and eddies of invisible force generated were complex indeed.

Kyra quite forgot she was supposed to be playing a part in the ceremony and stared blatantly at everything she could see.

She noticed that the people in the rings were placed alternately man and woman, boy and girl. The force they seemed to be trying to create this day was to come from the tension between, in a sense the friction between, differing elements. She knew that a mysterious energy was released when man and woman came together. She had felt the spark of it when she had been near the young desert priest. The priests of this community appeared to be using this force to build up energy for the use of the Lords of the Sun.

Curious about the people themselves who lived and worked in the presence of such a temple, Kyra began to look at individuals. There were people there she recognized as country villagers like herself, in roughly woven woolen garments, their bodies liberally browned by the sun and muscles well developed from work in fields. There were people she knew were metal workers, stone masons, flint miners, merchants. Others were stranger to her. Tall people. Elegant people. Dressed in flowing cloth, finely woven, the very way they held their heads different from the farmers and the villagers. The women of this type wore jewellery, some of which reminded her of her "travels". She saw necklaces of black jet, collars of sun metal, earrings and bracelets. The men wore studded belts and bands of leather on their heads and arms.

And then there were the Strangers from other countries, darker people, lighter people, dressed in different ways but all part of the ring moving with the same rhythmic movement.

Undeniable forces and vibrations were set up, currents and eddies of power. She could feel it. She could almost see it. The pulsing of the music added to the intensity of the feeling. The mist that moved with its own serpentine life about their feet added to the impression of detachment from the earth. Everything was charged and potent. She was on a level of reality that she had not known before. Her heart began beating loudly. She had finally reached the conjunction of the Lords of the Sun.

The figures of the concentrically moving circles began to dim for her and she became aware with greater clarity of the smaller Stone Circle within the greater, in which she herself was standing.

She was in the centre and around her in a ring but standing as still as the Tall Stones themselves were figures she could only think were the Lords of the Sun. They were impressive figures dressed strangely in the styles of their countries, each different from the other, and all different from the circling figures around them. The stillness of her Circle was astonishing in comparison to the movement surrounding them. It was as though they were enclosed in a capsule of great peace, the still point at the centre of ceaseless motion.

She felt the movement was generating power for them in some way, but leaving them undisturbed.

Within her circle there seemed to be no one in charge, no priest conducting the meeting. With a sudden tremor she realized that she was expected to speak, she had called them together and they were waiting for her to tell them what to do.

She looked around in despair. So many strangers! And

then her heart leapt. She saw first the girl athlete from the Palace of the Bulls, this time dressed like her country-women in long, flounced skirt and sleeved bodice open over the breasts, and then her young priest from the desert temple of the sandstone columns. Her face flooded with the warmth of a smile and she took a step forward. But the young priest shook his head slightly and she knew she had to stand in the centre and make a "speech".

She glanced up at the sky and she remembered that with the dawn her body would not be safe in the Sacred Circle of her community. She remembered also these Lords had work of their own to do and she must not waste their time.

She drew herself up to her full height and prepared to "think" the whole story of Wardyke coming to their village and what had happened since.

When she had done she stayed quietly, trying to keep her mind a blank, ready for their thoughts. The drumming and the movements of the people around them had become like a low vibrational hum and was no disturbance at all.

Slowly thoughts that were not hers began to come to her. She was not sure if they came from individuals, and if they did, from which ones. It seemed more likely that it was their composite thinking that was reaching her.

". . . It is true Wardyke has not received the final seal of the priesthood and so has no right to practice as a priest . . ."

She found herself wondering why they had not prevented him doing so.

". . . You are reminded that we are human and know only what is communicated to us. Before you had told us the story we had not known what was going on . . ."

She felt ashamed that she had questioned and doubted in this way and determined not to interrupt with her own thoughts again. She shut her eyes the better to concentrate.

". . . He must be stopped, but Maal was right to say that you must not do it with force . . ."

She smiled with pleasure at the warmth of their approval for Maal.

". . . It is the evil in Wardyke that must be destroyed, not Wardyke himself . . .

"To kill him would be to surrender onself to the same evil that ruled his life . . ."

Kyra agreed. But how?

". . . Confidence and belief are the strongest forces in a man's nature . . .

". . . It is here that you must mount your attack . . ."

In answer to Kyra's unspoken question the Lords of the Sun patiently explained.

". . . The key to Wardyke's power in your community lies in confidence and belief. He believes that he has the right and the power to do what he is doing, and you believe that too. This gives him his strength . . .

". . . No magician . . . (and here Kyra remembered Maal had said this too) . . . has power over you if you do not *believe* that he has . . ."

She understood this, but did not know if she would have the strength, faced by Wardyke, to doubt his powers. When Maal talked, when the Lords of the Sun explained, it all seemed quite simple. But meeting the burning eye of Wardyke was another matter. Then she *could not* doubt.

". . . We know it is not easy, but it must be done. You must return to your people and speak to them, make them understand that Wardyke has no power of himself. It is their *belief* that he has power that gives it to him. Without their belief he is helpless. You must render him helpless and thereby harmless.

". . . That way your community will be free without becoming the slaves of evil themselves . . ."

Kyra's eyes were open now and she was looking worried. She knew they were right but how she wished, how she had hoped, that they could do something sudden and dramatic to remove Wardyke from their midst. She knew it would be a long hard struggle to persuade the villagers to change their beliefs like this. In fact she did not think she could do it.

". . . You *can* do it . . . You can! You have powers within yourself that you are only just beginning to tap, and we will give you help . . ."

Kyra looked up hopefully at that.

". . . Before the Spring a new priest will arrive to work in your community. He will have the final seal and he will be a good man . . .

". . . When he comes, you will leave, your work there done . . ."

She looked startled. Leave her home?

". . . You will travel south through many trials and dangers and you will come, in the flesh, to this place and you will train to be a priest yourself . . ."

She gasped.

"Me?"

". . . Yes, you. You have been chosen. . . .

". . . But there is much still for you to do.

"When you return to your home this dawn you will go to the place where Maal is buried and you will find a small stone upon his burial mound. Yes, you will know which one it is when you see it. You will take it and keep it close with you until Wardyke is overthrown. Maal's help will be in that stone.

". . . Our help will be in the sky. Look at the sky and you will see a sign that is confirmation of our help . . ."

"Now?"

". . . No, not now. You will know when to look . . ."

"This is like Maal's advice," Kyra thought with a certain discontent, "always telling me I will mysteriously 'know' something and then leaving me by myself!"

But she was comforted that she would have definite help.

". . . You have already proved to yourself that you are capable of projecting images into Wardyke's mind. Work on this. Encourage your friends to help you. There is strength in communion of thought. Choose a time for as many as possible of you to project the same image into

Wardyke's mind. Never let him forget his crimes. Haunt him night and day. You will find that particularly when he is asleep it will be easy to influence the images of his dreams. His surface mind will be off guard and there will be no interruptions from superficial distractions . . .

". . . We will join with you in this work . . .

". . . Finally eroded by guilt and undermined in confidence, he will be helpless and will have to look for a new way to live his life . . .

". . . Believe it, child, for it is true . . ."

Kyra looked around the Circle. The thoughts of these great people were locked in her heart and she would draw upon them in the difficult days to come.

One by one she looked at them. Each the possessor of knowledge and skills far beyond the ordinary man, each from a country far distant from her own. She recognized the large man from the Temple of the Squares and Circles and beside him stood a woman of dark skin and hair of black silk streaked with silver flowing to the silver sandals on her feet. Beyond her a man clad in a magnificent cape of multicoloured feathers stood beside an old man dressed in rags, so thin and wasted that he seemed more of a skeleton than a living man, his hair wild and straggling, leaning on a gnarled and knobbled stick to keep himself upright, but his eyes full of light and fire.

Then she saw her beautiful athlete and could not help wondering at her youth. The girl met her eyes and smiled.

"Age has nothing to do with it," she said in Kyra's head. "We are all thousands of years old and yet still in our infancy."

Beyond her was a priest standing straight and tall, dressed simply in woven wool except for one magnificent pendant of green jade that he wore on a thong about his neck. She knew instinctively he was a countryman of hers. He was the high priest of this Great Circle. The host of this extraordinary gathering. She looked closer at his face and was impressed with its calm strength. In these people she had confidence. If they said she could bend metal

212

with a mere touch, she would believe it and she would do it. If they said she could be a priest, she would believe it and she would do it.

The task she had to do within her own community no longer seemed impossible. She would not be alone. She would have their strengthening thoughts with her in everything she did.

She began to think about her own powers and her own relationship to those around her.

"I cannot be too helpless," she thought, "otherwise I would not be here now. Otherwise I would not be chosen to be trained as a priest!"

And with that she had a surge of self-confidence that would see her through many a difficulty.

Pleased to feel the strengthening confidence that was coursing through her, the Lords of the Sun prepared to leave.

Kyra became aware of it when she suddenly noticed that the undercurrent of rhythmic sound from outside their small circle had risen to a crescendo and was beginning to deafen her.

Startled she looked around and noticed that the Lords who had looked so solid a moment before were beginning to dissolve in the air, whose visible vibrations were increasing every second.

"Oh no!" she cried, loth to let them go.

She turned to the young desert priest and had such an overwhelming feeling of yearning for him to stay with her that it was almost a pain.

As though her desire for him was holding him back in some way he was the last to go. She was sure his eyes were seeking hers as longingly as hers were seeking his. For a moment they seemed to melt together and Kyra had the strangest feeling that she was within his arms, although she knew she was not and could see him separate from herself across the Circle.

She opened her mouth to cry out in real words and at that second he and all about her disappeared.

Shaken and trembling she found herself on a slab of

213

cold stone, early sunlight streaming everywhere, and the anxious faces of Karne and Fern looking down at her.

"Kyra!" Karne was calling urgently. "We *must* go! Someone will find us here."

"Are you all right?" Fern put her arm around her gently and helped her upright.

Kyra looked dazed.

She could not answer. Everything was shaking and whirling around her. She felt as though she were going to faint.

"Kyra!" Fern cried, and Karne caught her as she fell.

"Oh you gods protect her!" he muttered fervently.

"We must take her out of here," Fern whispered anxiously. "Perhaps when she is out of this Circle she will be better."

Together they lifted her and carried her out and down the hill and as far as they could go from the Standing Stones.

In the valley the tired villagers were preparing for the funeral of the two young people. The fires of vigil that had burnt all night were nothing more than smouldering embers.

The Forest is Punished

As AUTUMN GRADUALLY CAME to the community Karne and Kyra worked hard to to change the villagers' attitude to Wardyke. As they had expected, it was not easy.

They explained much of what had happened to them to people they felt were ready for it, starting with their family.

Their father listened to everything they had to say with great attention and asked few, but pertinent, questions. Their mother was immediately horrified as the risks Kyra had been taking and the blasphemy of her entering the forbidden Sacred Circle. She was so occupied with fussing about these things that she did not seem to grasp the real implication of what they told her.

Thon was angry almost immediately and wanted action, arguing that the Lords of the Sun were soft and that there was only one way to deal with Wardyke, with force. He had had his eye on Mia for a wife and could think of nothing but revenge.

Patiently Kyra explained the reasons the Lords of the

Sun had advised against this. Patiently she went over the whole ground again. But Thon was not convinced. The only reason he had not already killed Wardyke was that he had not had the opportunity. The other villagers refused to rise again after what had happened, and alone he stood no chance against Wardyke. There always seemed to be some of his most unpleasant Strangers with him as bodyguard and Thon had noticed they were now carrying weapons, short bronze daggers tucked into the top binding of their sandal leggings and stone axes in their belts.

Kyra pointed out that Wardyke could not be such a powerful magician if he needed armed men to defend him. This made the people think and one by one they joined her in her efforts to discomfit him by projecting disturbing images into his mind. This was not easy, as they were not used to sustaining one image for a long time, nor to disciplining their minds so rigidly. Most of them found as they lay in their warm rugs at the appointed hour of the night that they started with great enthusiasm to project the image of Mia's death and the boy being stoned, and then one by one they drifted off the point, some to sleep and some to think of other things.

Many times Kyra felt close to despair. Weeks passed and though they tried projection every night Wardyke showed no signs of being disturbed. He strode about surrounded by his lackeys, more confident than ever.

He had set the villagers to work making battle axes from the hard granite of their local hills. Day after day they sat chipping and hammering and banging away, making weapons of war that they did not want.

He spoke to them of enemies about to invade, and remembering the fall of stars they obeyed his every command. Most of them were too afraid openly to oppose a man whom the gods had apparently set their seal of approval upon.

He told them flint was coming in great quantities from the south and that they would be able to make arrow and spear heads with it. Swords and daggers were on their way as well.

One evening, at her lowest ebb, Kyra sat upon the hillside feeling very much alone. There seemed no way she could carry out the instructions of the Lords. She, Karne and Fern were consistent and dedicated to the plan, but the others listened, agreed and seemed to want to help, but as soon as the slightest difficulty got in their way they gave up.

It seemed to her they had forgotten about Mia and the boy, were in fact deliberately trying to forget. It was so much easier to drift with each day, occasionally grumbling, but on the whole obeying Wardyke. If only she could show them some sign of success their resolution might be strengthened and they might be prepared to take more chances and make more effort.

She thought longingly about the Lords of the Sun. If only they were here to help! Perhaps she could summon them with her will as she had done before.

She shut her eyes to the pale gold of the evening sky, the red gold of the autumn woods, and thought about the Lords of the Sun. At first she could not get beyond the young desert priest, but her longing to see him was not entirely connected with the problem in hand and she forced her mind to visualize the others, one by one, and to call upon them with all her might for help.

She heard no voices, thought no thoughts that were not her own, and at last, defeated and depressed, she opened her eyes.

Before her in the sky, veil upon veil of shining light fell from the uttermost height of the heavens almost to the earth, in folds finer than the finest drapery she had ever imagined. Stunned, she gazed as it changed through every possible shade and finally faded.

"Look to the sky and you will see a sign that is confirmation of our help," they had said, and now as she called to them for help the sky was transformed beyond belief.

That night every person in the community, including Wardyke's Strangers, had dreams that kept them tossing and turning, groaning and sighing. Mia's death and the

217

stoning of the boy was played out in every detail, grotesque and horrible, within the minds of every sleeping person. If they awoke they would fall asleep soon afterwards and within seconds the ghastly scene would be enacted yet again in the arena of their minds.

Wardyke woke in sudden terror in his own house and cried out, fighting off imaginary stones and sticks as they came flailing at him. Around him, eyes wild with hate and accusation were closing in on him, and for a moment such fear took him over that he was powerless to withstand them.

He woke, sweating and trembling, and rose, lit torches and strode about his rooms the rest of the night. In the morning he looked haggard and tired, and Kyra was now slow to point this out to the villagers.

That day when Wardyke walked amongst the community there were many who dared look him boldly in the eye and there were many who looked and felt as though they had a secret knowledge that gave them strength against him.

For the first time he was uneasy. Something was going on over which he had no control. He tried questioning some of the villagers, but they pretended not to know what he was talking about. They became instantly humble, but in such a way that he was not sure it was real.

He alerted the Strangers to look out for any kind of disaffection and report it to him. If the villagers were beginning to turn against him, there must be a ring-leader. And that man he *must* have before it was too late.

In the afternoon he went again to Fern's house and surprised her sweeping the fallen leaves away from the entrance to her small home. She jumped slightly when he appeared and then gripped the branch she was using until her knuckles showed white. Her eyes were blazing and defiant.

He approached her, his own eyes like whirlpools of darkness.

"No!" she cried.

"I need you," he said, and his voice was filled with a strange kind of pain.

"No!" she cried again and lifted the branch to strike him if he took a step nearer her.

His mouth twisted slightly, and with a swift movement he knocked the branch out of her hand with one of his giant hands and struck her across the face with the other.

"I *need* you!" he repeated, his voice strained and menacing.

She reeled back with the force of the blow, but when she had regained her balance her expression was as defiant as ever. Indeed slightly mocking now, as though she despised him for having resorted to petty violence.

An ugly red flush began to creep across his face.

His hands began to rise and with a leap of fear in her heart she remembered Mia.

"Help me!" she cried deep inside her to all the forces of nature that she loved so much.

As though in answer to her prayer a sudden violent wind sprang up and Wardyke, who was standing near the door post of her house which was covered with creeper, was lashed in the face by its long and thorny tendrils.

With a scream he sprang back, covering his eyes as the thorns ripped and scratched at them. Leaves swirled everywhere and dust choked him.

"I cannot see! I cannot see!" he screamed, staggering and almost falling.

She stood looking at him, the wind swirling her long red hair like flame around her. Her eyes blazed with triumph as she remembered she was not alone.

"Go, Wardyke!" she cried with tremendous and surprising authority. "And never come to this wood again!"

A whirlwind pushed and buffeted him, he choked and spluttered with the dust, staggered and almost fell. He could feel blood on his hands and on his face. His eyes were stinging and painful, his chest aching with the effort of coughing.

He turned and half ran along the path, a fallen branch that he could have sworn had not been there when he arrived tripped him and he crashed to the ground like a felled tree.

As suddenly as it had started, the wind ceased. There was absolute silence as Wardyke picked himself up. He looked around at the bushes and the trees of the wood and he could *feel* the animosity, but he could see nothing.

He looked back at Fern and she had a strange grandeur. This was her kingdom, and he was banished.

He left, mopping the blood from his cheeks and thinking bitterly of the experience. He was shaken, but by no means defeated. He would be back.

That night Fern woke to a feeling of great unease. She sat up and looked around her, every sense alert, like a small animal. Something was wrong. Something did not feel right. As she listened she seemed to hear thousands of minute voices raised in pain and fear, clamouring for her help. Appalled, she leapt up and left the house, still not knowing what the trouble was. As she stood in the entrance an overwhelming smell of wood smoke met her nostrils, and her ears were filled with the cruel crackle of flames in dry twigs.

Fire! Her wood was on fire!

She could see it now, leaping scarlet from branch to branch, tearing at the dry leaves, devouring the delicate fronds of bracken.

"Wardyke!" she cried. Wardyke's revenge. She might have known he would not give in so easily.

Torn with pain to see her beautiful and living wood so tortured and destroyed, she could not see what she could do to rescue it. There was no way. The wind that had helped her before was now helping Wardyke. The flames were driven before it to wilder and wilder excesses and if she were not careful the fire would have her too. Weeping with pity for the trees she ran as fast as she could. Other creatures joined her and the ground was full of leaping frogs, deer, squirrels and hares. The luckier birds were screeching in the sky.

She called and called for help, but who was there to hear her?

Meanwhile in the village Kyra was having an uneasy dream in which the villagers had all been put in a deep pit by Wardyke and set on fire. She woke as the flame licked her own flesh and she could feel the pain. Once awake she lay puzzled. The feeling of fire on her arm had been so vivid and yet here she was, perfectly safe, in her sleeping rug. She was just turning over to sleep again when Karne tapped her on the shoulder.

"What is it?" she whispered.

"I am not sure. But I feel something is happening that should be stopped."

She sat up.

"Wardyke?"

"It must be. I am going outside to prowl around a bit to see if I can discover anything."

"I will come too," Kyra said, wide awake.

She pulled on her dress and her warm cape and slipped out into the night after her brother. The village was dead quiet and dark. Nothing was stirring but themselves.

"What is that?"

Karne pointed in the direction of Fern's home. There was a faint glow.

They both stared at it for a moment puzzled, and then the same conclusion hit them simultaneously.

"Fire!" gasped Karne and was off like a startled wild animal towards the red and ugly stain, Kyra close behind him.

If only Fern were unharmed!

The woods were dry at this time of year and would burn easily, and there was a wind blowing.

"Oh no!" thought Kyra, "all those beautiful trees and plants!"

But her main concern was Fern.

Karne covered the ground as though he had wings. He had reached the outskirts of Fern's valley before Kyra was within sight of it. He saw at once the smouldering devastation, the blackened husks of trees and beyond them the fire still raging, still tearing at the living wood. Scarcely noticing the pain in his feet he ran across the still smoking earth towards Fern's house, to stand appalled in sight of the pile of embers that marked the place where it had stood.

He knew now how a wolf must feel when it lifts its anguished head and howls in the deep hollow of the night. His heart was howling too.

He heard Kyra shouting, and looked back. She was on the rise just where the fire had begun. She was shouting and pointing but he could not hear what she was saying. He followed the line of her hand. She kept pointing and shouting, more and more desperate as he did not understand. At last she started to run in the direction she had been pointing, her feet less tough than his hurting against the hot earth.

"Go back!" he shouted, and ran towards her.

Within earshot at last he heard her cry, "Fern! Fern!" and look beyond at the woods still burning.

He did not stay to question further but ran towards the place.

On the way he came upon the stream and followed its merciful length for as long as he could. Before he left it he plunged himself in the water and made himself as wet as he could.

Through the flames and smoke suddenly he could see Fern. She was beating at the fire with branches, weeping and choking at the same time.

"Fern!" he shouted and without another thought plunged straight through a barrier of flame.

Startled, she saw him emerge from the fire as though he were the manifestation of some demon. She shrieked and fainted, the whole experience too fraught to bear another second.

Before she touched the ground she was in his arms and he was back through the wall of fire, smothering the sparks on her with his damp clothes. Staggering under her weight, he managed to get back to the stream and out on to the bare hillside where the stubble was almost burnt out.

Kyra was waiting for him and wept with joy to see them both safe, and from there they limped home on feet that were burnt and painful.

Kyra woke their sleeping family and within minutes they were being looked after. Karne's horrified mother rushed to put soothing animal fat upon the burns on her son's feet, and on Fern's arms and back. Kyra herself secretly rubbed some on her own soles. She was not blistered like Karne and Fern and did not want a fuss made of her, but her feet were tender and sore.

The dawn found Karne, Kyra and Fern fast asleep. The mother insisted the family should be quiet and leave them to rest as long as they could, so one by one they crept out and went about the day's business.

Most of the villagers went to see the fire, which by now was almost burnt out. They looked with sorrow at the blackened scar that had once been a lovely, leafy forest.

Wardyke came to survey the scene. Of course there was no proof that he had caused it, but more than one villager noted an expression of satisfaction on his face.

The Second Challenge

AFTER THE FIRE Fern stayed on with Karne and Kyra's family, but she did not recover as quickly as they expected. Karne's burns healed fast and although he probably would always have scars on his feet to remind him of that terrible night, he was soon back to normal. Fern's wounds took longer to heal and even when the skin was whole, she was so listless and pale that Kyra's mother insisted she rested most of the day. Fern, who was usually so full of energy that she rarely did nothing, sat now day after day beside the hearth or in the sun beside the wood pile, content to be inactive.

Everyone was anxious about her, but no one knew what to do. Karne particularly hovered over her and worried.

"What is the matter with her," he asked Kyra desperately. "The burns healed ages ago. She cannot still be in pain."

"It is something inside," Kyra said thoughtfully. "Perhaps she is mourning for her woods and her garden. They were like people to her."

Karne nodded and took Fern a present of some particularly beautiful autumn leaves and berries he found on the hill.

Fern accepted them in silence and lowered her head so that he would not see the tears that gathered in her eyes. But she was not quick enough. He stooped down and kissed the top of her head. With the touch of his lips she broke down completely and sobbed and sobbed. He gathered her to him and held her, not knowing what to say or do. But she did not need words or deeds. She needed him.

At last she had cried herself out and was still.

He sat down beside her and held her hand, she leant her head against his shoulder and, saying nothing to each other, they sat for a long time.

After that she began to take a small interest in things again and started to busy herself helping Kyra's family.

"In the spring the plants will all grow again," Kyra said to her one day. "You will see, your garden and your wood will be beautiful once more.

Fern nodded, but her smile was still sad.

"Shall we help you build your house again?" Kyra's little brothers Ji and Okan asked. They loved making things. They used the boat sometimes for fishing, but somehow it was not quite so much fun as the actual building of it had been, and it was such a long walk to the sea, carrying the boat the whole way, that they tended not to do it as often as they had planned.

Fern looked as though she were thinking about their proposal, and at last she made a decision.

"That is very kind of you. But we have to get the wood from somewhere else. All my wood is burnt."

"Wood is no problem," said Okan joyfully.

"We know where we can get plenty!" said Ji.

"And we can made a sled to haul it on."

225

"I do not want living trees chopped down heartlessly," Fern said warningly.

"Oh no," they said. "These were blown down in a storm. They have been lying all summer waiting to be used."

Fern smiled.

"I will show you how I want my house and when you are ready where there is more wood that itself is ready to be used," she said.

"Can we start making the sled now?"

"Of course."

They rushed off excitedly, delighted to have something else to make.

Kyra smiled at Fern.

"That is better," she said gently, "you are beginning to come alive again."

"I am sorry I gave up like that ... it was just that ..."

She hesitated.

"What is the matter?"

Kyra could see there was something still worrying Fern.

"Are you afraid to go back? Would you rather stay with us?"

Fern shook her head, but still could not bring herself to speak.

"Stay with us!" Kyra pleaded, suddenly sure this was the root of the difficulty. "We would all love to have you—particularly Karne!" she added with a mischievous smile.

At this Fern looked more miserable than ever.

"It *is* Karne!" Kyra cried in amazement.

"No," said Fern quickly.

"What then?"

"Oh, Kyra," said Fern in despair, "I am with child."

Kyra looked stunned.

"Karne?"

"No. Wardyke."

"Oh no!" Kyra was horrified. She took both of Fern's hands in hers and held them very tightly.

The relief of having told someone sympathetic was wonderful for Fern. She told Kyra everything, the visit she had had from Wardyke on the afternoon before the fire and the horror with which she had realized that he had burnt her precious trees in revenge for her rejection of him.

"I hate him, Kyra," she cried. "I cannot help it. I hate him and I fear him!"

Kyra did not know what to say. They both knew hatred and fear were self-destructive emotions and caused nothing but more evil to come from any situation, but she could not blame Fern for hating and fearing Wardyke.

"And what are we to do about Karne?" Kyra said thoughtfully.

Both she and Fern were loth to let him know the situation, and yet they also knew they should not keep it from him much longer.

Dumbly Fern shook her head. Hopelessly she shrugged her shoulders.

It was some days later that events forced an answer to this question.

Karne came briskly to Fern as she was helping Kyra shake out the sleeping rugs. It was a clear and shining day and before the long wet winter set upon them Kyra's mother liked to clear out all the dust and dirt of summer.

"Come," he said commandingly to her, his face the face of someone who has a happy secret he is longing to share, but is determined to make the most of it before he does.

She looked a question.

"I want to show you something special."

She shook her head.

"I cannot. Kyra and I must do these rugs."

"They can be done another time!"

"Oh no, they cannot!"

He was tugging at her now and she was laughingly resisting.

"Oh, go on Fern," Kyra said, "find out what it is. I can do these by myself."

"Of course you cannot! It is heavy work for one," Fern said indignantly, still holding back.

"Well, Karne will help us and it will be done more quickly."

"Oh, will he!" mocked Karne.

"I am not coming with you until it is done," warned Fern.

He shrugged.

"Women!" he exclaimed, but he was not unwilling to help them. He could spin out the delight of anticipation that much longer.

The work went faster with his help, but not fast enough for the two girls, who were by now much intrigued by Karne's secret.

At last they were through and Karne took Fern's hand. Kyra watched with tenderness and affection as the two people closest to her walked away.

But there was the shadow of Wardyke lying between them.

Karne took Fern a long way from the village. Somewhat in the direction of her former home, but carefully choosing the route so that the gloomy sight of the burnt wood did not intrude upon their mood.

He led her north, around the far side of her wood, but out of sight of it.

"What is it?" she kept asking.

But he would not tell her.

"You will see."

At last he paused on the ridge of a small hill and looked ahead of him in a way that made Fern realize that they had arrived. She looked to see what it could be.

What she saw was a beautiful little glen, trees of pure gold beside a stream, bracken- and heather-covered hills dipping down to join it, huge grey rocks covered with an exquisite patterning of lichen in orange and grey-green making a natural and almost circular sun trap just above the tree line.

"There," said Karne in triumph, pointing to the flat grassy patch of earth surrounded by the rocks, "is the natural place for our home!"

She gasped, her face a study of conflicting emotions.

It was truly beautiful. It was truly home!

But . . .

Karne was not looking at her. He saw only the future.

"We can use the rocks as part of the house," he said, "we can build on to them in some way. The garden can spill out through the gaps and run down to the stream. These are still your woods but on the other side . . . the fire did not come this far . . ."

"Karne . . ." she said at last, and there was something in her voice that made him look at her in surprise.

She was not smiling with joy and excitement as he had expected her to be. Her face was pale and drawn, her eyes dark. A sudden chill came to his heart. Surely she would not refuse to live here with him and be his wife. Surely there could be no doubt . . .

"Fern?"

She held up her hand as though to keep him from touching her. She shook her head sadly.

"Oh, Karne, you should have spoken to me before you started to think such things."

"But we love each other!" he cried.

She shook her head miserably.

"We *love* each other!" he repeated with force, seizing her arms and looking desperately into her eyes.

Her eyes were full of pain, but they did not deny what he was saying.

"It is not as simple as that," she said.

"It *is* as simple as that," he insisted.

"Let me go, Karne, there are things you do not know . . ."

"What things?" he demanded angrily, still not releasing her.

"Let me go."

He dropped his hands from her arms, but his eyes were burning into hers.

She was silent for a long time, her heartbeat almost stifling her, but she could not hold back forever.

"I carry Wardyke's child," she said at last, simply and flatly. Unable to say more.

He recoiled.

She dropped her eyes and could not look at him. She did not dare imagine what was going through his mind. She could feel his presence on the hill, feel the natural things around poised and waiting, the very air strained and tense.

And then the tension snapped. He moved.

She looked up but he was already gone.

She longed to explain, to tell him that she loved him, but the feelings that were conflicting in her heart were too strong and too complex.

She could not even call his name aloud, although in her heart it was called a hundred times.

She watched him as he strode away, and he did not look back.

Hours later Fern returned to the village.

Kyra met her with a bright and eager face and a question on her lips, but when she saw Fern's face the light went out of her own.

"You told him?" she said.

Fern nodded and walked past her to the house.

Kyra did not ask any more questions.

Fern spoke quietly but firmly to Kyra's mother, thanking her for the refuge in her home but saying that she must now return to her own.

"But you *have* no home!" Kyra's mother cried.

"I must be with my garden. I have been too long away. I am ashamed I left it when it needed me most. I should have been working there all this time trying to comfort it and to help it grow again."

Kyra stopped her mother's protests.

"Let her go, mother. It is important for her."

The woman responded to the sudden authority in her daughter's voice and let Fern go, but she insisted on giving her many things to help her start her life again.

When the kindly villagers who had helped Fern carry all their gifts back to the remnants of her home had left, the evening star was already out.

Fern sat in the midst of the ruined wood and tried to communicate with it. They needed each other. Both in pain and darkness. She laid her suffering close to the charred branches and asked for help as she now offered it. Small voices came to her. Sad voices, lonely. Tears fell from her eyes.

"I am sorry," she whispered.

And then she heard the voice of her little stream calling softly, and went to it. On the banks some tiny shoots of green were beginning to push up defiantly through the blackened earth. They had not even waited for the Spring.

She dried her eyes.

In the morning she would start work on the garden again.

For two nights Karne did not return home.

Kyra began to worry about him and on the second day she set off to visit Fern hoping to find out if she could what had happened to him. Her mother was convinced he was visiting Fern but Kyra was not so sure.

She came upon her friend trimming back the dead wood of the berry bushes they had enjoyed so much in the summer. She had worked hard since she had returned and the concentration on the needs of her plants had helped her to forget her own longings and uncertainties.

She was overjoyed to see Kyra and fairly flung herself at her, but her pleasure was soon snuffed out when she heard that Karne had not been seen since he had left her.

She recalled the whole scene for Kyra and they agreed that from the direction in which he had been seen striding off he had probably gone to the hills where Maal used to go to think.

There was a line of anxiety between Kyra's eyes. It had

been a cold night with frost upon the ground and Karne had not been dressed particularly warmly.

Fern thought of this too and her heart's pain returned.

"Will you come with me?"

Fern nodded.

The two girls packed away Fern's gardening tools and set off to look for Karne.

They searched the hills until they were exhausted but could find no sign of him. They called and called, but no sound other than the cry of birds disturbed from their nesting places returned to them. Hill beyond hill stretched into the blue, enigmatically holding to themselves any secret that they might have.

"These hills *feel* empty," Fern said sadly at last, and Kyra had to agree with her.

They plodded back to the village, too tired and dispirited to think where else to look. The evening mists were already beginning to gather in the marshy places of the valley, and the sun although still far from setting was staining the sky red and turning the hills from blue to purple. They could see the little groups of houses, each with its plume of smoke, settled comfortably and pleasantly at the foot of the hill of Sacred Stones. Cattle and sheep were coming in from the pastures. Everything seemed to be drawing inwards to a centre, except for the birds who were flying outwards towards the forests and the hills that lay distantly encircling the little community.

One lone sea bird flew above their heads, crying forlornly for all the world like a child in pain, winging inland as though it had lost its way. But when the sound of it had died down the two girls realized that what sounded like an echo of its lonely cry was something else, a thin and haunting thread of sound coming from the village itself . . . the horn that called the villagers together at the Meeting Rock.

Kyra and Fern looked at each other and then started to run. It was downhill all the way and they were not far behind the last of the villagers to reach the place.

Expecting to see Wardyke upon the platform rock everyone was astonished to see Karne, holding the horn to his lips defiantly and blowing again and again, the sound resonating through bodies and minds to generate a kind of wild feeling of apprehension and excitement.

As he blew the last note Wardyke came striding towards the platform, his face dark and angry.

The villagers drew back to let him pass.

Karne stood straight and proud, watching him come. A thrill of admiration passed through the villagers. For the first time they had hope that someone was going to be strong enough to stand up to Wardyke.

Wardyke reached the platform but before he took the steps up to it Karne raised his hand imperiously.

"No, Wardyke," he said, and the villagers noted that he gave him no titles of respect. "This meeting is of the people. You are not welcome here."

Wardyke's face was a study. He could not believe this slim, fair lad was daring to speak to him like this.

"Boy," he spoke with clipped and disciplined bitterness. "Step down or it will be the worse for you."

"No, Wardyke," Karne held his ground. "*You* step down!"

The people gasped.

A few of Wardyke's Strangers moved forward threateningly, but something in the situation, perhaps the very confidence with which Karne held himself, confused them and they were not quite sure what to do.

The villagers pressed closer to watch what was happening and the Strangers could feel the growing strength within them. If Wardyke did not strike soon it might be too late. Everything hung on the knife-edge of tension between Karne and Wardyke.

The air was fraught, silent, the villagers scarcely breathing as they watched to see what would happen.

Kyra and Fern at the back of the crowd clutched each other for comfort.

Wardyke took another step forward.

Karne, eyes blazing with a light of anger and determination that no one had ever seen in them before, took a

233

step forward and made one of Wardyke's own gestures towards him, thrusting his pointing finger dramatically at him.

"You *will not* step upon this stone! You are *not fit* to be our priest!"

His voice and his sense of command were impressive. He seemed to be a man much taller than his normal self.

By keeping Wardyke from reaching the platform he was insuring that he was above him and therefore appeared taller. If Wardyke, who was much greater in bulk and height, and who cunningly wore robes and headdresses to accentuate this advantage, once stepped on to the rock Karne would lose visual precedence immediately.

Wardyke tried to take another step, but strangely the passion in Karne was so strong, fed by the resentment and hatred of the villagers supporting him, that he found himself hesitating. This hesitation was his undoing. Kyra helped her brother in every way she knew, clutching the white crystal stone she had found on Maal's tomb. She used the powers she had to project into Wardyke's consciousness the image of the boy being stoned, but altered it so that Wardyke would feel he was the boy and everything that had happened to the boy seemed to be happening to him. As the image came pressing in on him, as Karne's accusing finger powerfully drove into his mind, he tried to fight with all his skill to regain control

Kyra's head seemed to be cracking with the pain of concentration. Karne's will was stretched beyond anything he had ever thought he was capable of. As he outstared Wardyke his vision seemed to split and shatter into flying angular shapes of black and scarlet. He could scarcely see the man before him, but he drove his will to concentrate and overthrow straight to the central point of the flying, splintering images. The three began to tremble with the strain, but not one of them would falter. There was no movement, no sound from the waiting crowd. Even Wardyke's Strangers were waiting for the outcome and did not think to touch their weapons.

Wardyke had been called and on the outcome of this encounter his future and the future of the community hung.

Suddenly Fern moved. She ran lightly and swiftly to the platform and leapt upon it. She joined her strength to Karne's and in that moment, unnerved by seeing the hate and disdain in the eyes of the woman he desired, feeling the pain in the burning of her trees, Wardyke momentarily faltered and in that moment Kyra managed to break through his defences.

The crowd saw him suddenly stumble, his eyes showing fear. He raised his arms to protect his face as though something was attacking him, and in that moment they realized they had won. It was possible to outface Wardyke, the magician.

With a roar they moved forward and Wardyke was lost.

Some of the villagers seized the Strangers and fights broke out among them, but the majority moved in on Wardyke. They might have torn him apart had not Karne, who was completely in command, managed to stop them in time.

"Hold him," he cried, "but harm him not. There are things we have to do, but killing is not one of them!"

Kyra moved back out of the seething crowd and sat down on the grass, holding her head in her hands. The pain in it was almost blinding her but at least she could relax now. Nothing more was expected of her for a while.

Karne was issuing orders as though he had done it all his life. His face was flushed with excitement and his eyes were very bright. It was not an easy victory he had just won and he was conscious of it, but he was also aware of the necessity to follow it up with action that would not allow Wardyke to regain his power. He had thought the whole thing through by himself in the hills and knew every move he should make.

When Wardyke and his Strangers were unarmed and held, some admittedly with bloody noses and black eyes, but none killed, he ordered an election of new Elders to

235

be held there and then, without the long ceremonies of the past, but at least with the justice of fair choice open to the villagers.

Names were put forward and the villagers stamped their feet to indicate approval. The seven who roused the most passionate stamping would be elected, among them some of the original village Elders, and some new ones to replace people like Thorn. Karne's father was one of the new ones chosen. Karne himself could not be elected as he was not a family man. Thorn's name was put forward by one voice, but the silence with which it was greeted gave clear indication of what the villagers thought of him.

When they reached the last name to be called, Karne held up his hand for silence and suggested that one of the Strangers should be proposed. A murmur of dissent went through the community.

"These people are living among us whether we like it or not. Most of them have behaved badly but some have not. I do not see that those who wish to live the way we live and work with out community should be penalized because of the viciousness of the others. Choose one among them and let your feelings be known."

There was silence for a few moments as everyone looked around and thought about it. At first they could see nothing but evil in the Strangers and then one or two of them remembered things about some of their new neighbours that were not so bad.

Ji tugged at his father's arm and when he leant down to hear what he had to say, the boy whispered the name of one of the Strangers. He had become friendly with the family and a boy of his own age had often come fishing with him and was helping him to make the sled to haul Fern's wood.

Karne's father proposed the father of this boy. There was silence for a moment and then gradually the stamping began, led by Karne. The man was brought forward looking awkward and embarrassed and installed as the seventh Elder. It was in his favour that he had not been noticeably one of Wardyke's men. His wife burst into tears of joy and one of the villagers' wives put her arm around her.

Kyra noted this and was pleased.

Fern meanwhile had left the platform almost as soon as she had played her part. She knew she must not distract Karne from his work. Everything depended on swiftness of action while the wave of self-confidence still lasted. Karne had become like a kind of god to them and could do no wrong.

She joined Kyra and the two watched with amazement and admiration how Karne handled the crowd, keeping its baser passions in check, drawing from it commitment to worthwhile action.

The Elders chosen with extraordinary efficiency were installed upon the platform almost immediately, in the positions corresponding to the Standing Stones. Faro, being the eldest, and the one who had served longest as an Elder under Maal, naturally became the leader. But Fern and Kyra noticed how he turned to Karne for guidance on what was to be done next.

"Wardyke has usurped the place of our true priest," the boy said, "and we will have to make our own decisions until the gods send us a new one. The first decision to be made is what to do with Wardyke."

With this Karne left the platform and took his place among the villagers. As he moved among the people many turned to him and smiled with gratitude and admiration. But he had only one thought in mind now. He had done half of what he had decided to do, the other half remained.

Torches were being lit and placed round the platform Stone as the darkness gathered close around them. Karne could barely make out faces in the dim light, but he had noted where Fern and Kyra were and was quick to seek out the place.

Wood was fetched and an enormous fire was lit to give warmth and light to what was now to be the trial of Wardyke. The villagers who were not taking part directly huddled round it for warmth. The Elders knew whatever decision was made must be made swiftly before Wardyke had a chance to gather his strength again.

He was bound with leather ropes and pushed forward to face the Elders on the platform. With stooping shoulders, his back half bent by the position of the ropes, his arms unable to make those deadly gestures they feared so much, he was reduced in every way. Even his eyes, usually his deadliest weapon, were veiled with fear. He was not used to failing, and failure came hard to him.

His crimes were listed and considered and while this was happening his one-time supporters crept away one by one, many of them to flee the valley without waiting to pack their belongings.

Some who could have left stayed and added their voices to the accusations against their one-time Lord.

Karne found Fern, firelight flickering on her long copper hair, her tired but lovely face. He emerged from the crowd and stood before her, his own face in shadow. She could not see his eyes but she knew they were upon her and she felt them almost like a touch upon her body.

She stood silently for a while. Strangely all the sounds of the crowd disappeared, as though they were in a pocket of reality that had no sound, no movement. She was aware of nothing, no one but Karne, and he of her.

At last he stepped forward and before she knew it had happened she was close in his arms and his lips were on her face and neck. She shut her eyes and the overwhelming feeling that she had longed for, of him enfolding her and loving her, was hers.

Kyra moved away quickly to leave them alone together, her heart full with love for them both and pleasure at their pleasure.

Wardyke's trial was not protracted. After the list of accusations, suggestions for punishment were put forward. Kyra joining the crowd was in time to hear that banishment was the most favoured, to be preceded by a ceremony at the Sacred Circle to call down the help of the gods to keep him from practising his evil ways again.

He was then stripped of his magnificent robes and made to walk naked and ridiculous, shivering in the night air, to his grand house, which was then set on fire, together with all the trappings of his power. As the flames roared upwards and lit the determined faces of the people gathered around, there could be no doubt in Wardyke's mind that he was finished as a magician-priest.

The fire lasted a long time and the night turned into a kind of weird celebration. Drums were brought, and other musical instruments. People danced and sang, lit fitfully by the red glow from Wardyke's house. He was clad in the oldest rags they could find and tied to a stake to watch the festivities. He had to endure many indignities. People spat in his face, people jeered at him.

Kyra watched for a long time, wondering at all that had happened.

The pivot on which the whole thing had turned was, as the Lords of the Sun had said it would be, confidence.

Karne standing so tall and proud upon the platform, sustained by the pain of his love for Fern, had *believed* that he could overthrow the magician. And in that moment Wardyke doubted, and he was finished.

Too weary at last to endure any more, Kyra crept back to her home and to her warm, soft, sleeping rug. She had seen no sign of Fern and Karne, but as she slipped into a deep and blessed sleep she knew they were all right.

The Invisible Binding

THE NEXT DAWN found Wardyke alone and shivering, still tied to the stake, beside the cold embers of his home. The villagers had all gone to get what rest they could before the excitement of the ceremony at the Sacred Circle and only a stray dog was abroad, sniffing and lifting its leg against the blackened stumps of the great columns that had once held up the grandest house that had ever been in this village.

Wardyke was tired, stiff, dirty and cold. No one was guarding him and yet not one of the Strangers had come to set him free. He saw some of them leaving with all their animals and their belongings in the early dawn, without so much as a backward glance. Bitterly his hungry eyes roamed the valley, trying to summon up some of his old will-power, his old command. But it is not easy to be commanding when you are cold and hungry, aching in every limb, and tied in a crouching position to a stake.

As the first rays of the sun began to melt the frost upon the grass the village began to stir again. Not one person seemed to notice him, seemed to remember him. They went about their business as though he were invisible. He could smell warm food cooking, hear cheerful voices talking, and tears of longing began to come to his eyes. He began to think about banishment and the fact that he would be travelling in winter, with conditions at their worst and food difficult to come by. He had never been a hunter. Everything had always been provided for him and to fend for himself in the hostile forests or the mountains, where certainly he would be driven by the malicious villagers, would be almost impossible.

"I will die," he thought gloomily, and the thought of death made him afraid. When he was riding high he had not thought of the consequences of his actions. Everything had seemed justified to magnify his power. But now that he was low, he began to realize that what he had done had no justification and would have to be faced.

At his lowest ebb he turned his face to the east and thought about the gods he had so mocked. He remembered the falling stars and knew now they had a different interpretation. He remembered how even in the Circle at the height of his power he had been unable to "travel". Not believing in the gods he had used them to fool his gullible people. Now he was not sure they did not mock him.

It could not have been the boy alone who overthrew the mighty Wardyke.

At this moment he heard his name called and looked round. A village girl holding a bowl of hot food was beside him. His eyes were those of a hungry dog. She fed him carefully and gently with her fingers. He gulped and swallowed thankfully, feeling warmth creeping into his cramped and icy limbs as he did so.

"What is your name, girl?" he asked when he was finished. He could remember seeing her in the village from time to time.

"Kyra," she said quietly, standing up, the bowl now empty.

"Thank you, Kyra," he said from his heart. "I will not forget your kindness."

She smiled and bowed slightly.

"I think there are many things you will not forget," she said quietly and walked away.

Was she woman or child? He could not tell.

The ceremony was held at noon. No one knew quite what to do as this situation had never arisen before, but on Karne's advice it was agreed that Kyra should enter the Circle and pray for help to the gods. It was hoped that the gods would give some sign that they had heard and that Wardyke would effectively have all his powers as a magician-priest somehow removed from him, like sand upon the beach that had pictures drawn upon it in the morning and by the afternoon had been washed clean and bare by the tide.

It was also agreed that until their new priest arrived Kyra would act as best she could, as it was unthinkable to them to live without the constant two-way flow of communication with the gods. She would not be able to handle all the winter ceremonial but at least they would not be completely alone through the long and dangerous months.

Just before noon the villagers began to gather round the Sacred Circle. There was a feeling of excited apprehension among them. They had heard of Kyra's adventures within the Circle, but were still not sure the gods would allow an untrained villager to meddle in their affairs. She had been safe before, would she be safe again?

When the sun was almost at its zenith for that time of year Kyra entered the Circle. She had no priest's clothes to wear, no magnificent regalia, but she walked with such dignity and poise it was as though she were fittingly clad. Her hair had been combed a hundred times by her mother and stood out about her shoulders like a fine golden cloak. She had tied the white crystal from Maal's tomb with a thin hide thong so that it could hang around her neck as she had seen the priest's jade in the Temple of the Sun. Before she appeared in public she held it against her forehead and said a silent and passionate prayer to Maal for help. After that she felt much calmer and as she walked she felt its comforting weight against her heart reminding her of the promise of Maal and of the Lords of the Sun.

Strangely she felt no fear as she entered the Circle this time. It was as though she had a right and it was as though she knew what to do.

The crowd was very quiet, holding their breath, as she took the step through the entrance Stones, but when nothing untoward happened to her they drew breath again and bowed their heads briefly in acknowledgement that she was speaking for them to the gods.

She walked with measured tread around the Circle bowing slightly to each Stone and each time calling on the unseen Spirits of the spirit world and the one great God who ruled over them to give her people council and help in this difficult time.

Since she had spoken with the young priest in the desert temple she had tried not to think of the gods in any kind of Form, and now standing within the Sacred Circle she saw them as influences used by the One who wore the whole magnificence of Existence as we wear our bodies, a cloak that gives appearance to our invisible Reality.

She knew that if All that existed in Material Reality were to be discarded as we discard our bodies in death, there would still be the One, Nameless, Formless, Power Source which could create another material universe in any form It willed, however many times It willed.

And if It willed to stay without a manifest form then It could and would.

She knew there was no necessity to Existence as we know it. But because it Is at this moment and we Are at this moment, we should accept it and enjoy its multifarious forms, not wasting a second of it, learning what we can from it while it lasts.

Knowing what consciousness means to us, that marvellous faculty imagination makes the leap to help us un-

243

derstand the Consciousness of God. But this leap is not easily made and happens only in splendid moments of illumination, hardly at all at the beginning of our journey, increasing as we grow in capacity to understand, and finally becoming a permanent state when we return to our Source, capable at last of taking our part in His kind of Consciousness, His kind of Will, Motive, Choice and Imagination.

At this point we add to Him as He has been adding to us and we play our part in the great cycle of Being and non-Being that turns forever.

Standing transfixed in the middle of the Sacred Circle Kyra saw these things with great clarity. But even as she grasped them they began to slip from her and she slithered back into her imperfect body.

"No," she whispered, "please do not go," and lifted her arms to plead with them to return.

But as she lifted her arms the watching crowd who were unaware of her inner experience took the movement as a sign for the ceremony to commence.

Wardyke was brought to the entrance of the Circle by the Elders and propelled by a deft push to fall at her feet.

Dazed she looked down and saw the man who had been so powerful and grand, clad in rags, bound with hide ropes, dirty and dishevelled, at her feet. Tears came to her eyes and she stooped down and raised him up. To their astonishment the crowd saw Kyra undo his bindings and brush the dust from his face and body.

Then she took his hands and stood looking deeply into his eyes.

Wardyke had been amazed to see the girl within the Circle and as he was pushed and chivvied along the path to her he had begun to hope that he could get back his lost control. Now as she lifted him up and released his bonds he was sure he could. Something of his old fire came back to his eyes and he looked boldly into hers, expecting hers to waver and fall before long.

But strangely the deep blue pools of her eyes seemed to draw his strength from him. He found too late he could not withdraw his gaze and she was compelling him in some way to follow her.

He seemed to be getting deeper and deeper into something he could not understand. But she drew him on. Visions of the sea came to him and he was sinking within it, seeing in great detail all its strange and varied denizens, its intricate and secret life. He swam among great beasts in the deeps and floated in the flickering light of sun on crystal sand in the shallows, seeing minute fish exquisitely shimmering with luminous blue and silver, creatures so small he knew he was seeing in a way no human eye had ever seen before. He knew in some magical way he was seeing within the creatures the curious and beautiful constructions of their inmost parts.

From this vision of the infinitely minute, his awareness seemed to expand and he was floating in the sky surveying mountains and plains, till they in their turn grew smaller and he was yet higher, amongst worlds and suns and stars . . . the infinitely huge was not beyond his vision . . . and all that he had seen was moving in constantly changing relationships, in patterns of perfect proportion and harmony.

When he had grasped this, Kyra and her spirit helpers allowed him to return. Dumb with awe at what he had seen he felt like an infant who was seeing the world for the first time and did not know what to make of it.

Kyra released his hands, released his gaze, and slowly and with measured steps began to circle round him . . . round and round and round . . . holding in her hand an invisible thread . . .

When she was done she looked at him and said,

"You are bound now with bindings that you cannot see. They will prevent you practising as magician-priest, but as you learn the meaning of the vision that you have just seen and begin to treat the Universe and its Creator with respect . . . the bindings will gradually disappear.

"When you are ready, you will be free."

He bowed his head, feeling very weak and very humble.

She pointed to the path leading away from the Circle.

In a daze he walked out of the Circle and on to the path.

No man touched him. In silence the villagers watched him go.

Kyra lowered her head once more to the Tall Stones that represented the different states of the unseen world, and she in her turn trod the path into the valley.

It was not until she was out of sight that the villagers shivered slightly and moved. They, although they had not understood all that had happened, had felt the presence of the spirit realm and knew that something very significant had taken place.

But enough was enough. With movement came release and within seconds they were all chattering and comparing notes, children were dashing about, mothers were hurrying home to prepare a meal and all was noisy but comfortable confusion.

The Wedding and the Call

WARDYKE WAS GIVEN warm clothes, good food and weapons for hunting and defence, and sent on his way. The last of his supporters left with him. Those Strangers who remained asked to be members of the village and showed every sign of wanting to settle down and be integrated with the community. The community accepted them.

A pleasant time of peace returned to the valley and as though to put the seal of the gods upon it the weather stayed bright and mild much later into the winter than anyone could remember it doing before.

The whole community helped Fern and Karne erect their little house on the new site among the rocks and within days it was ready for occupation. The day after its completion was declared the wedding day, and the whole village looked forward to a real festival. There would be no priest for the blessing, but every one was content that Kyra should say a few words. For the rest the wedding ceremony in the village community had never been very elaborate. It was enough that the community accepted a young couple setting up home, and celebrated with feasting and dancing the day they took up residence together.

Each family contributed food and ale and the cooking fires were laid in a great circle in the flat area near the Meeting Stone.

From a very early hour the village was alive with activity. The children were everywhere, running messages, carrying things, decorating a special place for Fern and Karne to stand during the blessing with arching boughs of gold and scarlet berries. Ji and Okan and their new friend had scoured far and wide to find leaves still upon the trees and in fact the best branch was from Fern's new glen which was sheltered and warm compared to the rest of the valley. They had been taught by Fern to treat the trees with respect and took only branches that the tree no longer needed, cut them swiftly and cleanly with their father's sharpest flint axe, warning the tree well in advance so that it could prepare itself.

The day of the wedding was still and golden and the wedding arch was beautiful. As the final touches were put to it by a triumphant Ji the village children cheered and danced around it chanting little jingles of love for Fern and Karne.

Karne was busy accepting presents of cows and sheep and goats from warm-hearted neighbours. He and some of the older lads set about building make-shift pens for them on the outskirts of the festivity area. Fern and Kyra lent a hand for a while until they were called home by Kyra's mother. As she turned to go Fern gave one big shaggy cow with soft dozey eyes a big hug.

"Welcome to the family," she said and kissed it on its hairy nose.

Kyra laughed.

"My favourite is that pure white goat," she said. "I know she is going to bear many kids."

Fern ran her hand across its soft and silky back.

"You are pretty enough to be married today," she

248

laughed, and then called on one of the little girls to decorate the goat's horns with little streamers of wool and feathery grasses.

Kyra's mother was fussing over what Fern should wear. Fern could not see the problem but Karne's mother insisted that it should be something special.

"You must wear the dress that I was married in," she said and brought out a dress the colour of Spring.

Fern gasped.

"It was specially woven for my wedding," Kyra's mother said proudly. "I think every woman in the village had a hand in it somehow." Her eyes looked misty as she gazed at it.

Fern and Kyra fingered the cloth gingerly. It was the softest, finest weaving Fern certainly had ever seen, and only on her "travels" had Kyra seen better.

"The colour!" Fern exclaimed in amazement.

"I know," Kyra's mother's face glowed with pride at this. "A travelling merchant sold it to us for a great deal of my father's best wool. He would not tell us how it was made so no one else in the whole village has a similar dress."

"You must wear it, Fern," Kyra cried. "It is the colour of new leaves and would be perfect for you!"

Fern stroked it lovingly.

"Could I really?", she said, smiling at Kyra's mother.

"Of course you must! Try it on now."

Kyra helped her take off her old dress, the two girls bubbling with excitement over the new. As Fern raised her arms above her head and Kyra pulled her dress over her shoulders, Kyra's mother caught her breath. The girl's slim figure was definitely showing signs of thickening around the stomach.

"Fern," she said sharply, "you are not with child?"

Fern lowered her arms and stood naked, looking at her with a shadow of anxiety across her face.

Kyra held her breath.

249

After a pause Fern said quietly and soberly, "Yes, I am."

The mother stared at her for a moment as though she was not quite sure how she was going to take the news, and then her face broke up into smiles.

At that moment Karne came in.

"You never told me Fern was with child!" his mother cried joyfully.

He looked at Fern standing forlornly in the middle of the room, clutching her dress. Kyra beside her with her face all worried.

His hesitation was barely noticeable and then he was across the room in two strides, his arm around his love, his lips warmly brushing the top of her hair.

"Yes," he said to his mother, "we were keeping it a surprise."

Kyra saw Fern's face lift to his and the relief in it was beautiful to see.

He laughed and looked at her all over.

"You will be a bit cold getting married like that!" he teased.

"Oh, get away with you," his mother chided, "Go on—get out! We have things to do even if you have not!"

She gave him a slap as though he were a small boy again and he laughingly left, giving a quick backward glance of amusement and love at his bride.

Kyra suddenly hugged Fern. They were both aware that in that moment when Karne had not denied the child was his the whole course of their life together had been made that much easier.

Unaware of the drama that had just been played out under her very nose, Karne's mother continued her fussing and bustling, dressing the girl in the new dress, chattering with joy about the prospect of the new baby, chivvying Kyra to make alternations on the dress before the ceremony while she rushed off to supervise the food.

A deputation of little girls from the village arrived with an exquisite crown of woven grasses, jewelled with green, orange and yellow berries, for Fern to wear. One of their number gave it to her shyly. It was obvious she was expected by the others to make a speech, but the words would not come. Fern stooped and kissed her and the child ran away happily with her friends.

Then Kyra gave Fern her present, a necklace of sea shells so long that it could be wound several times around her neck and still hang low across her breast. Kyra had gathered the shells from time to time since she had been a very small child. Her collection of sea shells was very precious to her and she had kept it all these years in a secret place. Now the whole collection was in the necklace, apart from the few she broke in threading them, and she gave the gift with great love to her new sister.

Fern gasped and gazed with wonder at the delicate and exquisite shapes and colours of the shells.

"Oh Kyra," she whispered and could say no more.

At last it was time for the festivities to begin. Fern was led through the village by a gay band of dancers and flute players to Karne who was waiting impatiently under the arch.

She caused a gasp of admiration as she appeared and Karne himself was stunned by her appearance.

Always a beautiful girl, now in the long flowing softness of the green dress, her hair red-gold and shining in the sun, the little crown proudly worn upon her head, she looked like some princess of the nature spirit world. He wondered if he dared take her in his arms as he saw her walking so gracefully among the admiring crowd, but when she reached him her eyes were shining so much with love for him he did not hesitate. A cheer of pleasure went up from all his friends and neighbours as he welcomed her into his embrace.

Kyra then moved forward and spoke simply and with dignity the words of blessing she had heard Maal use at weddings in the past.

After that the feasting and the merriment began. Kyra could not remember when she had known such a day of happiness.

The villagers were celebrating victory and release from the dark spell of Wardyke as much as the joyful union of two of their favourite people. Music was played the whole day long. Dancing and kissing and eating seemed endless. The children were never still.

At the high point of the afternoon grain was thrown into the air in great sweeping arcs, and all the birds from miles around came swooping down to enjoy it. The air was filled with the sounds of their flight, their cries of joy were added to the music and singing.

Seven times the grain was thrown. Seven times the wheeling, swooping flight of birds descended. On the seventh and final time a black bird dropped its feather as a gift at Fern's feet and Karne picked it up for her. As the sunlight caught it, every colour in the rainbow flashed from its jet surface. He kissed it before he placed it in her hair.

Kyra wandered off by herself during the afternoon and sat beside the deserted ring of Ancient Stones. She could hear the noise of the party clearly enough, but it was not obtrusive. The Circle itself was absolutely silent.

She thought back along the summer and all that had happened to her and could not believe that she was the same person who had lain with Karne that day so long ago to spy upon the old man, Maal.

She fingered the while crystal that hung about her neck and thought about Maal, his kindness, his wisdom, his death. She wondered where he was now and when she would see him again. She had kept her promise to him and had no doubt that he would keep his to her even if it meant only in another life.

She thought about the Lords of the Sun and her heart longed to see the young priest from the desert Temple once again. She was tempted to enter the Circle and attempt to call him to her.

One part of her mind gave her arguments for trying it, the other told her the Sacred Circle was not to be used for personal matters.

She buried her face in her hands and tried to stop the

conflict, but the discipline of mind she had managed to achieve with such effort lately seemed now of no avail. The tempter won and with beating heart she slipped into the Circle. Trembling with anxiety she made the rounds from Stone to Stone, trying to calm herself, but with every step becoming more agitated.

So determined was she to see if she could do it, she ignored all the warning signs within herself, and put herself against the Leaning Stone in the position she had learnt.

Nothing happened.

She remained exactly as she was.

Heart beating, conscious of herself.

There was no separation. No vision. No travelling.

Disappointed, she opened her eyes and stood up

The Circle felt dead in a way she had never experienced before.

She left, ashamed.

That night when Karne and Fern were happily in their new home, and all the village was sleeping peacefully, worn out by the day's activities, Kyra lay awake. She knew she had done wrong to go into the Circle for no good reason but her own selfish desires. She wondered if she would be punished by her powers being taken from her. It was certain there was nothing in her feelings or in the atmosphere of the Circle that afternoon to suggest that she had any powers at all.

She thought about the prophecy that she would travel south to the Temple of the Sun and be trained as a priest. She and Karne had talked about it a great deal and planned the journey between them. He and Fern were to go with her, first in the boat Ji and Okan had helped build on the great sea and then by river as far as they could, travelling overland when they had to, avoiding the forests as much as possible, resting at villages. The new priest who was travelling this route at this very time would give them advice.

Fern's baby would be born on the journey and live its first years within the influence of the Temple of the Sun.

Karne would have his greatest ambition satisfied. She knew that for as long as she could remember Karne had longed to see this famous Temple. He had even built the boat they were to use for the first stage of the journey for this very purpose.

She thought about that day so long ago when she had said to him, "The journey to the Temple of the Sun requires more than a boat . . . it is a journey on many levels . . ."

She knew now the journey had started on that day.

But had she forfeited all this now?

Tears came to her eyes and she felt very much alone and miserable. She had tried so hard to be worthy of Maal's trust and now she had let him down. It must have been because she saw Karne and Fern so much in love, that she began dreaming of the only man she had ever seen who roused her in the way Karne seemed to rouse Fern.

"It is ridiculous!" she told herself crossly. "If I cannot manage self-control, how can I expect it of other people? I would be no good as a priest anyway!"

She sobbed herself to sleep like a child, and as the moon rode above the village strangely vivid dreams began to come to her.

She saw herself in the Great Circle of the South, one among many initiates, bowing to the high priest with the kind face and the jade stone about his neck. He touched her head and pressed his thumb hard upon her forehead.

"You who now have my mark upon you will follow me and learn what I have to teach," he said in a flat ritualistic voice.

She saw him pass down the line of initiates pausing only at one or two, making the same sign to them and speaking the same words.

Her heart lifted. She had been chosen.

When he had passed out of sight the line of initiates broke up and went towards different parts of the Great Circle, where they gathered in groups around the particular priest-teacher who had been assigned to them.

As she passed one group she found her eyes drawn to it. She could not see the priest in charge, as he was hidden by his students, but the students were different from the others she had noticed. With a sudden jerk her heart registered that the clothing of these students was similar to that she had seen in the wall pictures in the desert Temple of Red Sandstone, and as she discovered this the group moved and the priest who was in charge of them stood clearly in her sight.

It was the young and handsome Lord of the Sun.

As she recognized him, he saw her.

Their eyes met.

But in that instant, before she could be sure what expression was in his eyes, she jerked awake and lay in her own house in the far cold north, wrapped in sleeping rugs and trembling from head to foot.

For the rest of the night she tossed and turned, unable to be sure whether it had been a vision or an ordinary dream.

The dawn found her pale and dark eyed. At first light she crept out, too restless to spend another moment trying to sleep. At the door she paused and then returned to her sleeping place to fetch Maal's stone. She had grown used to wearing it at all times, and particularly when she was unhappy and uncertain of herself.

As she came out into the cold light of the early morning she glanced down at it before she put it round her neck.

And then she paused and stared.

The stone that had been white as frost before was now unmistakably green as jade.

Trembling, she turned it every way in the light, afraid to accept too soon its miraculous transformation.

Jade!

"You who now have my mark upon you will follow me and learn what I have to teach."

It had not been a dream.

255

FREE
Fawcett Books Listing

There is Romance, Mystery, Suspense, and Adventure waiting for you inside the Fawcett Books Order Form. And it's yours to browse through and use to get all the books you've been wanting ... but possibly couldn't find in your bookstore.

This easy-to-use order form is divided into categories and contains over 1500 titles by your favorite authors.

So don't delay—take advantage of this special opportunity to increase your reading pleasure.

Just send us your name and address and 35¢ (to help defray postage and handling costs).

FAWCETT BOOKS GROUP
P.O. Box C730, 524 Myrtle Ave., Pratt Station, Brooklyn, N.Y. 11205

Name_____
(please print)

Address_____
City_____ State_____ Zip_____

Do you know someone who enjoys books? Just give us their names and addresses and we'll send them an order form too!

Name_____
Address_____
City_____ State_____ Zip_____

Name_____
Address_____
City_____ State_____ Zip_____